Return of the Sagan

By:
Neil O'Donnell

W & B Publishers

For information:
W & B Publishers
9001 Ridge Hill Street
Kernersville, North Carolina 27285
www.a-argusbooks.com

ISBN: 978-0-692367766
ISBN: 0-692367764

Book Cover by AMYGDALA DESIGN
Printed in the United States of America

Dedication

This book is dedicated to my brother, Francis Aloysius O'Donnell. We love you, Francis, and we will never forget you.

In Memoriam

I have been blessed with having family and friends who have taught me much about life and about trying to be a better person. Three individuals in particular I wanted to remember here, three individuals whom were always kind to me and all others and will always be remembered: Clarence Counts, Christy Fornoff, and my uncle, Paul Leary. I miss you all.

I also wish to take time to remember those who serve(d) in the United States armed forces. For the remainder of my life, I will always remember the following heroes:

Marvin 'Joe' Curry – Chief Warrant Officer, US Navy
Wilbur Curry, Jr. – Staff Sergeant, US Army
Lambert (Bert) Danhof – Seaman First Class, US Navy
Scott M. Dennison – Chief Petty Officer, US Navy
James F. Metzger – Sergeant, US Marines
William Sullivan – Second Lieutenant, US Army

Chapter 1

"Saturn Alpha? Saturn Alpha, please respond," the U.S.S. Drake's copilot, Martin Kalowitz, called into his helmet microphone. The activation of the shuttle's maneuvering thrusters remained the only sound to resonate throughout Martin's headset. Hope was fading. "Still no response, Captain," Martin said, turning to his left where the pilot, Rebecca Sanford, sat.

"Roger that," Rebecca replied. "Sagan Actual, please respond." Rebecca waited while the crackling of the radio reached out to their base ship over one hundred seventy kilometers behind. Rebecca's melodic voice belied her gruff nature in adverse conditions. Her cool command presence had guided Rebecca's teams through multiple emergencies during her five years in service to the American Navy, a demeanor and collectedness that earned Rebecca her captaincy and call sign: *Frost*.

"Shuttle Three, this is Sagan Actual. Report." The commander's firm voice, even over the radio, evoked calm amongst the crew. Rebecca, like every colonial, drew strength and courage from that voice, willingly executing any command that followed.

"Still no response from the platform, Commander; requesting permission to dock and explore," Rebecca said, her cool tone masking her eagerness to explore Earth's most remote space station. It was an eagerness shared by the whole crew; a colonial setting foot on the first structure of Earth-origin in nearly three hundred years.

"Permission granted, Shuttle Three. Make for the station's lower hatch and deploy the Marines. I want the flight crew to stay put. Understood?"

"Roger that, Actual." Rebecca cut off her reply quickly, her disappointment shared by Martin and every crewmember back on the base ship, the U.S.S Carl Sagan. Without another word, Rebecca guided her shuttle, the U.S.S. Drake, to the station's main docking hatch, specifically designed for the class of ship Rebecca piloted. The shuttle, a miniature version of the U.S.S. Sagan, served as a troop transport. Like the base ship, the Drake was named for one of the pioneers who guided the first steps of S.E.T.I., the organization that helped design their ship and mission, or at least the mission of their predecessors. After leaving Earth 293 years earlier, the Sagan carried S.E.T.I.'s initial crew of 20,200 to a distant planet deemed suitable for human occupation. With the Earth's population breaching ten billion, the distant planet, *Maximus Prime*, offered hope for a way to gain the space and resources Humanity desperately needed. The journey took ninety-three years, three generations, and ended better than anticipated. Maximus Prime, roughly the size of Earth, was the fourth planet in a system of ten, which circled a yellow star ten percent larger than the sun. With one large continent reminiscent of *Pangea*, Maximus Prime offered more land area than Earth and a water supply with twenty percent more readily accessible fresh water. Humanity's future was assured.

After landing on the planet, the ever-growing crew, now at well over 40,000, settled along the equatorial zone of Maximus Prime and built a city while teams of scientists explored the planet. Like Earth, Maximus Prime had temperate, tropical, and arctic zones as well as a plethora of new species for the scientists to study; species including mammals, reptiles, fish, birds, insects and flora. The richness of opportunities Maximus Prime offered was tempered by the loss of contact with Earth.

Incoming radio transmissions from Earth ceased eighteen months into the Sagan's mission. As per protocol, the mission was to continue *unless ordered to return*. Years passed and no messages came, though the Sagan crew continued to transmit reports to Houston Control. After the fiftieth anniversary of the landing on Maximus Prime, the elected representatives of the colony commissioned a retrofit of the Sagan and organized a return flight. Eighty-seven years after the Sagan set out from Maximus Prime, the ship was now within months of orbiting Earth. Yet, this close to terrain space, communications sent to Houston Control remained unanswered. Now, as the Sagan's crew looked to dock with the Saturn Alpha space station, hope of answers grew.

"Colonel Leary, we are a go," Captain Sanford called into her helmet microphone. Without another word, she skillfully guided the shuttle with maneuvering thrusters to the station's lowest access hub. All the while, Colonel Paul Leary and his platoon remained alert and cognizant of the coming mission, the first they would ever commence outside of drills. The seconds counted down as the Marines listened to the shuttle's bulkheads knocked into position aside the space station, which resembled a spark plug adrift in space just a few hundred kilometers further from the end of Saturn's belt of debris. Seconds passed as the shuttle docked, Colonel Leary's eyes never diverting from the indicator light positioned above the shuttle's main hatch, a light that suddenly glared with a startling amber hue.

"Make ready!" the colonel commanded as he and his team unlocked their safety harnesses and maneuvered into formation, Gunnery Sergeant Thomas Fernel taking point. Outfitted in pressurized, dark-gray suits akin in design to snowsuits, the platoon appeared *unsuited* to action in space. The thin design of their outfits, however, belied the fact the construction included polyamide fibers and a Kevlar-micrometeoroid shell, which would resist possible abrasions from space debris. Also armed with M4 carbines and a variety of sidearms, these Marines were far from vulnerable.

"Colonel, the station's artificial grav units are offline," Sanford called over the com system. "Prepare for depressurization."

"Activate grav-locks and prepare to move!" Colonel Leary commanded. In turn, each of the Marines, the colonel included, pressed a button on their shoulder guard, which activated magnets embedded in the souls of their boots. Then, after the hatch light flickered, the shuttle evacuated all pressure from the hold. Seconds later, the hatch light turned green; following Sergeant Fernel, the Marines entered Saturn Alpha.

***

Separated into squads of five, Colonel Leary's platoon marched into the entry room with weapons drawn and readied. With no lights emanating from the space station, the Marines relied on the small lights fastened to their weapons for illumination. The view was ominous.

Odd pieces of furniture and a variety of smaller items including pens, clipboards, computer tablets, and clothes littered the room, every item floating about aimlessly in the zero-gravity. All that was missing was the station's crew.

"Gunny, take your squad and check the aft control room," Colonel Leary commanded. Nodding his acknowledgement, Sergeant Fernel led his squad to the pre-determined location in hopes of firing up the station's main generators. Meanwhile, Colonel Leary tasked two squads to stand guard while he led the remaining platoon members to the upper decks via the central stairwell.

The climb to the other decks took considerable effort as the grav-locks made for clumsy movements. Meanwhile, floating office-like debris continually hampered the Marines' progress. Yet, meter by meter, Colonel Leary's platoon progressed onward, but inspections of each deck revealed no sight of recent human occupation.

"I thought this was supposed to become an active space port?" a private asked as she ducked under a floating desk. "I doubt anyone's been here in a hundred years."

"Definitely could use a thorough cleaning, maybe a fresh coat of paint," commented another private as he wiped a layer of dust from a monitor mounted to a wall.

"Cut the chatter, Marines!" Colonel Leary scolded as they finished a sweep of the entry room of the station's highest deck. "Lieutenant, check the remaining rooms."

"Yes sir!" Lynn Suya replied. With a curt wave of her left hand, her squad moved forward to inspect the rooms behind the only two doors remaining.

"Gunny, report!" the colonel called into his headset. For several long, anxious seconds, he waited for a response.

"We're all set here, Colonel. The power grid is beyond repair. We've secured the hard drives from the main computer as well as a stash of flash drives. Making our way back to the shuttle now."

"Roger that," Colonel Leary replied, his disappointment evident. *Where was the crew?*

"Colonel!" Lieutenant Suya's voice cried out over the com system. "Starboard antechamber!" The lieutenant's call grabbed everyone's attention instantly, and with a wave of the colonel's left hand, all converged on the antechamber.

"My God," Colonel Leary whispered into his microphone as he entered into the room. Floating about the room were the remains of seven astronauts, clad in the space suits familiar to the era of space travel that immediately followed the U.S.S. Endeavor's final flight. Bulky, white and capped with a dome-like helmet, the suits contained an eerie sight: skeletons whose visages reflected terror.

***

"Roads go ever, ever on, …under cloud and under star," Francis's voice sang out the classic Tolkien verse to an audience of fan-blown fruit trees, cornstalks and bean plants, the latter scaling the cornstalks upwards, ever reaching for the network of fluorescent grow lamps that fed the U.S.S Sagan's plant population with the requisite ultra-violet radiation to fuel growth. Here, hidden amidst the rows of plants, Francis read away his days free from the cold steel and technology that surrounded the crew of the Sagan. Crippled by fears of contact with the ever-present people, germs and mercury-laced technology he shared space with, this was the only place where Francis felt alive, comfortable. Even now, as every other human on the U.S.S. Sagan anxiously awaited news of the mission to Saturn Alpha, Francis dreamed bigger. Holding tightly to his well-worn copy of J.R.R Tolkien's *The Hobbit*, Francis dreamed of adventures through the forests of Earth in search of an existence freed from the stale air of space.

At twenty-three, Francis's blue eyes and raven-black hair hid a soul aged by anxiety. Every day was a struggle to continue on and survive. Now, with Earth only months away, Francis saw an opportunity to break free of the trap he grew up in. Now, he would leave behind fears of the known for awe of the unknown.

"This is Governor Counts," a deep, baritone voice called out over the Sagan's com system. "We've recovered the search teams from Saturn Alpha. While the base was unoccupied and we still have not made contact with Earth, we did recover logs, which should answer some questions we have. Presently, we are continuing on towards Earth. I will update everyone as soon as we have more details from Saturn Alpha's records. Governor, out."

"To Earth," Francis said in response to the governor's report. His hope of adventure rekindled, Francis continued on singing the verses from Tolkien's masterpiece, telling of a hobbit traveling over a larger world.

"Yet feet that wandering have gone, turn at last to home afar."

Chapter 2

The U.S.S Carl Sagan's hull was tired, a condition born of nearly three hundred years of interstellar travel. The first and only generational ship ever constructed, the Sagan, propelled by three gargantuan fusion engines, took nearly a century to bridge the distance between Earth and Maximus Prime, the planet considered most suited to Humanity's needs. The journey took a heavy toll.

The ship's design, reminiscent of America's shuttles, included titanium-reinforced bulkheads built to repel most space debris, everything from comet fragments to small asteroids. For larger obstacles, the Sagan's crew relied on long-range sensors and an array of thrusters positioned to help avert collisions with surprises that came along. Fortunately, none of the Sagan's commanders ever needed to give the order to fire thrusters. Yet pitting and charring resulting from smaller space debris left indelible reminders of the taxing nature of space flight. The commander knew this was the Sagan's last trip.

Back on board, secured on the bridge behind the titanium-reinforced hull and windows made with layers of fused silica and aluminum silicate panes, Commander Taryn Southern sat in her command chair looking through the shuttle's windows at Saturn Alpha.

"He's right," Commander Southern murmured as she considered Colonel Leary's earlier assessment. "The station does look like a spark plug." The commander smiled as she continued to contemplate the vacant spaceport. The commander's attention then turned to the com station just three meters to her left. Manned 24/7, the com officer's responsibilities included a continued attempt to contact Earth.

"This is the U.S.S. Sagan calling Houston Control. Houston Control, please respond," the current com officer called into his microphone. "Houston Control, do you read." The tiring endeavor had long ago lost meaning to many on the bridge. Yet, Commander Southern held out hope for her ship's signal reaching some terrestrial outpost or community. Staring back out the Sagan's windows at Saturn Alpha, with Saturn's outer rings just kilometers beyond the station, Commander Southern sat in awe at the footprint of Humanity against a backdrop of the Milky Way's sixth planet. From the bridge, immersed in a sea of computer indicator lights, Taryn marveled at the smallness of Humanity versus the enormity of the universe's creations.

"So far have we yet to go," the commander whispered as the hum of the bridge's main door motor drew her attention towards Colonel Leary. The colonel stopped and saluted, waiting for the commander to respond. "Let's do this in my quarters, Colonel," Commander Southern replied as she stood and walked past the colonel and on towards the hatchway. "Captain Lorin, you have the con."

***

The two officers, clad in the everyday dress of the military - tan trousers and tan short-sleeved oxfords, marched side by side along the metal-tiled hallway, the stomping of their well-polished shoes proclaiming their approach. Aside from occasionally saluting a passerby, Commander Southern and Colonel Leary made no effort to communicate, offering no hint of their respective moods; military commanders to the end. Reaching the hatchway to her quarters, Commander Southern punched her entry code into the console beside the hatch. After a series of beeps and mechanical knocks echoed through the ship's hull, the hatch opened, closing abruptly after both officers entered.

"Home sweet home," Taryn said as she walked to a recliner not far from the entry hatch and sat, her limber movements belying her nearly thirty years of service. "I take it the news is far from promising?" she asked the colonel who had marched over to the commander's bar. Pouring himself a glass of whiskey, Colonel Leary downed the curt beverage before answering.

"We secured the hard drives from the base's main computer," Colonel Leary replied before pouring another glassful of whiskey. "Hell, we pulled the hard drives from every computer we could find." Taking just a sip this time from his glass, the colonel turned and walked to a nearby leather sofa. There he sat, sighing before staring into the depths of his glass.

"What is it, Paul?" Commander Southern asked, uncertain she actually wanted an answer. After seconds passed, Paul Leary looked to his friend, ready to relay their initial discoveries.

"Preliminary analysis of the main computer's hard drives indicates the last added file dates to about two years after the Sagan departed for Maximus Prime."

"Six months after we lost contact," Taryn said. She then rubbed at her short crop of red hair as she contemplated the report. "Could we actually be all that's left... of Humanity? Is that what you're telling me?"

"At this range, we should be able to pick up some type of transmission from Earth, Taryn. Hell, we should be able to watch football games on Sunday, but we're picking up nothing. I think it's time we reevaluate our strategy, Sir. This is no longer a contact mission." Colonel Leary's words might as well have come from the commander herself. As the colonel drank deeply from his glass, the commander stood, walked over to her desk and picked up her phone's receiver.

"Com, this is the commander," Taryn called into the receiver after which she awaited a response from the watch.

"Go ahead, Commander," a young voice called back hesitantly.

"I want sensors adjusted to look for any nuclear signatures emanating from Earth, and tell Dr. Walken to meet me on the bridge in twenty minutes."

"Understood, Sir."

"Commander out," Taryn replied before hanging up the receiver. "Better switch to coffee, Paul. I think this is going to be a long day."

***

"Was Edmond Dantés justified in seeking vengeance?" Professor Francis Burns asked his students, his well-worn paperback copy of *The Count of Monte Cristo* resting gently within his young hands. At 1.81 meters, Francis towered over most of his students, their ages ranging from seventeen to twenty-two. In age, Francis was not their elder by much, but the shoots of white hair that traced through Francis's short, black hair made the twenty-three year old seem ancient. Then, there were Francis's eyes.

His blue irises themselves were youthful enough. However, the well-defined crow's feet emanating from the corners of his eyes only added to Francis's aged appearance. Francis's worn exterior matched his exhausted heart, all consequences of the daily battle he fought with Obsessive-Compulsive Disorder. That battle temporarily subsided when he taught classes, a time when he seemed able to push aside the intrusive thoughts and focus on more creative, more positive concerns.

"I think he should've taken the money and run," David Thompson, one of the gathered students replied to Francis's query. A series of giggles raced through the two dozen students, all garbed in military attire; blue trousers and white shirts for naval cadets and brown trousers and tan shirts for Marines.

"So, you think revenge wasn't warranted?" Francis asked, energized by the continuing debate. As always, Francis moved to within a meter of the student to give undivided attention. Participation from students was rare.

"He had all the money he would ever need, certainly enough to take care of himself and his true friends," David continued as he squirmed a bit under the stare of the anthropology and liberal arts professor. The cadet could feel the sweat gathering under his arms and soaking into his white shirt.

"So, you're thrown in prison, locked away for years for a crime you didn't commit, and you wouldn't seek retribution?" Francis asked as he paced about in a circle, eager to have the debate spread throughout the class. Eagerness then led to heartache.

"Professor, how is this even relevant to our majors?" David asked, a question Francis often heard from students and parents alike. A sharp tone cast over the intercom system, noting the end of the hour, prevented Francis from his defense of literature.

"Remember to read and be prepared to discuss Poe's *The Cask of Amontillado* for Wednesday," Francis called out to his fleeing students, who noisily placed their tablets into an array of bags. Then, after the last student exited through the automatic doors, Francis was left alone to consider David's question, or rather the *Truth* Francis clung to dearly. *The arts are what make life worth living.*

***

The most taxing part of Francis's day followed the brief respite that class offered. After placing his books into his satchel, Francis looked to his 22cm by 17cm tablet computer. The device offered wireless access to the Sagan's stores of books, movies, journals and other information sources, which Francis relished. Yet, touching the device always proved difficult if not impossible at times. Francis dwelled on the traces of lead, mercury and cadmium found in most electronics. He spent hours each day thinking about possible contamination, particularly from mercury, questioning whether he would in turn contaminate the Sagan's entire population. Francis washed his hands repeatedly to quell the obsession over contamination, which worked for only short amounts of time. Then, as if he never bathed before, Francis washed again.

Placing his tablet in its own separate case, Francis quickly made his way to the room's doors, which opened at the professor's approach. There he stood and turned, gazing at the room's central computer console. He counted each of the lights, making note of their respective colors; green meant on and orange meant off.

He then left only to return seconds later to check once more. Fearing that leaving a computer on would cause a fire and destroy the Sagan, Francis usually returned four to five times to check the console lights, actions that took upwards of twenty to thirty minutes each day. Once satisfied the computer was off, Francis continued through the halls to his quarters, a cell of cold metal walls eight meters by five meters in dimensions. Equipped with a toilet, shower stall, cot and desk, Francis had little room to move about, especially since he built a bookcase from wood scraps he secured from the ship's botanical department. The wood brought a little peace and warmth to the otherwise Spartan enclosure, but that was of little importance since Francis spent little time there.

Once inside, he took a quick shower before donning a fresh, white oxford and khaki trousers. Then, slipping on his hiking boots, Francis grabbed his paperback copy of McKiernan's Iron Tower omnibus and headed to the ship's arboretum, the only place onboard where Francis found true peace.

Chapter 3

With Saturn Alpha now in its wake, the venerable U.S.S. Sagan continued on towards Earth, her crew eager to distance themselves from the disappointment of the Saturn base. For the first time, everyone, the commander included, seemed as tired as the ship. Then, after two weeks of long-range sensor sweeps of Earth and its surrounding space, Commander Southern convened a meeting of senior officers and the governor, the latter of who remained ever hopeful of the Sagan's mission and the crew's return to their home world. Crammed into the commander's ready room, hope for answers was dwindling.

"Xenon isotope levels are within norms as are all other detectable particulate densities in the atmosphere for that matter," Dr. Tom Campbell reported to the gathered leaders. The leading astrophysicist onboard, Dr. Campbell coordinated the effort to contact Earth. The effort had so far failed.

"What does that mean in English, Doctor?" Governor Clarence Counts asked, his irritation evident. The governor, though only thirty-five, was an accomplished leader and diplomat whose patience was legendary. Yet, after days of little sleep, the governor's patience was in short supply.

"At this range, we should be able to pick up some radio transmissions, Governor. We've been operating under the assumption that... a catastrophic event occurred that wiped out all communication networks."

"Nuclear war," Governor Counts said to voice what many long suspected happened to cease communications between the Maximus Prime colony and Earth.

"Or an asteroid collision," Dr. Campbell continued. "Both would cause a disruption of communications, but both would also have left telltale signs in the atmosphere."

"The xenon isotope levels," Governor Counts interjected. Dr. Campbell nodded.

"Xenon isotopes should be elevated, but our sensors indicated the levels are near where they were when the Sagan first left."

"And the impact of an asteroid?" Commander Southern asked. All heads snapped towards the commander; when she spoke all listened.

"An asteroid strike would have kicked up enough debris to choke the atmosphere with a mix of minerals that would be reflected in our scans," Dr. Campbell replied. "We'd also expect high levels of iridium, ash and…"

"Bottom-line this for us, Doctor," Commander Southern interjected.

"There's no indication that Earth is inhabited by any human society." A murmur quickly spread amongst the assorted brass as the commander and governor, seated at opposite ends of the conference table, exchanged looks of alarm. Then, with a word, the governor restored order.

"Enough!" Governor Counts exclaimed. "Dr. Campbell, are you saying Earth is no longer inhabitable?" he asked the science chief as all attention returned towards Dr. Campbell.

"No, Governor. I'm saying… we're saying that all indications are that Humanity has vanished from

Earth. We're saying that when we arrive in Earth's orbit, there likely won't be anyone to greet us." Again, chatter enveloped the room as the governor and commander contemplated the doctor's report.

"Wait!" the commander exclaimed; silence reined once more. "How can you be absolutely certain no human populations remain on the planet, Doctor?"

"We can't, Commander." The doctor leaned forward, rested his elbows on the table and folded his hands, his eyes ever focused on the commander. "Yet, we've been gone for nearly three hundred years. With communications having ceased not long after the Sagan's initial departure, it seems logical that some kind of cataclysm occurred centuries ago. Commander, I have to believe that if anyone survived, we'd be picking up some sort of transmissions by now."

"What if an environmental factor, a virus or contagion, wiped out Humanity?" Commander Southern asked. "What if the Earth *is* uninhabitable?"

"It's possible, Commander, but we won't know that for sure until we've put boots on the ground."

"If it wasn't nuclear warfare or an astcroid strike, we have to assume that a toxin or virus of some kind is responsible," the governor added, drawing eyes to his end of the conference table. "I can't see a conventional war claiming all communities."

"I would agree," the commander said as she focused her eyes on Dr. Campbell. "But again, we won't know anything until we land and run environmental tests on the air, water and soil."

"So, how do we proceed, Doctor?" Colonel Leary asked, cutting through the veil of queries.

"I recommend we land a research team near the Great Lakes. They're the largest source of readily accessible fresh water, a good place to start. Since the Sagan's water reserves are in dire need of replenishing, that's our first priority anyway."

"I take it you have a location in mind?" the governor asked.

"I'm beginning to feel like a ping pong ball," Doctor Campbell said as he turned to face Governor Counts. "I think we should land along the Niagara Frontier in western New York State. If there's any contamination of the water supply, it would be most evident in the lower Great Lakes region."

"Then why not just land near the juncture between Lake Ontario and the Saint Lawrence?" the governor asked.

"If there is any contamination, Lake Ontario is more likely to be a hot zone since all other lakes channel into it. We are hoping that any water contaminates have been carried along to the Saint Lawrence seaway and that the elevation at Niagara Falls created a barrier, which allowed Lake Erie and the upper Great Lakes to filter out any remaining toxins."

"That's a lot of guess work, Doctor Campbell," Commander Southern said as she punched in a series of codes into a tablet resting in front of her. The series of projection screens positioned on the wall to the commander's left lit up, an isotopic map of the Niagara Frontier region replacing one dark screen.

"It's as good a place to start as any, Commander," Dr. Campbell replied as he stepped up to the central projection screen. Then, after tapping the screen near the confluence of Lake Erie and the Niagara River, the map expanded to project details of the Buffalo and Niagara metropolitan areas. "We should arrive in September, barring any significant delays. Even without human supervision, a variety of edible plant species and animals should be available for harvesting, unless they too were eradicated. What's more, the rapids of the Niagara River will serve as the perfect stage for placement of power generators. Fresh water, food and energy, main staples we'll need to start a new colony."

"I sense there's a catch?" the governor asked. Doctor Campbell, his facade grim, nodded.

"The testing and engineering tasks will be easy enough, but our knowledge of the environment is considerably outdated. We need to spend the next few months designing field equipment. My team doesn't have time to gather intel on the region's resources and history."

"Perhaps I can help with that task," Colonel Leary said, his face now beaming with a sly smile.

***

"You cannot escape!" the voice exclaimed as Francis ran through the unfamiliar woodlands. Exhausted, Francis meandered around the endless blanket of trees and brush, the fading sunlight making it difficult to find any sense of a trail. All the while, the calls of birds and crickets resonated through the woodlands, as did the call of wolves and coyotes. Then, just when he felt he was gaining distance from his stalker, Francis's trek ended at the edge of a ravine; all sounds vanished and midnight took hold.

A horrid chuckle from the depths of the woods came from behind, and Francis turned to see if the beast would finally show itself. Yet, instead of a monster or villain, all Francis Burns saw were multiple sets of red eyes staring back at him. Set for the coming attack, Francis unsheathed the sword belted against his left hip.

"The Foe Hammer will not stop me, boy," the stalker said as a large, hairy form started to take shape within the darkness. "You are mine!" The dark form lunged at Francis before he could ready his sword"

"No!" Francis exclaimed as he jumped up from his blanket, sweat covering his face and torso.

"You're all right, Francis," a familiar voice said as a figure emerged from the shadows of a nearby spruce. "You are safe."

Comforted, having awakened from the ever-present nightmare, Francis wiped the sweat from his brow and stood to greet Colonel Leary.

"Same nightmare, I take it?" Colonel Leary asked as he embraced Francis, patting the young professor on the back to ease Francis's fears.

"I almost saw the beast this time, Uncle Paul. Almost." Francis lowered himself back to his blanket as Colonel Leary picked up Francis's copy of the Iron Tower trilogy.

"Do you ever get sick of reading these?" he asked as he sat next to Francis. The colonel then scanned the area where Francis spent most of his time. This section of the arboretum was mixed with species of conifers and deciduous trees, mostly pines and maples. Fan-generated winds coursed through the area, batting branches together, adding nature to an otherwise desolate existence of metal and machine, of mercury, iron, copper and lead.

"The books help ease the attacks," Francis replied before drinking from his water bottle. "It's hard to notice the anxiety when you're running from Mordru or Sauron."

"It's only a temporary fix though, Francis," his Uncle Paul replied before handing back the book to his nephew.

"Something up, Uncle Paul?"

"I came to tell you that an operation is being planned for an initial landing on Earth when we arrive. The plan is to land near Buffalo." Francis's eyes lit up at the city's name.

"We're going home?"

"We're going home, though the team is in need of someone with extensive knowledge of the region's history and landforms."

"Nobody on the Sagan knows the region better than me, Uncle Paul. I can help." It was a truth that the colonel did not question.

"You're the first one I thought of, Francis, but this won't be easy. To prepare, you will have to leave the arboretum behind, train and bunk in the barracks with the other team members. It'll be nearly three months of immersion in everything you fight to avoid. There will be no time for fantasy novels. Are you ready for that?"

The plants of the arboretum kept his OCD at bay, allowing Francis to maintain some peace in the darkness and cold of space. Earth offered the same soothing atmosphere only on a grander scale. Once there, Francis knew he could dwell within woodlands for the rest of his days. Yet, Francis questioned whether he could last during the three months of training, avoiding the only space on the Sagan that offered him true sanctuary.

"I'm in," Francis finally said as visions of gigantic trees and a menagerie of myth-like animals pulled him through his moments of anxiety. "I'm in."

Chapter 4

Francis owned little besides seven books, a set of rosary beads from his first communion, a modest assortment of clothes and a sword, the latter an heirloom passed down through over ten generations of Burns's. The sword never served in war, nor was it part of a military uniform worn by a service man or woman who died centuries earlier. Yet, the sword was well known and once heralded around the world. Standing in his room, his possessions in a large, navy duffle bag, Francis lifted the sword and fingered the etchings along the flat of its blade.

"*Glamdring,*" Francis whispered as his fingertips traced along the Elvish script noting the sword's name. "The Foe Hammer." The blade was long, a combined 1.3 meters of hilt and blade, the blade itself forged of high-carbon steel. Francis had read the collected works of J.R.R. Tolkien and watched the *Lord of the Rings* movies endlessly, those crafted under the guidance of Peter Jackson. The sword was designed after the movie's depiction of it, the very sword carried by the wizard Gandalf. "Made for the goblin wars," Francis said as his mind strayed to his remembrance of the scene in Tolkien's *The Hobbit* when Elrond spoke of the blade's history. Eyes closed, Francis recalled the very words Tolkien wrote pertaining to the ancient weapon, which '*the King of Gondolin* once wore.' Warmed by the memory, Francis sheathed the sword before enclosing it within the now stuffed duffle bag; it took a bit of convincing to get the zipper to work. Finally packed, Francis walked about the room checking over every centimeter to ensure he missed none of his possessions. It would be another twenty minutes of checking before he would leave the room behind for the last time.

Shouldering his duffle bag, which weighed more than 100 pounds, Francis walked through the Sagan's labyrinth of passageways, ever mindful of the air vents overhead, which he perceived as spewing mercury-laced air into the ship's atmosphere.

Only have to put up with those for a few more months, Francis thought as he tried to keep his face from the path of the warm air bellowing from the vents. The fear he would contract illness from the air and then pass it on to others, wiping out the Sagan's crew, would end the day he left the ship behind, or so Francis hoped.

Francis's trek through the Sagan entailed a myriad of turns and going up and down endless staircases. With space equivalent to three Nimitz-class aircraft carriers, it took a great deal of effort to travel from his previous quarters to the flight deck, which was literally on the other side of the ship. Forty minutes of walking, carrying the heavy duffle bag, finally brought Francis to the deck where thirty or so deck hands ambled around securing pallets of munitions, aluminum ductwork, scaffolding, copper pipes, and spools of wire. The flurry of activity reminded Francis of video footage of ants constructing a new colony: efficient, organized and tireless. The scene soon faded from his view as he gazed upon the fighter craft.

Eight in all, the design of the planes reminded Francis of those flown in some of his favorite classic movies like *Top Gun*, *The Final Countdown* and *Independence Day*. Yet, the coloring, glossy white with red striping, reminded Francis of something entirely different.

"Vipers," Francis said while now motionless. With his mind spinning visions of the triangular fighter craft chasing down Cylons, the Battlestar Galactica ever in the background, Francis stared longingly at the aircraft. "Frak me," he whispered as he maneuvered around the stains on the deck, ever fearful of chemical contamination, inching towards the closest fighter. A blend of aromas, mostly oil and torched metal, enveloped Francis as he came within reach of the fighter. He stretched out his hand to touch the ship's hull, but fear halted his reach. *What if the hulls, long exposed to spaceflight, were radioactive? Would touching the fighter contaminate him? Would Francis then go on to contaminate Humanity?* For ten minutes Francis stood there without moving, wondering if he had already crossed the line of no return.

"Professor?" a voice from behind him asked. "Professor, are you all right?" Slowly Francis turned and looked behind. There stood a woman with shoulder length black hair and deep, brown eyes that warmed Francis's spirit. He smiled.

"Are you finished?" the woman asked, which snapped Francis back to reality. "I'm Captain Rebecca Sanford," she announced as she extended her hand. He clasped the hand while shaking off the last bits of his delirium.

"Captain. I'm Francis Burns…"

"Burns, I know. Colonel Leary sent me to greet you and show you around. You want to take a closer look at the fighter?"

"Is it okay to touch it?" Francis asked, suddenly overwhelmed once more with fear of touching the plane.

"As long as you stay clear of her guns, you'll be fine, Professor," she said as she moved off. "Come with me." He followed without question while still shouldering his duffle bag. Rebecca led him to a nearby fighter whose canopy was open. She patted the plane on its underbelly as she walked underneath. "How are you, old girl?" Rebecca asked the fighter. "Here's my bird, Professor, an F15-E Strike Eagle, retrofitted for space-flight. The best of the best." Francis walked under the plane and reached out to touch the fighter's paneling. His hand stopped centimeters shy of making contact.

"For crying out loud," Rebecca said as she pushed his hand onto the fighter. "It won't bite you." The metal was cold and textured, textured by tiny dents attained from collisions with miniscule space debris that pummeled the fighter during every flight.

"It's not radioactive?" Francis asked as his con-tamination fears screamed at him.

"Not in any way, Professor. Each fighter is scanned after reentering the lower flight deck. Fighters showing any positive signs of contamination are cleaned before they're allowed back in this hanger. No worries," she said as she examined the landing gear. Francis, meanwhile, felt along the fighter's side.

"How fast does she fly?" he asked, Francis's eyes fixed on the fighter's body panels.

"Fast enough, Professor. Do you want to check out the cockpit?" Francis snapped his head towards Re-becca and nodded. *Was he going to be a Viper pilot?*

"Most definitely," he replied before following Rebecca to the narrow ladders, which reached up to the fighter's cockpit. While Rebecca walked to the rear ladder, Francis grabbed onto the rungs of the forward one.

"Nope, you're back here, Professor," Rebecca said while extending her arm to point at the rear seat in the cockpit. Disappointed, Francis climbed up the other ladder, checking for blood, oil or other contagions as he proceeded upwards. He then climbed into the cramped space, the respective chair encircled by monitors, pow-ered-down indicator lights and a keyboard. Rebecca was up the ladder and peering in just as Francis began his survey of his space.

"You'll serve as my REO as we fly down to Earth's surface.

"REO?" Francis asked.

"It means Radio Electronics Officer."

"Oh. On Battlestar Galactica the position is called 'E.C.O.,' short for Electronics Countermeasures Officer," Francis said as he looked over the control panels that would be at his control. Rebecca just shook her head and contemplated her new flight partner.

"Look, Professor, nobody is looking for you to do any flying. You'll just be along for the ride. Under-stood?"

"Understood. Will I at least get some basic train-ing in the safety features?" He asked, ever hopeful.

"Very basic training, Professor Burns."

"My name is Francis, Captain Sanford," he re-plied, his stern eyes letting Rebecca know there was no option in that regard.

"Fair enough," she said. "You can call me Frost. That's my call sign." Francis suddenly smiled.

"Do I get a call sign?" he asked enthusiastically. She shook her head.

"Civilians," Rebecca said as she climbed down the ladder.

***

After his exposure to the cockpit, Rebecca led Francis to the pilot quarters. Placing his duffle bag on his assigned bunk, Francis made a dash for the bathroom to wash his hands to cleanse away the germs and chemical compounds he envisioned having touched while in the cockpit. Twenty minutes later, he emerged from the bathroom.

"You ready?" Rebecca asked, clearly frustrated at the loss of time.

"I'm all set, Frost."

"Good, then follow me." She led Francis through a series of corridors to a well-sealed chamber from which popping noises emanated. They entered what was one of two firing ranges on the ship. At the moment, three other pilots were target practicing. Each in turn eyed Francis with seeming contempt.

Rebecca and Francis walked to the end of the range where a pistol rested on a table; the weapon was in pieces.

"You want to fly with me, you gotta be able to shoot, because I need to know you have my back and the back of my pilots. Understood?" she asked. Her posture and tone were as cold as the gazes of the other pilots. Francis simply nodded while he thought of the residue that firearms emitted with every discharge.

"I'm gonna teach you to assemble, disassemble, clean, load and fire a pistol," she said as she stood up to the firing line. First putting on earphones, Rebecca quickly assembled the 9mm pistol, aimed and fired at the distant target, her round striking the target's outline of a human head and torso between the eyes. Without a word, she quickly disassembled the weapon, placing all its components back on the table where she found them. "Any questions?"

"No," Francis replied. He walked up to the line and picked up a set of earphones. After looking at the earphones in disgust, he returned them to the table after which he assembled the pistol quicker than Rebecca had. Francis then loaded the weapon and fired four rapid shots at the target before disassembling the weapon and turning back to his would-be instructor. Each of his shots struck the target equidistant from Rebecca's leaving the bullet holes to look like a *five* on a die. "OORAH!" Francis exclaimed while reminiscing about the instruction he learned from his friend's father, a Marine, more than ten years earlier.

"Any questions?" Francis asked in return.

"Why me?" Rebecca asked herself as Francis walked away to wash off the invisible gun residue on his hands and all the contagions he envisioned the residue contained.

Chapter 5

Bunked in a remote part of the ship, Francis and nineteen other crewmen hunkered down for the night after a day of drills, which included maneuvering in zero gravity, administering field dressings, and operating aircraft systems. The latter instruction provided Francis with some much needed alone time. Tucked into the rear seat of the F-15E Strike Eagle, Francis ran through the onboard programming while fighting off concerns of toxic fumes he envisioned spewing out from the overhead air vents. In 'hunt and peck' fashion, Francis hammered at the REO keyboard operating targeting, scanning and navigation software. After three hours, his eyes tired, Francis retired to his bunk where sleep overwhelmed him quickly. It was the first sound sleep Francis had in days.

In the morning, Francis woke refreshed. After a quick breakfast of coffee and toast in the mess, he headed back toward the flight deck where another day of flight training awaited.

"Not so fast, Francis," a woman called out as he neared his fighter. "Dad needs you at a meeting, ASAP," the woman said as she emerged from an adjacent hallway. Standing a few centimeters shorter, the dark-brown haired woman was one of the few individuals on the ship whose presence eased Francis's anxiety: his cousin Kathleen Leary.

"I think I've had my fill of meetings, Kathleen," Francis said as he ran his fingers along the wing of his fighter. Kathleen stood and watched her cousin as he carefully examined the ship's lines, inspecting every centimeter.

"Did you name it yet?" she asked.

"Ert. Its name is Ert."

"Why the hell would you name…"

Francis pointed to the nearest vertical stabilizer, emblazoned with the ship's id: ERT 332.

"Ah," Kathleen said, nodding in understanding. "Come on, Dad wants you to listen in on to some political blowhards trying to BS the governor." Francis turned and smirked.

"You didn't tell me there'd be entertainment."

***

The room Francis sat in was cold, void of any carpeting or chair cushioning. It looked like a steel box populated by gray, steel folding chairs, the room's only warmth provided by the three oak tables set in the center arranged like a giant, capital 'T.' Governor Counts, Commander Southern and Colonel Leary sat side by side at the end table, which was perpendicular to the other two. All three of the Sagan's leaders looked worn, as if they spent the last week in non-stop meetings with no sleep. The surrounding officers and politicians appeared no more energized as each grabbed chairs as close to the senior officers as possible, which amused Francis to no end. For his part, Francis selected a seat at the opposite end of the collected tables, patiently checking out his chair and the table surface for chemicals, blood or questionable stains he feared might be a virulent contagion. Rebecca Sanford entered the conference room just in time to see Francis's dance about his chair.

"Did you lose something?" she asked, sitting in the chair directly opposite Francis. He looked up at her and stood. *How could he explain his obsessive thoughts of contamination or the rituals he employed to assuage those thoughts?*

"No," Francis replied as he glanced around one last time before taking his seat and setting his clipboard on the table. Kathleen showed up seconds later, taking a seat next to Francis.

"One big happy gathering," Kathleen said as she spread out a number of reports, several pens and a legal pad on the table space before her.

"Surprised to see you here, Lieutenant," Rebecca said as she looked at a map Kathleen placed on top of her reports.

"You shouldn't be, Sir," Kathleen replied. "We Seabees are always the first on the ground."

"Order!" the governor exclaimed drawing everyone's attention while simultaneously ending all discussions. Clad in a gray suit, the governor stood out from military personnel who wore a standard short-sleeved khaki shirt with forest green or khaki colored trousers; the latter for Marine personnel, the former for naval officers. The other politicos, meanwhile, wore suits as well, mostly in a variety of dark blue hues.

Francis, neither a politician nor military personnel, enjoyed some latitude with his clothing. As usual, he wore khaki pants, a white, long-sleeved shirt and a pair of brown shoes that resembled moccasins. Francis hated that he stood out, but the familiar dress helped ease his anxiety.

"All right," the commander said drawing everyone's attention. "This morning, we launched a probe towards Earth. It should reach the planet's orbit within twenty days… at which time we'll be able to scan the surface and receive high-res images. Those images along with a series of scans should provide us with an idea of what awaits us." The room remained silent in the wake of her words, save for the sound of pen on paper as several officers wrote down notes. The commander flipped over a sheet of paper placed in front of her before continuing.

"An hour ago, the probe passed Mars and conducted a scan of the planet's surface, focusing on the Terradome erected in the years just prior to the Sagan's launch. It was to be the first terraforming operation on the red planet, but it appears that construction ended after the superstructure was completed." Copies of a surveillance photo, taken by the probe, were passed around the table. After looking over one of the copies, Frost moved to hand it over to Francis. After reaching out his hand, Francis pulled back, his eyes fixed on a brown stain on the edge of the photo. Kathleen reached over and grabbed the photo with her left hand while patting her cousin's hand with her right. She showed the image to Francis before looking it over herself and passing it on.

"Commander? Wasn't the superstructure completed just before the Sagan's launch?" one of the naval officers asked; all eyes remained fixed on Commander Southern.

"It was," she replied. "It appears no additional progress was made. What's more, the probe detected no transmissions from Mars. The Sagan itself will be in Mars's orbit in three weeks, and a plan is underway to investigate the Terradome. However, our expectations are low with regards to finding settlements or answers to what happened on Mars or Earth." Again, a number of the gathered officers jotted down notes while the remainder of the room's occupants kept their focus on the commander.

"Governor?"

"Thank you, Commander," Governor Counts said as he glanced around at his constituents. "The Sagan received a transmission from the congressional delegation on Maximus. Should we find no settlements remaining on Earth, they've implemented a plan to restore the United States. For now and always, adherence to the Constitution remains. Our nation will carry on." Nods from the gathered officers sparked fervor through the throng. Governor Counts looked on, comforted by the patriots. "Order," the governor said, tapping his fist twice on the table after doing so. Every head snapped to his call. "At issue will be the reconstruction of the three branches, if indeed the government is no more. A plan is already set for such a contingency... plans that call for elections within the year." Nods from several of the gathered and murmurs of agreement passed for seconds. Governor Counts, meanwhile, looked for any dissent, which soon came from the Sagan's Senator and House rep and their aides.

"Governor, will we have no say in the efforts to restore Constitutional authority?" Representative Maria Harding asked?"

"As we will be the only representatives on Earth, we should determine the course of action," Senator Antonio Torres interjected before the governor could answer. Every civilian present, except for Francis, nodded at their representatives' words.

"I have not received any specifics regarding the plan," Governor Counts said, his voice quieting the room for at least the moment. "I'm sure that the final course set for reestablishing government..."

"Will the military be placed in charge?" Senator Torres asked. Governor Counts snapped his head towards the Congressman. Torres immediately looked down at the table in deference. "My apologies, Governor Counts."

"As I was saying," the governor said shifting his gaze to the others around the tables. "I know of no specifics, but I already made clear the fact that the Sagan's passengers, military and civilian, would share equally in the decision making."

"And the military would not take over," Commander Southern added. "I assure you of that." The officers nodded in agreement.

"You haven't really assured us of anything, Commander," Representative Harding said. "Neither you nor the Governor seem willing to address…"

The slamming of a fist on one of the tables turned everyone's attention toward Francis whose eyes seemed focused on the tabletop.

"Are you all mad?" Francis asked as he lifted his head. "Are you all truly that daft?" He gazed at the others who stared back, like mischievous children caught unaware. "Three hundred years without contact? I think it's likely that Humanity is extinct, at least as far as Earth is concerned. Think about it! Generations of animal species have occupied Earth… without any human interference. These animals would look upon any landing party as a mere curiosity, nothing more. Worse off, new apex predators will have filled the void left by our ancestors. Those species will see us as a threat, and they will attack in little time." Francis took a moment to scan those around the tables, his eyes finally resting on the two members of Congress present.

"You two are so fixated on getting your flags to the top of the mountain that you're likely to rush efforts… have us recklessly venture forth. What if whatever contagion or creature or disaster that killed off Humanity is still there, still virulent? Do you two want to be the first to set foot on the planet?" Neither representative spoke. They simply glared at Francis until his eyes darkened, his forehead now furrowed in anger. The representatives turned away from Francis as did everyone who met his anger. "I didn't think so."

"Professor Burns?" Commander Southern asked, clearly amused at the dressing down the professor just delivered; smirks from Colonel Leary and Governor Counts assured the amusement was universal. "What would you have us do?"

"We land at Fort Niagara as planned," Francis replied as he looked at his hand, now reddened by contact with the table. Frost watched as Francis's attention shifted between his hand and the spot on the table where her REO's fist hit. Francis retracted his hand and looked over every centimeter of it as if in search of a bruise, dirt or something else entirely.

"Professor, you were saying?" Commander Southern asked. Francis did not look up.

"Land at the fort, with a small contingent of Marines and scientists," Francis replied, his eyes cast down towards his hand, which he was now rubbing against his shirt. "We keep on our flight gear while we test the air and water. Then, if everything checks out, we build up the fort's defensive embankments and installations and move on from there." Francis then stood up and looked towards the head table.

"Governor, Commander, Colonel," Francis said, bowing towards the respective leaders in turn. He then turned and left the room in search of the nearest restroom.

Chapter 6

"So this is the person you picked to guide us?" Commander Southern said as she poured whiskey into three glasses, handing one quickly to Colonel Leary who smirked before taking a drink.

"You need to trust me on this, Taryn," Paul said as he sat in one of the felt-covered recliners in the commander's quarters. "Nobody on the ship knows more about the Niagara Frontier than Francis, and we desperately need that intel."

"And the thing with his hands?" Taryn asked as she set one of the other glasses on an end table between two empty chairs before sitting and sipping from the remaining glass of whiskey. Paul took an additional swig before responding.

"He has his OCD in check. Francis has gotten a bit stronger every day since moving to the barracks. I have no doubt he'll serve us well in the field."

"He seemed quite rattled in the meeting, Colonel," the governor said. Standing on the far side of the room, staring out the quarter's solitary window at the sun, Clarence contemplated the questions of the Congressional representatives as well as the concerns and plans of the Sagan's senior officers. "My God... I'll never tire of this view." The governor then turned and walked to the remaining chair and sat before lifting the last glass of liquor. "To coming adventures," Clarence said as the three leaders lifted their glasses in a toast and drained every ounce of whiskey.

"He won't fail us," Paul said after moments of silence passed. "I promise you that."

"Relax, Paul," Clarence said as he set down his now empty glass. "I'm just yanking your chain. Frankly, I quite enjoyed watching your nephew put the representatives in their place. It's something they've had coming for a long time, something the rest of us could not do without making an already tense situation worse."

"While I'm not as enthusiastic as the governor here, it was quite refreshing," Taryn commented as the three chuckled for several moments. "With all seriousness... Professor Burns's assessment is spot on. We have no way of knowing what we're walking into," Taryn said as she stood up and walked over to the window. "To think that we left Earth overpopulated... and now we may be all that's left." The commander's gaze gravitated to a soft glow set against the backdrop of stars, planets and nebulae. "Earth," she whispered as she contemplated resettlement options. "Governor Counts?" she asked aloud, suddenly quite formal, which the others noticed immediately. She turned to face the governor and colonel, her outline illuminated by rays of the sun.

"Yes, Commander?" Governor Counts asked, standing up and turning towards where Commander Southern stood.

"I understand you have a job to do, but right now..."

"Understood, Commander," Clarence said before nodding. "I'll keep the reps out of your hair, though I may need to borrow a cell in the brig from time to time." He smiled at the commander before moving to the door, patting Colonel Leary on the back as he passed. "Let me know if you need me," the governor said before exiting the room.

"That went better than expected," Taryn said as she returned to her seat. "I wouldn't want to trade places with Clarence, having to restart the government while balancing the egos of politicians here and on Maximus."

"I wonder how we'll fit into the new scheme of things?" Paul asked as he turned to look towards the window. "The battle for equal representation all over again," he said as he then looked towards Taryn. "Any word from Naval command?"

"Just an addendum to our previous orders. We've been tasked with establishing a moon base as soon possible."

"All right then. After landing on Earth, testing the environment for toxins, building a settlement and transporting the bulk of the crew to the planet's surface, I'll get right on that," Paul said; they both chuckled at the colonel's jest.

"You're taking it better than I did, Paul. I got a little pissed and had some choice words for the admiral. Frankly, I don't think he's calling the shots anymore. I'd guess that the Congressional delegates on Maximus are already setting up a new government. Bloody politics, which will likely spill over into the Sagan, at least if Senator Torres has his way."

"Do you think the governor will be able to keep the peace between the Sagan and Maximus delegations?" Paul asked before getting up, filling his glass once more and taking another sip.

"Harding and Torres won't push Clarence too far; they know we support the governor, not that Clarence needs any help."

"And what if Maximus sends new orders, orders given by a new president and Congress?" Colonel Leary's question pulled at the heart of their dilemma.

"We are required to answer to Maximus Prime as long as we are in transit, but once we land…" Colonel Leary smiled as he recognized what the commander and governor had already determined.

"If there is nobody left on the planet, we become the Earth-based representatives of the United States."

"And Maximus Prime no longer pulls the strings," Taryn added before leaning back in her chair and sighing."

"You okay, Commander?" Paul asked. An accomplished translator of Commander Southern's expressions and mannerisms, he knew something weighed heavily on her.

"What if we've come all this way only to be forced to head back to Maximus?" Paul had no answer. "At least we'll have a few more answers when we land at Mars," Taryn said. She then rose and walked to the table where the whiskey bottle rested. Pouring another glass, she downed the liquid in a gulp before turning to Paul. "I want a full detachment of Marines on this and half the fighter squadron for support. Understood?" Paul nodded before standing and walking towards the room's exit.

"I want Francis in on this mission, too, Colonel. I want him tested before the mission to Earth." The colonel stopped in his tracks.

"I understand, Commander," Colonel Leary replied, turning his head back, a smirk on his face. "And when he shows his worth, you owe me a bottle and a vacation." Without another word, Paul exited and headed for his quarters for some desperately needed sleep. Taryn, meanwhile, stood and walked to the window.

Her gaze reached beyond the star Earth circled, towards blue, lavender and crimson hues she envisioned supported life yet discovered.

"And all the science I don't understand," Taryn sang, her melodic voice quietly soaring through verse immemorial: Elton John's *Rocket Man*. "It's just my job five days a week…"

"Bridge to commanding officer," a voice called out over the intercom.

"Go ahead," Taryn replied in her command voice, her longing for exploration falling to the shadows.

"We've detected a faint transmission emanating from the orbit of Mars."

"I'm on my way," the commander replied as she left her quarters and dreams behind."

***

Francis hated mornings. His old routine was simple enough: a cup of coffee while reading a chapter of a book followed by a shower. In the barracks, now a quasi-member of the military, he bunked with others and used a public shower, the latter sending Francis into a tailspin as he fretted over the limitless contaminates his mind conjured. Francis entered the showers every morning at 0500, always the first to arrive. Arriving at the locker room, he stripped off his clothes and placed them in the same locker, but only after he thoroughly checked to see that the locker itself was clean. As for his clothes, he folded them in peculiar folds, arranging the pile to make it easy to determine if someone touched the clothes while he was in the showers.

His procession to the showers entailed an intricate dance around scattered drains, Francis's eyes ever on the lookout for hair, bandages or clothing left by previous bathers. Then, after finding one of the central showers and inspecting its head and lever, Francis washed while holding onto his bottles of shampoo and body wash ever fearful of germs inhabiting the shelves reserved for cleansers, razors and other personal items. Francis generally finished just as the rest of the Marines and sailors awoke and started straggling into the showers, which required Francis to navigate a circuitous route to his locker all the while avoiding any contact with his shipmates. Any contact with another sent Francis back to the showers to start over with a fresh shower. Once clothed, Francis headed to the mess for oatmeal and coffee before morning maneuvers that commenced at 0630. In the days after Francis's outburst at the meeting, fewer military personnel seemed happy with the professor's presence. Francis heard several of the officers refer to him as "Civy," which only increased his dread of participating.

"Just a little longer," Francis muttered to himself often as the prospect of setting foot on Earth helped ease the anxiety that seemed to build while in maneuvers. Weeks after his outburst in the meeting, as Master Sergeant Karen Zavack scheduled hand-to-hand combat tactics for an entire week, even the thought of Earth failed to assuage Francis's fears on day one of the exercises.

"Line up!" one of the gunnery sergeants commanded as the twenty Marines Francis trained with filed into the training facility. They rapidly formed a long line and stood at attention with eyes fixed on the master sergeant. Nearly as tall as Francis, Master Sergeant Zavack likewise towered over most of those present. Donning a black tank top and MMA fighting shorts, the barefoot Zavack stood in stark contrast to Francis and the others, all of whom wore padded green bodysuits, sparring helmets and fighting gloves. Whispers of Zavack's fighting prowess reached Francis days before, but rumor fell aside to his own observations; her well-toned arms, abs, and calves reminded Francis of the marble statues that adorned the ancient Greek and Roman sites he'd lectured about. Zavack's long brown hair, with highlights that glistened like threads of gold, moved Francis to think of Aphrodite. Yet, the sergeant's movements, both graceful and stately, turned Francis's memory to Athena, Goddess of Righteous Battle.

"Good morning, grunts!" Master Sergeant Zavack shouted after assuming an at ease posture in front of the assembly. Her voice woke Francis from his memories.

"Morning, Master Sergeant!" the gathered Marines replied with equal vigor; Francis remained silent.

"You'll all be engaging in close quarters combat tactics this week. We'll start with hand to hand sparring and move on to weapons by…"

"Attention on deck!" yelled one of the nearby gunnery sergeants. Everyone, Francis included, stood at attention awaiting the officer that entered the facility. Seconds later, Captain Sanford marched into view before stopping five meters from the Marines.

"Master Sergeant, a moment," Rebecca Sanford said before distancing herself from the ears of the others; Master Sergeant Zavack followed quickly. Francis watched as Sanford and Zavack spoke, Master Sergeant Zavack nodding repeatedly before saluting the captain and returning to her position before Francis and the others.

"Break up into your squads," Zavack commanded. "Your squad leaders will then partner you up for sparring. Move!" The Marines wasted no time moving to separate corners of the facility. Francis watched as the squads left him behind, alone with the master sergeant. "So you're our esteemed guide," Zavack said as she approached Francis. Tying her hair back into a ponytail, she then proceeded to look at Francis from head to toe, just as he assessed her. "You'll be sparring with me, professor. Follow me." Francis did as instructed and followed Zavack to the center mat; both noticed the multiple glances from the others.

"If you're going to stand with us, you'll need to fight with us, Professor," Zavack said as she turned to face her impromptu student. Francis nodded in reply, but his concentration was elsewhere. Karen Zavack's hazel eyes were a stark contrast to any he ever saw. One moment they appeared as a deep brown, warm and strong. The next her eyes looked like emeralds, brilliant and bold.

"Are you all right, Professor?"

"Sorry," he replied realizing he remained silent for almost a minute. "Your eyes are quite hypnotic, Master Sergeant."

"Flattery will get you nowhere, Professor." Francis smiled.

"It's not flattery, Master Sergeant. It's merely an observation, as is the fact that I see steel in your eyes." Karen Zavack quickly noticed the serious tone in Francis's voice. "This battle will be over in a minute." Francis suddenly took a fighter's stance, fists raised.

"So, you believe you'll take me down in a minute?" she asked as she too assumed a fighting posture.

"Hardly, Master Sergeant. I fully expect that I'll be bruised and breathless and collapsed at your feet in less than sixty seconds." Without another word, the two began their contest while all others in the facility watched. Both launched tentative swings to gauge the defensive preferences of the other. After ten seconds, the battle fully commenced. Francis spent the majority of the time on the defensive, and Master Sergeant Zavack remained impressed with the professor's ability to deflect her fists. Yet, after one of Francis's attacks lightly connected with her shoulder, the reality of Francis's ability sunk in. His effort was all in. Zavack smiled at the realization that this man, a civilian, saw beyond gender. Her smile then vanished, replaced by the stern grimace of a Marine entering battle. The Marine released a swarm of fist blows, which Francis deflected away from his face and torso. Soon the combatants seemed in rhythm at which point Francis knew it was over; she had his timing.

Master Sergeant dropped and kicked Francis's legs from under him. Before Francis regained his senses, Zavack was standing over him, her foot now resting on his throat.

"Fifty-one seconds, almost a minute," Zavack said before extending a hand to the exhausted professor. He gratefully accepted her help in standing. "How did you learn to fight so well?" she asked as she held him upright while his breathing slowed.

"My dad got me a book on karate when I was a kid."

"You got that from a book?" she asked amidst a series of chuckles. "Must have been one hell of a book?"

"It was, Master Sergeant." At that point they realized the full attention of the facility was on them.

"What are you grunts staring at? Start sparring or your next!" The other Marines immediately started their matches.

"Why don't you hit the showers, Professor," Master Sergeant Zavack then said to Francis. "You've earned a break." He nodded and turned towards the exit when he noticed Frost looking on. She smiled and nodded at Francis before exiting.

***

After showering, Francis went to his locker and put on a fresh set of trousers and a clean shirt. Still exhausted, he inspected the nearby benches before sitting at which time he pulled a journal out of his bag and scribbled down some notes.

"Quite a feat you pulled out there," Frost said as she sat next to Francis.

"I'm sure you enjoyed watching me get my ass kicked about," he replied never turning away from his journal.

"Not true, Francis." She said as she reached into his bag. He stopped writing and watched her pull an object out of the bag.

"Hey!"

"What the hell is this?" she asked as she examined the stuffed animal, a fist-sized turkey, she removed.

"It's a turkey."

"No shit, Sherlock," she replied. "Wow, this thing's certainly seen better days."

"Be careful with that," he said as he pulled it from her grasp. Covered with a patchwork of red and tan felt, the ragged turkey looked a few stitches away from falling apart. "This has been in my family for hundreds of years."

"Wait a minute. You recoil from every stain you see, yet you carry around that disgusting piece of stuffing?"

"Don't mess with Turkey," he said before smirking at his tormentor.

"What the hell do you do with it?"

"Every Thanksgiving we tie it to a ceiling fan and let it fly."

"Why?" Her question caught him off guard. He truly never considered the purpose of Turkey's yearly flight.

"It's tradition," he finally replied before donning a fresh pair of socks.

"You were great out there today, Francis." Her use of his given name brought a smile to his face. "You gave it your all."

"I didn't have much choice, did I," he replied as he slipped on his shoes. "Another test, right?"

"I'm the one who had no choice, Francis. We're dependent on you for a great deal, which means we need you ready for the tests yet to come."

"And fighting a skilled Marine? What does that test?" He now stared at Frost with heated eyes.

"It tests whether or not you would accept any of us as an equal."

"Did I pass?"

"Well, you didn't fail," she replied before smiling wryly at her copilot. They both broke into laughter, the tension gone. "Come on, let's get going," she said as she stood and marched towards the nearest exit.

"Where to now?" She turned and smiled before responding.

"Now, my dear copilot, we fly."

Chapter 7

"Commander on deck!" an ensign exclaimed as Taryn entered the bridge.

"As you were," she replied. Commander Southern's footfalls echoed through the room as she marched towards First Officer Lorin. "Report!" Taryn exclaimed as she halted in front of her chair.

"The com system picked up an encoded transmission emanating from the orbit of Mars. We're processing it through the descrambler, but we've not been able to crack the code as yet." Lorin, a stellar pilot, in time became the most accomplished administrator on the Sagan. His adeptness at cutting to the heart of matters while also leading with integrity and evenhandedness made him the perfect candidate for her First Officer. Taryn knew she would never need to verify the captain's reports.

"How the hell did the probe miss it?" Taryn asked in a whisper, a question she knew was pointless at this moment. "Let me hear it," Taryn said as she sat and eased back into her chair, the center location on the bridge around which all action stations were positioned. The com officer punched at his keyboard until a series of beeps and static cried out over the speakers.

"Commander, none of our ciphers have been able to decode the transmission," the com officer said as he turned to face Taryn. The commander never turned towards him, her eyes remaining fixed on the lights of distant planets visible through the Sagan's bridge windows. For long moments, Taryn just listened to the transmission without reacting to any sound or movement by the crew.

"Commander? Commander Southern?" Captain Lorin asked as all stared at their commanding officer. Still Taryn remained silent, her attention fixated on the series of sharp beeps that pierced through the bridge air.

"Com, reply to the same frequency with the code 'Omega 113' and play any response over the bridge loudspeaker." The com officer turned his gaze back to his communications equipment. Taryn, meanwhile, leaned back in her chair, her eyes ever focused beyond the stars and on the dot of red light she knew to be Mars. Moments passed as the com officer tapped at his keyboard, long moments where only the hollow echo of depressed keys sounded. The silence suddenly ended, annihilated by a series of ear-shattering beeps after which three separate amber lights positioned around the deck pulsated with obnoxious exuberance: one above the com officer's station, one above the helmsman's station and the last above the commander's chair.

"Red Alert!" a chilling computer voice exclaimed through the wireless. "Red Alert! All personnel to action stations! Red Alert!" The com officer, after a nod from Commander Southern, repeated the code over the wireless as the bridge crew hurried about in well rehearsed motions.

"Contact Colonel Leary, the governor and our Congressional delegates; have them meet me in my quarters immediately," Taryn said as she stood and turned to face Captain Lorin.

"And if the delegates refuse?" Lorin asked, his face ever dispassionate.

"I need them alive, but you can lock them in irons if they resist," Taryn replied. Then after flashing a smile, the commander turned and exited the bridge.

***

The blaring alarms proved more than enough to convince the Sagan's Congressional delegation to hurry along to the commander's quarters, which left Captain Lorin a bit disappointed. Both nearing 40, Representative Harding was the elder by a few years. Her long brown hair, offset by locks of white, matched her tired, brown eyes. Senator Torres, meanwhile, was bald save for the black goatee he'd donned for over a decade. His cyan blue eyes, though youthful and vibrant, showed signs of stress as if the senator failed to get a good night's rest in several days. Neither showed the tenacity constituents had grown accustomed to, which immediately told Captain Lorin the representatives understood what the alarms and code 'Omega 113' meant.

Captain Lorin and the representatives found the Sagan's governor as well as Commander Southern and Colonel Leary standing at the room's main console. After a quick nod from the commander, Captain Lorin departed leaving the leaders to contend with what Captain Lorin assumed was the first of many crises to come.

"Welcome," Commander Southern said as she approached the representatives with her hand extended. After an exchange of nods and handshakes among those gathered, Taryn directed everyone back over to the console. "As our resident Federal authorities, I would ask that you enter your codes first." Without more than a nod, Senator Torres approached the console and positioned his head within centimeters of the camera mounted on top of the console.

"Recognize Senator Antonio Albert Torres, Sagan District, code Omega 113 authorized," the senator said after which an azure light emanated from the camera and scanned his left retina.

"Authorization verified," a droll voice replied via the computer's speaker system. The computer appeared not the least bit excited or agitated by the alerts, which bothered every human in the room. After the response, the remaining political and military leaders similarly input their information ending with the commander, whose ultimate responsibility was to activate the 'Omega 113' program.

"Computer, enable program Omega 113, authorization Delta-Zulu 5."

"Program enabled, standby," replied the computer. The leaders took seats positioned around the console while the computer went through a series of packet downloads. Then, after minutes passed, an image appeared: three women and one man sitting at a table. The Sagan's leaders instantly recognized one of the women in the image for she was the President of the United States at the time of the Sagan's launch centuries earlier.

"Greetings to you all as the Sagan enters the final leg of its journey home," the president said. Her coal-black, curly hair and youthful visage made the president seem out of place amongst the others, but history itself shattered that illusion. Only the second female president of the United States, she managed an expansion of NASA while also instituting the first budget surpluses in fifteen years all while orchestrating peace treaties that ended three separate conflicts around the world.

"I am President Sandra O'Sullivan and am joined by Chief Justice Laura Wilcox, Senate Majority

Leader Francisco Lorenza and Speaker of the House, Jennifer Carlito. On behalf of the citizens of the United States, I congratulate the Sagan's crew for their resolve and accomplishments. I only wish I could be there to see your return. I only wish someone could be there to welcome you home.

"This beacon was meant as a precaution. Yet, as the Sagan is now well within earshot of any number of Earth-based communications networks, it seems our fears proved all too true. Regardless of the tragedy that unfolded, Humanity's time on Earth has ended." The president's words, while not totally unexpected, pulled at everyone's heart. "As the remaining members of our nation, a great burden now rests upon your shoulders. Should you land on Earth and find no remnants of the United States, it will be up to you to reestablish our nation. To the Sagan's governor, by the authority of Congress, you are hereby elevated to the rank of President of the United States. Your term shall run from the day you receive this message until the end of the next full election cycle." The governor's elevation elated Commander Southern and Colonel Leary; Representatives Torres and Harding were clearly not so enthused. President O'Sullivan's voice cutoff any debate.

"The Sagan's Federal representatives likewise are elevated to the positions of Senate Majority Leader and Speaker of the House and tasked with conferring with the delegates from Maximus Prime to ensure that the Constitution remains the guiding principle for our people. You and the Maximus Prime representatives are additionally tasked with arranging for fifty applicants to the Supreme Court, from which the president will consider seven for nomination. This will set the basis for our Nation's rebirth. I wish there was more we could do for you. Please know that we are with you in spirit and wish you all success in your endeavors for you are the only hope for the United States and Humanity itself. God bless you, and may God bless the United States."

"This is unconscionable!" Representative Harding exclaimed as the image of President O'Sullivan vanished from the console's screen. She has no right..."

Clarence rose from his chair and walked to the window whereupon he gazed out at the distant stars within view. Senator Torres stood and joined in with Harding's protest, but Taryn and Paul blocked those arguments out. After moments of remaining silent, Taryn stood and approached Clarence. Once standing within the governor's peripheral vision, Taryn stopped and saluted.

"Commander Taryn Southern, reporting for duty... Mr. President. What are your orders?" Colonel Leary likewise stood and saluted the new president as Clarence turned towards the commander.

"Commander, you have a lot to do in the coming weeks," Clarence said as he turned and saluted the military's top brass. "Perhaps more than any of us, but you are not suited for that task. Well, at least not as a commander. I hereby promote you to the rank of Admiral of the Fleet." Her eyes wide in surprise, Taryn found the president's words a heavy weight.

"Colonel Leary!" Clarence then commanded as he turned to face the Marine. You too will have a lot to tackle as you assume complete command of the Marine Corps. You are promoted to the rank of brigadier general. Make note of you rank changes in the ship's logs and send word to Maximus immediately." The new president then turned to the now silent representatives. "I believe you both have quite a bit to accomplish; I recommend that we meet this evening for supper and plan out a meeting schedule for the week." They nodded their agreement sensing no arguments would work for the moment. President Counts finally turned back to Admiral Southern. "Take us home, Admiral."

"Yes sir," Taryn replied with a quick salute before she reached over to the wall and picked up the nearest phone's receiver. "Commanding officer to the bridge."

"Bridge here, Sir," came the reply in seconds.

"Tell the commander of the air group I want a CAP set ASAP, and set the ship at DEFCON 1."

"Yes Sir," the bridge officer replied. Seconds later a new sequence of alarms sounded throughout the ship.

"All hands to battle stations," sounded the deck officer's voice over the com system. "I repeat, all hands to battle stations."

Chapter 8

A transmission. The whole ship was abuzz about some transmission. Francis didn't care. His movements were set to bring him to the hanger bay and his first trip outside the Sagan's hull.

All crewmembers participated in spacewalks, a part of training whether part of the United States Navy or Marine Corps. Francis, afflicted with OCD since childhood, was not permitted to serve in any military capacity. Hence, Francis was forbidden from participating in military exercises including spacewalks. Things were about to change.

After changing into his assigned flight gear, Francis marched along the ship's corridors oblivious to all but the coming flight and the metallic sound reverberating thru the floors, an echo of combat boots against the metal decking spread throughout the ship. A number of science fiction films and television shows played through Francis's memory as he walked: *Battlestar Galactica*, *Star Trek*, *Aliens*. All science fiction franchises where spaceflight played an integral component of the storyline. Francis was excited by the prospect of joining the ranks of Viper and X-Wing pilots who fought for the freedom and survival of Humanity.

"Identification?" a deep voice asked, jarring Francis from his daydreaming. At the entrance to the flight deck stood three Marine privates along with a corporal, the latter of whom seemed all too eager to hold to protocols.

"Don't make me ask twice," the corporal said; Francis quickly fumbled about with the id tag strapped about his neck on a Star Wars themed lanyard.

"Enough of that, Corporal Tipton," said a voice from beyond the collected Marines. "I'll take it from here." The corporal and privates immediately snapped to attention and saluted as a brick of a man stepped into view. Standing twenty centimeters taller than Francis and with biceps that dwarfed Francis's legs, this Marine, a lieutenant, appeared capable of defending the Sagan's crew all on his own.

"I'm Lieutenant Mario Williams," the man said as he extended his hand out to Francis, which the professor grasped in turn. Francis's kept his grip firm, but his hand still seemed to collapse under the pressure of Lieutenant William's fingers. "As you were!" the lieutenant then said as he looked to the posted Marines. "Follow me if you will, Professor."

Francis did not delay in keeping step with his guide. Moving beyond the entryway, Lieutenant Williams led Francis down a corridor to a doorway that was marked as 'Med Lab'.

"This can't be good," Francis said as they entered. His OCD immediately kicked into high gear, the professor's boot-covered feet quickly becoming his means of holding open doors while his hands took up residence under his armpits.

"Just need to draw some blood, Doc," the lieutenant said; Francis's attention had already wandered. He scanned every surface for signs of blood or other possible contagions. Meanwhile, Lieutenant Williams updated the attending medical staff. "Last one of the day, Petty Officer Fischer," he said as a young woman with long, brown hair and crystal-blue eyes walked out from behind a curtain that surrounded one of the room's beds.

"I was beginning to think you wouldn't show, Lieutenant," she said. She smiled as she picked up a clipboard and approached Francis. "Good morning, Professor," she said as she pulled back the curtain to another bed in the room. "If you'll just take a seat on the end of the bed, we can draw some blood." She seemed friendly enough, pleasant even. Yet, Francis could only grasp the words "draw some blood," which made him stop all movement save for the quivering of his lower lip.

"Professor, are you all right?" she asked as she rested her left hand on Francis's shoulder. He didn't move. The petty officer looked to Lieutenant Williams, who just shrugged in response. "Come on, Professor," she finally said as she escorted him to the bed. Francis sat while his eyes scanned about erratically over the bed, the floor and all surfaces in between. Petty Officer Fischer looked over the file clamped to the clipboard; realization set in. "OCD?" she asked. Francis nodded. "You're in good hands, Francis," she said before setting the clipboard down and gently grasping Francis's upper left arm. "Trust me. Would you please open your jacket and pull out your left arm?" Francis nodded before carefully unzipping the top half of his suit and pulling his left arm out from the sleeve. The petty officer then disappeared into a back room before returning, now accompanied by a man nearly as large as Mario.

"Hi Professor, I'm Chief Petty Officer John Williams, senior medic," the man said; Chief Williams then moved about organizing tools for drawing blood.

"You can call me Ashleigh," Petty Officer Fischer said as she returned and began searching Francis's left arm for a vein from which to draw blood.

Francis nodded, still unable to speak. He carefully watched as the medics donned gloves and opened up a needle. In little time, Ashleigh had one small vial of blood drawn. "That wasn't so bad now, was it?" she then asked as she opened a new bandage in front of Francis before covering the skin where the needle pierced. "We're all set, Chief," Ashleigh then said as she wrote a few notes on the side of the vial.

"Run that to the lab ASAP," Chief Williams said. The petty officer disappeared while Chief Williams handed Francis a protein bar and a glass of orange juice. "You'll have to finish this before you leave." Francis, still silent, looked over the glass for stains before chugging the contents. He then tested the protein bar wrapper; a pocket of air remained trapped inside - it was sealed. Opening the bar, Francis sniffed at the foodstuff before quickly consuming it. "That wasn't so bad was it?" the chief asked before taking the empty glass and wrapper away from Francis at which time Ashleigh returned.

"Tox screen was negative for alcohol, but there were some anomalies," she said as she handed Chief Williams a printout with the results of Francis's blood test.

"Prozac and Keppra?" the chief asked as he looked to Francis.

"The Prozac is for my OCD, the Keppra for my seizures," Francis replied, breaking his silence.

"How the hell did you get flight clearance?" Chief Williams said as he looked through the rest of the results.

"He's not a pilot, Chief," Mario said. "He's an observer, nothing more. Let's go, Professor." Mario helped Francis get his flight gear back on while Chief Williams shook his head as he read.

"Take this, Professor," Ashleigh said as she handed Francis a small package. "If you get nauseous in the next hour or so or you get stressed, take one of the pills in here. Then let us know."

"Thanks, Ashleigh, and please call me Francis," he replied as he looked over the package for stains of blood or chemicals.

"All right, enough pleasantries," Mario said as he pulled Francis by his arm towards the entrance. "We got a plane to catch, Professor." As the two departed and Ashleigh cleaned up the area, Chief Williams picked up the nearest wall-mounted receiver.

"Put me through to the CAG."

***

Walking onto the aft flight deck was an experience in and of itself. A wave of industrial fumes from fuel, grease, solder, and miscellaneous cleaning agents infiltrated every nook of Francis's nose as he navigated around unidentifiable floor stains, seams in the decking, toolboxes, engine parts and weapon-packed crates. A mechanical-like voice blared over the flight deck's loud speakers directing crews to various areas of the Sagan to handle routine repairs on the hull as well as the ship's environmental systems. Francis overlooked all the flight deck's environmental stressors as soon as he saw the fighters.

Four F-15E Strike Eagles were hoisted above their respective hanger bays while crews inspected each for electrical or structural defects. For a moment, all other concerns disappeared as Francis considered the present. He would soon ride in a fighter.

"I'm gonna be a Viper jockey," Francis said as he stopped by the nearest craft and reached out to touch the underbelly.

"Let's go, Professor!" Mario exclaimed as he continued on. Mario's gruffness masked his joy over seeing Francis get to fulfill what obviously long remained the professor's dream: spaceflight. Few ever got a chance to ride in a fighter, let alone someone with medical constraints. A close friend of Captain Sanford's, Mario knew much about the professor's efforts and importance to the mission. Getting to fly in a fighter was the least they could do for a civilian willing to join in such a dangerous mission. The two continued onward to the far side of the flight deck where Captain Sanford stood speaking on a receiver.

"I understand, Chief Williams," Francis heard her say. "He just needs to survive the flight down to the planet."

"So much for flying," Francis whispered while the captain hung up the receiver. Mario, for his part, nodded towards Rebecca before turning to face Francis.

"Take care, Professor," the lieutenant said before walking off out of sight.

"I take it I am not fit to fly," Francis said as he approached Rebecca. "I understand."

"The chief is concerned about the seizures mostly, which is understandable." For a moment, Rebecca considered the restrictions placed on Francis. *What must it be like to be prevented from pursuing a dream?*

"So, are you ready to fly?" she asked as she threw Francis a helmet.

"But I thought…"

"Let's go, Professor," she said walking by Francis towards her fighter. Like the others, it was white with red striping along the tail and wings. Rebecca's name was emblazoned in black lettering under the canopy, her call sign included underneath her true name. Francis's eyes then diverted to the section of the canopy where the REO sat. 'Francis Burns' was written there above what he knew could only be his call sign – 'Recoil'.

Chapter 9

Climbing up the ladder towards the REO's position, Francis stopped his ascent to touch the ship's hull where his name appeared. Gently, he traced his fingertips over his call sign while euphoria coursed through his body. For a few mere seconds, he envisioned flying in formation with a host of vipers, x-wings and Veritech fighters. A brilliant flash of light jerked Francis from his dreams.

"Good morning, Professor," a young woman said. Her voice, while soft and elegant, hinted that she was truly made of grit and steel. The smears of grease upon her cheeks and forehead only added to her rugged persona. Francis, after fully emerging from his daydreams, gazed at the young woman whose short, brown hair and blue-green eyes reminded Francis of a number of his cousins. In her hands rested the most impressive camera Francis ever saw: an SLR camera with manual settings, a long zoom lens and large flash attached to the camera's body. "Sorry if the flash bothered you," she said as she drew closer while examining the captured image. "I'm documenting the coming missions for the archives."

"You think I'm worthy of note in the histories?" Francis asked as he scaled down the ladder. Once on the ground, he looked back up towards his name.

"Everyone is important to history, Professor Burns," she replied as she extended her hand so Francis could view the photo. He looked down at the camera and the captured image of him touching the fighter. Francis smiled.

"You think I could get a copy of that?"

"Certainly, Professor."

"Please, call me Francis…"

"Corporal Leigh Dennison," she replied grabbing his hand enthusiastically. "It's a pleasure… Francis." She seemed to hesitate at the lack of formality.

"The pleasure is mine, Corporal. So, are you joining the mission to Mars?"

"Yes, and the Earth landing as well," Leigh said as she looked down and made adjustments to her camera's settings.

"My girl all set?" Captain Sanford asked, her unnoticed presence startling Francis.

"She's all set, Captain," Corporal Dennison replied as she patted the underbelly of the fighter. "We tuned her up and loaded the ordinance. You'll be ready for whatever action the cosmos sends your way." Setting the camera down on a cart laden with tools, Leigh picked up a clipboard, which she handed over to Captain Sanford. "The chief signed off on each test, found no problems."

"And how's your girl doing?" Rebecca asked as she scanned the list of work done to the fighter, Leigh pointing out major work requested by the captain.

"You have a daughter?" Francis asked, surprised. The captain and corporal looked at him quizzically.

"Civvies," Leigh whispered, shaking her head in jest while Rebecca laughed. "The captain is referring to my tank. She's all right, captain," Leigh said turning to Rebecca. "A few more engine adjustments and she'll be ready for Earth."

"Glad to hear it, Corporal. Tell the chief I appreciate the second look."

"Will do, Captain," Leigh said before saluting Rebecca and walking off."

"Is she a photographer or a mechanic?" Francis asked as Rebecca zipped up her flight suit.

"She's both. Why? Don't think a woman should repair engines."

"Hardly, Frost. You know me better than that," Francis replied as he checked over the zippers to his own suit. "I'm just surprised we have tanks on board." Rebecca laughed then as she moved over to Francis and spun him about to check over his suit.

"We were shocked, too. The tank was found in a sealed-off storage room, its hull full of rust. Leigh rebuilt the entire thing from the treads on up. We hope we don't need it, but happy it'll be there if we do."

"I'll tell you what, flyboy," Leigh said as she walked back to the fighter to unhook the fuel hose. "When your ass is on Earth surrounded by an enemy, just remember what you said when my tank shows up to save the day." She smiled wryly as she walked past Francis to unhook a cable securing the fighter's ordinance.

"You ready for flight?" Rebecca asked, her question ramming home the reality that Francis was about to have a dream fulfilled.

"Yes Ma'am!" Francis said, a smile beaming across his face.

"Never call me Ma'am," she then said after which she jabbed her thumb into his gut. "Call me Sir!" she exclaimed as she picked up her helmet. Francis, meanwhile, coughed for a few seconds. Rebecca was smiling at him when he regained his breath. "Let's go,

Francis," she said before patting him on his shoulder. "You okay with the call sign?"

"It definitely fits," he said as he walked towards the rear ladder.

"Hold it, Recoil," Rebecca said, her words causing a shiver to run through Francis. "You're up front, Professor."

"What... me... launch the fighter." She laughed as she started climbing the rear ladder.

"I will be able to control the bird from the REO's seat. Once we're airborne, you'll get a turn at the controls. It's the best way to learn."

Francis turned and looked up at the ladder to the pilot's seat; it looked like a much longer climb. Hesitantly, he put on his helmet and climbed up until he was staring at the empty chair.

"Get in, Francis!" Rebecca ordered as she strapped herself into the REO's seat. Francis climbed in, maneuvering his feet and legs into the cockpit and around the control stick and assorted pedals.

"Don't touch anything until I tell ya to!" Rebecca exclaimed as she punched at the keyboard adjacent to her seat. Leigh and several other crewmembers, meanwhile, busied themselves around the flight deck moving equipment from the area. Leigh gave a wave before giving a thumbs-up to Rebecca.

"Air Boss, this is Frost... requesting permission to activate systems," Rebecca called into her helmet's microphone.

"You're all clear to begin final flight checks and enter the hanger," a crackly voice called back over the com system.

"Roger that," Rebecca replied before activating several levers one of which closed the canopy. "Check your seat belts, Recoil. Things are about to get bumpy."

Francis quickly pulled at his belt connections and braced for flight. Fear and exhilaration fought for control of his soul. Suddenly, a series of red lights, embedded in the ceiling, activated and flickered while an alarm sounded.

"All hands, launch in progress," another voice called out over the com system. Francis sat impatiently as the fighter was jerked about by the frame securing it. He could hear a variety of motors operating, but he had no clue as to all the actions underway.

"All set, Sagan... good to go," Rebecca called into her microphone after she finished her checks of fuel, oxygen and power gauges. Bulkheads lowered from the ceiling moments later, boxing the fighter in with only the craft's indicator lights for illumination. Francis looked below in anticipation, awaiting his first glimpse of outer space, which wasn't from behind one of the Sagan's windows. The view did not disappoint as the flooring retracted exposing the distant lights cast by stars, planets, moons and nebulae.

"Frak me," Francis whispered, his breath and heartbeat now racing. The fighter then jolted about as the hoist started to lower. "This reminds me of the drop ship from *Aliens*."

"What?" Rebecca asked, angered by the distraction. Francis did not reply as the hoist lowered the fighter until it was suspended about a meter below the bottom hull of the Sagan. Seconds ticked away, Francis anticipating the coming thrust of power while Rebecca again punched away at her keyboard. Suddenly the hoist's clamps opened; the fighter drifted off as the Sagan continued on.

"Well, that was anticlimactic," Francis said as Rebecca used the fighter's thrusters to turn away from the Sagan's main thruster wash. Finally, after stabilizing their ship, Rebecca called into her microphone to relay a series of data to the Sagan's air boss, but Francis failed to notice any specifics. Now calmed, the sci-fi fan's memory cycled through the books, television programs and movies he had encountered throughout his life. *Star Trek, Star Wars, Space 1999, Starblazers, Robotech, Space: Above and Beyond, Contact...* every memory flew by in an instant until Francis finally recalled the two *Battlestar Galactica* series, where Humanity traversed the cosmos in search of Earth. Thoughts of Lorne Greene's wise, grandfatherly 'Adama' quickly gave way to Edward James Olmos's 'Admiral William Adama' and the story's re-imagining until all that remained were the orders Francis longed to answer to.

"Launch vipers!" Francis exclaimed as he punched the fighter's systems into high gear.

Chapter 10

"Francis!" Rebecca exclaimed as the fighter's sudden thrust threw her back hard against her seat. "Francis, stand down! Power down! Professor! Recoil!" Her words proved futile. Francis's memory was awash with the main theme from *Battlestar Galactica, the 'Colonial Theme'*, and images of Cylon fighters and colonial vipers battling for air superiority. The first moments after activating the main engines proved hardest for Francis as he adjusted to the controls for pitch and yaw, but his control quickly quieted his passenger as the fighter stabilized. The calm was short-lived as several indicator lights erupted along with an ear-piercing alarm.

"Incoming!" Rebecca cried out as the fighter's radar detected an incoming meteoroid. Francis's reaction was simultaneous. Activating the fighter's vernier thrusters, Francis rolled the fighter out of the meteoroid's path. Calm restored and their flight path cleared, Francis guided the fighter towards the once vanishing Sagan.

"DRADIS is clear... heading for the Sagan," Francis said in a matter-of-fact tone.

"DRADIS... what the hell... how?" Rebecca struggled to figure out where to start her inquiries. "Who taught you how to fly, and what the hell is a DRADIS?"

Francis chuckled a bit before responding.

"DRADIS is the *Battlestar Galactica* equivalent of radar," Francis said as he piloted the fighter within a few hundred kilometers of the Sagan. "As for flying, I probably have more hours of flight simulator training than you and every active pilot combined."

"How the hell did you get access to the flight simulator?" Rebecca asked as she typed commands into the REO keyboard. "You locked me out!" she then exclaimed, her irritation palpable. "Return control, now!" Francis heard his copilot slam her fist into the REO control panel.

"Take it easy, Frost. As for accessing the flight simulator, well... it's a small ship, relatively speaking. I've been friends with a lot of pilots who let me take a turn at the simulator."

"Who?"

"Spare me, Rebecca," Francis said, a sharp tone evident in his retort. "I have no doubt you've bent the rules for your own gain just as many have. The point is, I am capable to pilot this craft. Now landing, that's a different story."

"What?!"

"Don't worry, I'll return control to you shortly. I just wanted a turn at the stick."

Rebecca relaxed a bit and leaned back in her seat as Francis piloted the fighter alongside the Sagan.

"My God," Francis said as he looked at the gigantic hull of the ship generations called home and took in every seam, divot and scratch. Even battered from centuries in space, the fatigued exterior plates still retained some luster. It was a view Francis longed to behold, a view he never believed he would see. The experience didn't disappoint.

"I've waited my whole life for this," Francis said after moments of silence. "She's beautiful."

"She's definitely seen better days, but this view never disappoints," Rebecca replied as she too stared in awe at the ship. "A lifetime onboard… can't believe it's almost over." Francis didn't miss Rebecca's despondent tone.

"You're not excited about Earth? I would think you'd enjoy exploring the planet after a lifetime in space."

"It'll be hard to let go… being part of the Core, flying."

"Nobody said you had to give this up, Frost… at least not your military service. For me, the inside of the Sagan was nothing but a cage…"

Francis's voice trailed off, thoughts of his endless battles with OCD overwhelming joy-filled memories. Haunted by retracing countless steps and breathing the Sagan's stale air he envisioned laced with contagions, Francis could not wait to leave the generational ship behind. Rebecca sensed her copilot's distress, which made her quickly forget her own troubles.

"What's it like, I mean, is it just an organizational thing?" she asked. Rebecca didn't know where to begin; Francis chuckled just a bit. "I'm sorry, I didn't…"

"No worries, Frost. That's usually the first thing people say to me. I think they'd be shocked to see how much of a slob I actually am. OCD is more like having random, ridiculous thoughts pop into your head, thoughts of some impending doom. Like, a family member or friend will die because of something I said or did."

"What's with the checking and washing stuff then?" Rebecca asked, not certain if pushing was necessarily the best idea, but still wanting to know what she signed on for with Francis as a partner.

"They're little rituals I go through that relieve my anxiety… at least to an extent." Francis's explanations confused Rebecca even more.

"I take it there's not some manual of rituals you refer to," she said perplexed by the revelations Francis provided. Francis chuckled again as he maneuvered the fighter under the Sagan and up till the craft was positioned eye level to the Sagan's bridge.

"Yeah, there's no manual. I just get… thoughts of things I need to do to prevent disasters from happening. Washing my hands a certain number of times, checking locks repeatedly… it must sound like absolute nonsense to you."

"It sounds like a rough way to get through life," Rebecca replied as she considered Francis's description of life with OCD before remembering her jest in selecting his call sign. "I'm sorry, Francis… I didn't mean to make light of what you're dealing with."

"What the frak are you talking about, Rebecca!"

"Recoil. I can pick a different call sign if you want."

"Good God no, Frost. I love Recoil; it fits. Besides, making light of my OCD helps me cope with it."

"I'm sorry you have to deal with it at all."

"Don't be. Look, there are lots of worse things I could be dealing with. Okay?" He then chuckled leaving her more confused. "I mean, I spend hours each day checking doors, locks… to make certain I turned off the electric burner on my stove; all because I'm fearful my actions or inaction will cause the destruction of the Sagan. It's happening to me and I… I can imagine how ludicrous it all is. Making fun of my OCD? Some days, that's all that keeps me going."

"Would it help if I checked your stove and doors for you?" Rebecca said after moments of silence passed.

"No. That would just make things worse. Your checking stuff for me just enables OCD to linger on. If I ever ask you to check something, just say '*BT Steps says no answer*' and walk away."

"What?" she asked, clearly exasperated. He chuckled again.

"Sorry. I found a program in the archives called BT Steps. It's a self-guiding program that helps me manage my OCD. Its protocols are that anytime I ask someone to check something for me or assuage any fears, he or she should simply say 'BT Steps says no answer' and nothing more. Otherwise, your '*helping me*' actually allows OCD to maintain its grip on me."

"Fair enough," Rebecca replied as she typed away at her keyboard until a readout of radar scans displayed on her monitor; her thoughts, however, remained fixated on Francis's struggles. "You know, you're doing these rituals to prevent disasters? It sounds like you're pushing yourself to be a superhero."

"I always saw it as I was performing the rituals to prevent my becoming a super villain."

"*Sagan to CAG, Sagan to CAG,*" a voice called over the com system. "*Please respond.*"

"This is the CAG, go ahead," Rebecca replied bluntly; *Frost had returned.*

"The commander has ordered a CAP set for the remainder of the journey to Earth, effective immediately."

"Roger that," Rebecca replied. "Get Starling and Talon up here ASAP; they'll fly CAP with me and Recoil the next three hours. Tell Butch, Hellfire, Gorgan and Stretch they're on deck for the second shift. I'll call in the complete schedule in thirty minutes; two birds each shift. Understood?"

"Roger that, CAG. Sagan out."

"CAG?" Francis asked as Rebecca again typed away at the keyboard.

"It means commander of the air group whereas CAP means Combat..."

"Air Patrol... I know what they mean, I just didn't know you were the CAG," Francis said as he maneuvered the fighter until it was out in front of the Sagan by nearly twenty kilometers.

"Let me guess? You learned it from *Battlestar Galactica?*"

"Actually, no. I learned that from the movie *The Final Countdown.*"

"What?"

"You've never heard of *The Final Countdown?* It's where the aircraft carrier Nimitz is transported back in time to days before Pearl Harbor..."

"Enough, Recoil! The point is, this isn't *Battlestar Galactica, Star Wars or Star Trek*! This is real life combat! Return flight controls to my station."

"I have five names for you," Francis called back to Rebecca. "Alex Jacobson, Sam Frank, Joseph and Sam DeRose, and John Boyer."

"The pilots' names written on the side of the flight simulator?"

"Yep! Five *Battlestar Galactica* fans who built a flight simulator modeled after the colonial Vipers from the show. The Sagan's flight simulator and all the controls in this fighter craft were based on their designs. So in many respects, this *is* very much like *Battlestar Galactica*! Now, just sit back and relax. I have the con."

"And what the hell am I supposed to do then?" In response to Rebecca's question, she heard Francis wrestle with a zipper on his flight suit.

"Heads up!" Francis exclaimed. A book flew over the back of the seat seconds later, hitting Rebecca in the head. She picked up the book and scanned its cover.

"*The Hobbit*?" she asked. "What the hell is this?"

"You didn't want to fly with anyone who couldn't fire a gun. Well, I don't want to fly with anyone who doesn't know who Bilbo Baggins is."

Chapter 11

CAP duties, munitions training and Mars mission-related briefings consumed Francis's days. Much to the chagrin of the other fighter pilots, however, Francis woke each morning eager to embrace their collective duties, because every day culminated with air patrol. Nearly every second spent aboard the fighter provided a break from Francis's obsessions and fears, even if Frost didn't let him sit in the pilot's seat again.

After each shift in the cockpit, Francis and Rebecca checked over their fighter along with the deck hands. It was an exercise that showed just who ruled the flight deck.

"Your bird looks like you flew through a meteor shower, Captain" Corporal Dennison quipped as she felt the divots along the fighter's nose. "Are you trying to blowup?" she asked while jotting down notes onto the form affixed to her clipboard.

"Gotta give you grease monkeys something to do," Rebecca replied as she studied the fighter's tail section. "Just hammer out any large dents; she'll hold together."

"Oh, believe me Captain, your flying leaves us with more than enough work to do," Corporal Dennison said as she continued to write down diagnostics she planned for the fighter. "As it stands now, I've already had to redo several of the hull's panels. Perhaps you should let your REO take the stick. At least he brought it back with just minor dings."

"I'm with her," Francis called out from his seat in the cockpit where he continued his scan of sensor readings from their last flight.

"Did I say you brought it in spotless, Rook?" Leigh asked, her eyes never diverting from the clipboard.

"The last thing I'm gonna do is give you the reins again, Recoil," Rebecca said as she climbed the ladder to the REO seat.

"I said I was sorry," Francis jested as he typed away at the keyboard and scanned images they captured of the Sagan's hull.

"What'cha doing, partner?" Rebecca asked as she peered at the REO's computer monitor.

"Taking a look at the Sagan's hull. Figured I'd actually do something while we flew CAP."

"You mean aside from scaring the hell outta me, Francis," Rebecca asked as she looked closer at the images splayed across Francis's monitor. "Wait... go back to the last image."

"I got this, Frost. Why don't you go and, I don't know, cleanup your side of the cockpit."

"Why don't you two get a room?" Leigh whispered as she walked off.

"What?" Francis and Rebecca asked simultaneously before looking back to the images. They looked quizzically at one another before returning their eyes to the image of the Sagan.

"She's seen better days, but she's still beautiful," Francis commented on a close-up of the Sagan's cockpit.

"Roger that," Rebecca replied as she too saw past the clearly visible fissures and scorch marks marring much of the ship's nose to see the ship's sleek and elegant design, which shone through the countless blemishes caused by space debris and age.

"*CAG to the Admiral's quarters, CAG to the Admiral's quarters*," a voice called out over the ship's com system.

"This can't be good," Rebecca said as she slid down the ladder and rushed towards the hanger deck's nearest exit.

***

"Make a hole!" Rebecca repeatedly exclaimed as she power-walked through the Sagan's people-clogged hallways and up and down stairwells during her trek to Admiral Southern's quarters. Rebecca's footfalls, which resonated through the metal decking, provided a cadence to guide her thoughts. *What travesty cast shadows over the Sagan now? How would she confront the situation?*

Rebecca halted abruptly the minute the admiral's hatch came into view, her concentration broken by the sight of four marines, resplendent in full dress and well polished M-1 rifles. As one, the Marines, all gunnery sergeants, shifted their rifles until the weapons' stocks were uniformly repositioned to rest on the Marines' left shoulders. The sharp sounds of the Marines' actions preceded their collective salute to Rebecca, their superior officer. After her responding salute, three of the Marines pivoted to allow Rebecca to proceed while the fourth knocked sharply at the admiral's hatch.

"Enter!" replied Admiral Southern.

"Captain Sanford is here, Sir," the Marine replied after opening the hatch. The Marine then assumed a similar stance as the others allowing Rebecca space to carry on. Once inside, the Marine pulled the door closed, a resounding metallic thud verifying that the door was tightly sealed.

"Captain Rebecca Sanford, reporting as ordered, Sir!" Rebecca exclaimed as she stood at attention and saluted her commanding officer, the only other person in the room. *Why the heavy guard?*

"At ease, Frost," Admiral Southern said as she walked over to the nearby bar and poured a brown liquid from a carafe into a glass. "Ice?"

"Neat, Sir. Thank you, Command..., I mean, Admiral. Sorry, Sir." Taryn smirked as she handed the glass to Rebecca.

"Relax, Rebecca. I'm still getting used to the title myself. A lot of changes in such a little time, wouldn't you say?"

"Agreed, Admiral," Rebecca replied as the two raised their glasses before drinking.

"Well, enough pleasantries, Frost. Follow me." Taryn turned and walked towards the far side of the room to a doorway, which led to a sitting room. Rebecca followed and then again stood at attention as three others came into view, including President Counts.

"Mr. President!" Rebecca exclaimed as she switched her glass to her left hand before reverting to attention and saluting the new president. Clarence, sitting in a leather chair set against the room's picture window, stood and saluted.

"As you were, Captain," he said before sitting again. "Please, take a seat." The others, General Leary and a navy lieutenant, sat as well after having stood when Rebecca entered. "We have quite a bit to discuss. Admiral?" The president nodded towards the Sagan's commanding officer, the only one who remained standing.

"When it rains, it pours," Taryn whispered as she walked to stand at the room's window. "Part of me will miss these views." While her eyes were focused on a distant nebula, Taryn's concerns drifted towards her ship. "Captain, this is Lieutenant Shawn Morris... who has a ship update everyone needs to hear. Lieutenant?"

"Thank you, Admiral," Lieutenant Morris said as he stood and handed out file folders to everyone present. "I was recently assigned oversight of the Sagan's water treatment facilities and food storage units." Lieutenant Morris paused to look at President Counts.

"Ah, damn," Clarence said as he saw the deep concern in the lieutenant's eyes. "Spill it, Lieutenant."

"I transferred into the unit yesterday and immediately inspected all water reserves."

"Please tell me we are not out of water, Lieutenant," General Leary said fearing the worst.

"No Sir," Lieutenant Morris replied quickly, assuaging the senior staff's main concern. "We definitely have sufficient reserves for the journey to Earth, but I'm concerned with the growing salinity levels in our water. It's been over five years since we've located a viable water source with which to replenish our reserves."

"The Legop Asteroid," General Leary said, his thoughts returning to the difficult mission to land on and extract the limited water resources the asteroid contained. It was a mission that cost two mission specialists' limbs.

"Most of that asteroid and the other water sources we've encountered contained mostly hard water," Lieutenant Morris said. "The minute traces of usable water could only be treated and recycled so many times before new reserves would be needed. We're now at that point."

"Why are we just hearing about this?" Rebecca asked, her frustration evident. "I thought the moons around Saturn and Jupiter…"

"The Sagan's inaugural crew extracted most of the viable water from those moons; all that's left now is hard water stores," the lieutenant replied, his tone unphased by the captain's tirade

"Lieutenant Morris has been more than diligent in monitoring our water reserves, Captain," Admiral Southern interjected. "He's monitored potential water sources since he was in the academy. If there was any water left on Titan or Vulcan or any of the other moons, we would've stopped." The admiral's tone and glare ended further inquiry by the CAG. "Lieutenant, please continue."

"Thank you, Admiral," Lieutenant Morris said, turning until Rebecca was only in his peripheral line of sight. "Since there's a concern of possible contagions in Earth's atmosphere and hydrosphere, the Sagan's water reserves are our sole water resource, at least for the foreseeable future. As for replenishing our water tanks, we are running out of options."

"And what options do we have, Lieutenant," President Counts asked, hopeful there was at least a slim chance of obtaining water before reaching Earth."

"The Mars base, Mr. President," Lieutenant Morris continued as he approached a laptop positioned on a coffee table near the president's chair. Seconds after Shawn typed away at the computer's keyboard, the laptop's camera projected an image of three bunkers upon the far wall. "These structures present the next hope of fresh water," Shawn said as he walked over until the image was within arm's length. The bunkers, outlined in a brilliant, dark blue hue captured everyone's gaze. "Under each were erected large reservoirs, which were meant to contain a total of thirty thousand gallons of water. The reservoirs were connected to a filtration system capable of extracting waste, chemicals and other contaminants. That water would be sufficient to sustain us for an additional eighteen months, if each tank is full."

"How likely is it for those tanks to have survived these past three hundred years, Lieutenant?" asked President Counts. "Surely their hulls would be corroded by now and the water drained." Shawn poked his finger into the image of the nearest tank projection, an action that caused the image to triple in size and slowly spin counter-clockwise.

"The tanks were made from a rust-proof alloy, which was then coated in a polymer resistant to vibrations, rust... most conceivable hazards," Shawn replied before tapping the image causing it to cease spinning.

"Could the polymer itself have contaminated the water?" Admiral Southern asked. "Plastics of the time were noted for their carcinogenic components."

"Admiral, we won't know until we set foot on Mars and test whatever water is present."

Chapter 12

Light from the quarter moon glared through the leaf-less branches of the trees providing enough light for Francis to hold true to the path through the mountains. Hooded and cloaked, Francis moved along in the bitter autumn night uncertain where to go and of what he sought. The growing wind tossed fallen leaves about the path while knocking the barren branches together overhead, which orchestrated a creaking echo to accompany the shrill wind. It was as if Francis was embedded in any one of a hundred horror films he'd watched throughout his life. All he needed was for a driver-less, coffin-bearing carriage to overtake him or for the howl of a wolf to pierce the air. Instead, a crow's cawing jarred Francis from his thoughts and stole his breath.

Francis turned abruptly towards the direction from which the bird's call originated, suddenly aware that he grasped a staff. Snow started to fall around him, swirling about the air harmoniously with the leaves. Francis realized he was lost, unable to speak... to call out for help. It was then he spotted the amber light emanating from farther up the path.

A way out?

Francis pushed on towards the light, which suddenly darted away as if fleeing from him. The Burns pressed on, darting through the woods, ever at the edge of the light's radiance. Unable to gain ground, Francis had but enough depth into the light to guide his feet away from fallen limbs, bushes, boulders, and exposed tree roots. While he ran, voices in whisper cursed at him, taunted him. Exhaustion set in and Francis's breathing grew haggard, yet no amount of effort seemed to help close the gap. Then, an unseen mass of pine roots, exposed by previous rains, ended his pursuit; Francis tripped and fell hard to the unforgiving ground, and all lights vanished.

For uncounted minutes Francis laid there, his staff cast into and hidden amongst the darkness, hope all but gone. He simply turned over onto his stomach and listened to the torrent of winds that coursed through the trees. The eerie howls of the air chilled Francis even though the winds themselves seemed quite warm against his face and hands. His ears reached outward in search of any information or warning, yet no footfalls registered.

"What do you seek, Mortal?" a cackling voice asked from the shadows. *"Passage?"* As if suddenly summoned, an amber-hued specter appeared before Francis. Garbed in shredded robes, the specter appeared to hover above the ground, its actual feet obscured by the tatters of cloth rustling in the wind. The specter seemed human enough, though its gaunt skin bespoke of a life tortured through starvation and disease. *"You will find no welcome here, Mortal,"* the specter said as its illumination grew, providing dim light through which Francis could see the landscape about him. *"Why have you come? Speak!"* At the specter's final words, three additional figures emerged from the shadows. All glowing in an amber hue and similarly garbed, Francis's mind immediately pulled at thoughts of the Four Horsemen of Death.

"I do not seek anything!" Francis declared. "I am simply leading my companions home." Francis stood as the four specters surrounded him, though they stayed nearly seven meters from him. The specters' hands, once hidden within their robes, reached forth grasping scythes. Francis reached under his cloak to *Glamdring* and unsheathed the blade, which was not there moments before. The fabled sword reflected not a bit of the specters' light. They laughed at Francis's action, a cold laugh that disarmed all hope. Then, as their laughter grew and their amber hue ignited further, *Glamdring* crumbled into metallic ash within Francis's hand.

"*There will be no light but ours,*" the lead specter said as they inched closer to Francis. "*You and your kin... will die!*" At the last word, the specters flew at Francis, forcing him to the ground. Every time Francis made an effort to stand and confront them, the specters and a host of winds pummeled the human down to his knees. All was dark but for the specters circling above Francis, their hue now radiating in a piercing white light. Francis buried his eyes into the crook of his left arm while stretching forth his right to find balance. Instead, he found his staff.

"Trust in this, Francis," two new yet familiar voices uttered. "You are stronger than you realize," the two voices, the voices of his parents, said. With that, a pale blue light bathed the staff, and Francis grasped it without question. The maple staff then erupted into a light source that obliterated the darkness.

"*The Istari are not welcome here!*" the specters cried out, their voices now draped in fear. Francis ignored their cries and focused instead on rising to his feet. As if burdened by a suit of chain mail, Francis slowly, clumsily stood. The staff, his only support against the torrent of winds and specters that sought to destroy him, grew brighter until even the specters were outlined in its brilliant casting.

"Fall with your species, fall into night!" the specters shouted. *"Embrace the midnight!"*

"I am more than you can possibly imagine, witch-lings," Francis said as he braced against the potent winds. "We... have returned." With his final words, Francis slammed the butt of his staff into the ground. A light, greater than any star, burst forth and incinerated the specters while Francis, his robes now gleaming white, embraced the warmth of his parents' memory.

***

"Dad... Mom...!" Francis exclaimed as woke from his dreams.

"You're safe, Francis... you're all right," Rebecca said as she cradled Francis in her arms. Seated on the edge of Francis's cot, the CAG held her REO while gently petting his hair out of his eyes. "Just a dream, Francis. It was just a dream." She then lowered him back to his cot while Francis struggled to break from the dream's grip and calm his breathing.

"What is Istari?" Rebecca finally asked when Francis's breathing finally relaxed. He thought over her question at length before answering, his grasp of the present still tenuous.

"They were powerful spirits created by J.R.R. Tolkien," he said as he sat up and looked about. He was in the pilots' quarters on the Sagan, his latest home. He finally looked back into Rebecca's eyes where he saw worry. "The Istari were sent to help Humanity battle a growing menace... to drive evil from Middle Earth." Francis leaned back into his cot and stared at the ceiling as he considered the dream.

"Why are you doing this, Francis?" Rebecca asked as she pulled his left hand into hers. "What have you lost?"

"Tolkien wrote that 'not all who wander are lost', a proverb to which I hold. I seek but to wander the roads ahead... I seek the prize of wonder, of knowledge and experience," Francis replied as he rested back deeper into his pillow, his gaze turning towards the room's sole window beyond which a host of stars radiated. "I wish for every breath to touch a new wind, a new taste of life. I go to wander, knowing that I will never be lost." In silence they remained, both Rebecca and Francis gazing out at the distant stars until he finally fell back asleep while she considered his words.

Chapter 13

Francis jarred to consciousness at the crescendo of snores that echoed through the pilots' quarters. Wrapped tightly in a Navy-issued, steel-blue cotton blanket, Francis found himself precariously perched on the very edge of his cot. Francis tried to edge back, but a still body prevented his retreat to a more secure position. He turned his neck to see what obstacle was there. Rebecca slept peacefully, her back to his, and her breath was barely audible; Francis smiled. While Francis failed to recall much of the previous night, save for the nightmare, he remembered Rebecca being there to comfort him. Rebecca's body suddenly quivered, ending Francis's remembrances; she was cold, clothed only in a tank top and sweats. After extracting himself from the blanket, he wrapped Rebecca in it without disturbing her sleep. He took a moment to watch her, to make certain she stayed in deep sleep. Covered and now warm, Rebecca smiled and appeared contented.

"Sleep well, Frost," Francis said as he gently brushed her hair away from her eyes. It was then he noticed the book on the floor, the copy of *The Hobbit* he had given Rebecca. "What's this?" he asked aloud, though in whispered words and a brief, silent chuckle. Francis flipped the book open to where Rebecca had placed a bookmark; she's made it through to the end of chapter two. "Read about Bilbo's trolls have you?" He put the book on the cot near Rebecca's waist before looking once more at his partner. "Perhaps like Bilbo, we should outfit you for your coming adventure, Frost."

Without another word, jest, smirk or chuckle, Francis left the quarters.

His first stop was the showers, always empty at that hour. Once stripped, soaked and lathered, Francis stood long under the stream of hot water while considering his coming adventures. After decades of pacing the Sagan's decks, Francis relished the idea of real forest paths under the sun and moon. The wonder of Humanity's seeming disappearance aside, he was excited to breathe *fresh air* and hear the call of birds against a backdrop of water dancing amidst the cobbles and boulders that populated the streams of his homeland. Above all, Francis dreamed of treading mountains carpeted by trees, pine needles, leaves and shrubs, where an array of micro climates offered shelter and sustenance to animals large and small.

"Morning, Professor?" called out a high-pitched voice, which dispelled Francis's dreams. A female cadet had called out to him, one of many individuals starting to filter into the showers.

"Good morning," Francis replied before lowering his head under the flow of water one more time. He then shut off the valve to his shower and returned to the locker where his towel and clothes waited. It didn't take Francis long to dry off and put on his clothes, and soon he was walking along the Sagan's corridors towards his destination: Corporal Dennison's workshop just off one of the ship's maintenance bays. Francis's trek proved difficult as he fixated on the rendering he conjured right after he finished dressing, which he held open with both hands. He ignored the seams in the flooring, which he always avoided until then, and bumped into more than a few Marines and naval personnel along the way. It was not until he smelled air mixed with grease and fuel amidst the sounds of hammering that he realized his destination was at hand. After questioning a few deck hands, Francis finally located Corporal Dennison's workshop. Tucked away, as far from the main hanger bays as possible, Dennison's domain sat far from the incandescent lanterns that lit the rest of the ship. Instead, this part of the Sagan depended on the light of electric torches spaced where needed most. To one side of the large room rested a tank, whose dark torso glimmered under the light of one of the larger lanterns. The other side of the room, meanwhile, glowed orange, the space lit by a forge set against the wall itself. There Corporal Dennison stood hammering at a piece of metal oblivious to Francis's presence, or so he thought.

"What do you want now, Professor Burns?" Leigh asked, her eyes never diverting from her hammering. Her hammering seemed in sync with a song Francis could not hear.

"A favor, Corporal," he replied as he held out the rendering towards her. Leigh stopped mid-swing and stared at the offered drawing. She then set the hammer on an anvil and wiped her hands off on a dirty rag before grabbing Francis's rendering.

"Small design... like a combat machete. What do you need this for?" Leigh asked as she continued to scan over the dimensions Francis included.

"It's a gift, of sorts," he replied.

"Why don't you just get the captain a ring and be done with it?" Leigh asked; she looked at Francis and smirked.

"Can you make it?" Francis asked, ignoring the corporal's jest.

"It'll take some doing, but..."

"Hold the light still!" a deep voice exclaimed. Francis turned towards the tank and noticed a wavering light emanating from under the metal monstrosity.

"It is still!" a female voice replied.

"You two better not be messing up the fuel lines," Corporal Dennison said before turning back to Francis. "The blade will be easy enough. The hilt and the etchings along the blade are a different matter entirely. Hold on a second." Leigh moved to the front of the tank and ducked down to peer under the mechanized weapon. "Sarge, you got a minute?"

"Yeah, hold on a second," the female voice said. "Here, you take the light," Francis heard "Sarge" say before the sound of wheels creaked from underneath the tank. A mechanic's creeper cart rolled out from under the tank seconds later bearing a woman in fatigues with long blond hair tied back into a ponytail. She stood and walked to a nearby stool where she grabbed and drank from a water bottle before moving to within a meter of Leigh and Francis. "So this is the professor," Sarge said before taking another draw from her water bottle. Her sea blue eyes scanned over Francis for a quick moment before she walked up, her hand extended. "Sergeant Sarah Beauchamp; it's a pleasure to meet you, Professor Burns. Francis shook her hand and felt as if Sarah's grasp would crush his hand easily.

"What do you think of this, Sarge?" Leigh asked, handing over Francis's rendering. "You think you could handle making the hilt?"

"Shouldn't take too long I imagine. I take it you want it high carbon steel and battle-ready? Of course, a nice display model of 440 stainless steel would be a lot easier and quicker."

"Battle-ready, Sergeant Beauchamp," Francis replied. She nodded before looking over the depicted blade.

"What language are these markings in?" Sergeant Beauchamp asked as she turned the rendering about several times.

"Elvish," Francis replied. Sarah and Leigh exchanged a quick look, but neither said anymore about the design. "Can you two make this sword?"

"The sergeant and I can get it done, Professor," Leigh said. "Though, it won't be ready for the Mars mission, if that's your hope."

"I need it for the mission to Earth. Is that possible?" Leigh looked quickly to Sergeant Beauchamp.

"We'll get it done, Professor," Leigh said after she exchanged nods with the sergeant.

"Am I the only one working today?" questioned the man under the tank. Preempted by the sound of his shuffling along the decking, and the dancing light cast by the torch he held, President Counts emerged from under the tank. "You're up, Corporal." President Counts handed the torch light to Leigh before moving off and grabbing a rag from the main workbench in the area. "Can't wait to see how bad you two messed up my baby," Leigh said as she shimmied along the deck and under the tank to where repairs were being made. "I just realigned that!" Francis, Clarence and Sarah heard Leigh curse amidst the clanking of unseen tools the corporal wrestled with to secure a series of bolts.

"Sarge," Clarence said as he wiped grease off his hands.

"I'm on it," Sarah replied as she ducked down and crawled underneath the tank to assist with the repairs. Francis, meanwhile, remained silent, uncertain how he was to address the president. He finally chose a military approach and saluted.

"At ease, Professor," Clarence said before setting down the rag and drinking from a nearby water bottle. The president then picked up the rendering of the sword Francis drew. "This doesn't appear to be standard issue equipment."

"No, Mr. President… just something…I,"

"Take it easy, Francis. With all you'll be doing for us, not to mention all you've done for us already, small requests like this are the least we can do."

"I appreciate that, Mr. President." Francis nodded towards the chief executive, a man who long ago earned the respect of the Sagan's entire crew. Then, turning, Francis walked away towards the nearest exit.

"One thing, Professor," President Counts said, words that caused Francis to halt mid-step. "Why did you agree to this?" Francis's visage reflected puzzlement. Why had he agreed? What did he hope to gain? Would the others understand?

"I…," Francis uttered, clearly flummoxed.

"You know, I did some research into OCD after you were assigned to the mission," Clarence said as he sat on a nearby work stool. "I can't imagine what you are going through, what obsessions haunt you. But, leaving this ship? Even you must realize that isolation from Humanity, hiding in the wilds of Earth, will not stop OCD. It will find new chinks in your armor, Francis."

"I don't know what you're…"

"Spare me, Professor Burns. I'm an investigator, and I know perfectly well what your plans are once you've carried out your mission." Clarence stood again and walked to within centimeters of Francis. "Before you disappear into the wilderness, I ask that you consider truly embracing your anxiety and give us a chance to help you confront it. This may be your last, best chance to do so."

Chapter 14

Was he running? The president's words stung and held tight to Francis's memory for days after their conversation. Earth once seemed like *The Promised Land*, where OCD would fade into history. Now, reality set in; new obsessions and compulsions would surface.

"At least Humanity will be safe from my actions," Francis had said after he first considered his oversight of the insidious nature of the disorder. He soon realized that those fears, however, would likely return. *Would he ever be free?*

Francis and Rebecca continued their CAP responsibilities while a veil of melancholy washed over him. Each night, while on patrol, Francis found some respite. With her responsibilities as CAG, Rebecca often let Francis pilot their fighter while she monitored the complex of gauges spread across the fighter's panels. She said it gave her a chance to keep her skills sharp, but her questions made Francis suspect Rebecca had ulterior motives.

"You sure you're all right, Francis?" she asked almost every night shortly after they took flight.

"I'm good to go, Cap," he'd always reply. *How could he explain his fears, his visions?*

For his part, Francis devoted his energies to taking in the splendor of space. The light of distant stars and planets, spread against the backdrop of nebulae and black holes, brought solace. Francis also kept a close eye on the panels covering the Sagan's hull. The pilots and core of ship engineers ever maintained a constant watch of the panels; there was no indication of catastrophic failure, which Francis knew well. For the anthropologist and sci-fi fan, the scars and divots covering the hull were instead a story of crews past whom were now but a memory. *What had the original passengers encountered? What asteroids and comets had accompanied the Sagan en route to Maximus Prime?*

"What will you remember most?" Francis asked in whispers during the last patrol before the scheduled Mars mission. The Sagan never answered.

***

"Should we go help send off the Mars team?" Senator Torres asked as he and Representative Harding finished up the second draft of legislation to organize a temporary capitol in the Buffalo metropolitan area.

"Be my guest if you want to go stand and look subordinate to the Governor," Maria replied. She never diverted her eyes from the draft.

"You mean President…"

Maria shot Antonio a glare that ended his remark. "If you're gonna stay, stay on task," she said before returning her gaze to the second section.

"All right," Antonio replied as he took his seat and opened his copy of the legislation to the appropriate pages. "Well Buffalo certainly makes for the best option. At least at the time the Sagan left it was a central hub for high-speed rail and had the most extensive network of cement highways. That alone would make it easier to expand any settlement."

"You're acting as if everything is intact, something that is rather doubtful," Maria remarked dryly. She'd never considered Antonio to be overly bright.

"Still, I imagine the highway system should have endured relatively intact."

"Niagara Falls should certainly be accessible for power generation," commented the Senator. Maria was impressed that he actually added a logical point. "It's a shame we'll not be able to continue on much longer." Maria shot another death stare at her compatriot.

"How does reminding me of this help?" she asked.

"When the elections are held... we can't, I mean," he stumbled for the words. "The thirty-second Amendment forbids more than eight years. You and I have just over a year left. Unless... you're thinking of the Presidency?" Maria laughed at that comment.

"Clarence and his support would squash any such effort. Our esteemed president's allies would make certain we didn't win. Our support would only gain us Congressional positions."

"Then why don't we change the rules?" Antonio asked. Maria looked up; a smirk spread wide across the representative's face. "President Counts has enough on his plate right now, overseeing our progress and the landings on Mars and at Niagara. I say we rework this Bill to start with things he seeks most, and then add text nullifying the thirty-second amendment."

"The repeal of an Amendment is too noticeable," Maria replied after first leaning back in her chair and smiling. "But, if we reworded provisions as to what constitutes a term..."

The representative shook her head; she could not see a way to implement Antonio's plan. Frustrated, Maria stood and walked to the room's kitchen area. After pouring a cup of coffee, she maneuvered to the window and looked out into space as she considered her predicament. Antonio, meanwhile, flipped through a paperback copy of the American Constitution, flipping pages until he reached the text regarding the thirty-second amendment. Using his finger as a guide, he quickly scanned the amendment for a loophole. He found one and laughed.

"Yes?" Maria asked, not expecting much. She never did when ideas came from Antonio.

"No one shall serve as a Senator and/or Representative, for one or more States, for a period of over eight years, whether the years are consecutively served or not," Antonio quoted before lifting his eyes to meet Maria's.

"You damn fool, I know the law!" she exclaimed before halting her tirade. She laughed, too.

"To my knowledge, Representative Harding, we've only served as elected officials for a United States colony," Antonio said as he closed the book. "We could run for New York's seats and then get rid of the term limits altogether." Maria considered the Senator's words, looking for a kink.

"The president would veto any attempts at lifting the term limits. And since Maximus would remain a colony, what incentive would they have to help us override the veto?" Colonial bylaws also limit terms to eight years?"

"Everyone is feeling lonely right now given the likelihood Earth is unoccupied," Antonio replied. "If we proposed establishing Maximus Prime as the fifty-second State and the Sagan's crew as official representatives of New York, I'm willing to bet people would feel better. Wouldn't you agree?" Maria smiled. Perhaps Antonio was not the fool she once thought.

Chapter 15

Every member of the Sagan crew tried to imagine Mars as the weeks ticked away. Yet, no one, not even Francis, was prepared for the enormity of the celestial behemoth. Far from the giant red orb most expected, a condition of an atmosphere choked with iron oxide, Mars appeared as a mottling of red-orange, green, beige and white from the Sagan's current orbit.

"So much for the 'Red Planet'," Admiral Southern said as she peered out the bridge's windows from the comfort of her chair. "Any signals yet?" she asked the com officer.

"Nothing, Admiral," the com officer replied.

"Blind as a bat," Taryn whispered as she stood and approached the com station. "Try the probe in Earth's orbit. Anything?" The com officer tapped away at the com panel's keypad for several seconds, seconds that seemed like hours.

"The signal is still too weak, Admiral," the com officer replied. "Engineering believes we won't have a clear connection until the solar flairs subside later this week."

"It's as if the universe is conspiring against us," Taryn said as she picked up the com station receiver. "This is the admiral; connect me with General Leary."

***

The pilot's briefing room was packed with Navy and Marine corps personnel, the pilots and infantry who would land and investigate the Mars facilities. Francis twitched as men and women passed by and filled in the seats surrounding him, removing breathing room he secured earlier. The sight of his uncle, Rebecca and President Counts entering the room and standing by the podium provided a respite from his bout with claustrophobia.

"Ten hut!" a nearby Marine exclaimed as she stood at attention. The whole room responded in kind.

"As you were," General Leary commanded as he stood behind the CAG's podium. "The admiral has given the order; you are a go." Nods of approval and excitement spread throughout the room, but not a sound broke the silence. "Having received no response to our hails, the ship will remain at DEFCON 1 until we have secured all the planet's facilities." General Leary, now holding a remote, stood back from the podium. The image of the Mars base appeared on the screen seconds later, which nearly covered the entire wall behind the podium. "Scans of the Mars base show that the landing strip is relatively intact; the strip itself is half a kilometer west of the main facilities. Lieutenant Morris will lead the investigation of the water storage tanks, which are south of the living quarters. Sergeant Beauchamp, meanwhile, will supervise inspection of the fuel storage tank." General Leary crossed in front of the screen and tapped on the fuel storage tank positioned on the northeastern side of the Mars base.

"The fuel will not be needed for the mission itself. The inspection of the tank is for safety purposes; we want to ascertain if the base is a viable option for a colony should Earth prove uninhabitable. Any questions?" No one questioned the general's plans. "Special Agent Harrington?" In response, a stocky man with a relaxed stride made his way to the podium.

"Good morning," Todd Harrington said as he picked up a laser pointer and turned towards the projected image. "NCIS will spearhead the investigation of the living quarters," he said as he projected the pointer around the edges of the largest base structure. "Additionally, we will investigate the greenhouse off just to the east. Scans show the greenhouse remains intact, which is surprising to say the least if in fact the base has remained abandoned for the last century." Todd put down the pointer and turned back to the gathered crew. "Whatever team you are on, assume the structures are unstable. Combat engineers and EOD team members will join in the inspections; listen well to their commands. Understood?" No questions were raised. "Thank you, General," Todd said before taking his seat.

President Counts then strode forward, beyond the podium, to stand right before the assembly. "You are our heroes," he said as he scanned the faces in front of him. "Beyond the coming adventure, beyond the excitement of exploration, you are our first, best line of defense. I am honored to be your president and, as your commander in chief, I have but one order to give beyond the directives already mentioned; stay safe. God bless you all." The assembly then stood and saluted their president, a response Clarence answered in kind before nodding to General Leary and returning to his seat.

"You have your orders," the general said after retaking the podium. "Now go out there and get it done. Dismissed!"

"Ooh-rah!" a number of Marines exclaimed as they stood and broke into their teams for final instructions from squad leaders. Francis remained seated as he continued to look over the projection of the Mars base until he blocked out all but the greenhouse. For long moments, all sound from the room vanished as Francis remained fixated on the rectangular structure. Gradually, Francis perceived the sounds of a growing wind, which sounded more and more like the prelude of a hurricane.

"*Francis*," sounded a chilled voice from within the wind. Francis shivered as if he felt the cold of space for the first time. "*Istari*," whispered the voice as the wind intensified.

"Francis?" Rebecca asked, rousing her copilot from the waking nightmare. "You okay?"

"Yeah, I'm okay," he said standing and following behind as Rebecca treked onto the flight deck.

"You'll be teamed up with NCIS in the investigation of the living space," Rebecca said; she went on to explain the mission objectives, but Francis's thoughts were on the fell voice he'd heard. He remained oblivious to Rebecca and the host of people and objects that he maneuvered around until finally reaching their fighter where a stone wall of a man blocked their path. With short, red-blonde hair and a broad, muscled chest, the man appeared as a hulk. Francis doubted the man had any equals in hand to hand combat.

"You ready, Frost?" the man asked as he reached out and shook Rebecca's offered hand.

"As ready as I'll ever be, Red," she replied as both Frost and Red stood at attention.

"I relieve you, Sir," Red said, his tone serious and formal.

"I stand relieved," Rebecca answered back. The two then hugged briefly before Rebecca turned back to Francis.

"Francis Burns, this is Captain Joe Mosher," Rebecca said as Joe and Francis shook hands. "Regs require I step down as CAG while on 'landing' missions; Red here is replacing me."

"Nah, I'm just keeping the kids outta trouble while you're away, Frost," he said. "See you two in the air." Joe 'Red' Mosher walked off while Rebecca checked over her flight suit.

"Wow he's got a hell of a grip," Francis said as he rubbed at his right hand.

"He was an MP; I wouldn't mess with him," she said as she started to climb the ladder to her seat. "He'd frak you up…"

Rebecca stopped midway up the ladder and looked down at Francis who was smiling.

"Did you just say… frak?" he asked amongst his chuckles.

"Oh God, I'm spending way too much time with you," Rebecca said, shaking her head before finishing her climb. Francis chuckled incessantly as he ascended to his seat and brought the fighter's systems online. Seconds passed as individual indicator lights blinked across the REO's terminals.

"It must be hard to relinquish command," Francis said as he adjusted his seat restraints.

"The squadron's in good hands," Rebecca replied. "I trust Joe more than I trust anyone."

"What about me?" Francis asked. Rebecca didn't need to turn around to know Francis was flashing a sarcastic smile her way.

"My comment speaks for itself. Let's go thru prep."

"Ouch," Francis said as he scanned the indicators for the fighter's systems, searching out any orange or red glows. Rebecca quickly went through system priorities: engines, navigation, fuel, weapons. Francis replied "check" to each.

"The board is green, Frost," Francis replied seconds before Joe Mosher's voice called out over the com system.

"This is the CAG; all fighters check in," Captain Mosher said against the sounds of the bulkheads moving into place and the hoists powering up.

"Eagle one, good to go," Rebecca responded, her acknowledgement followed by declarations of readiness from Eagles four, five and eight.

"Air boss, this is CAG; all fighters set."

"Roger that," a voice called out over the com system before the deck flooring retracted and the hoists lowered the fighters.

"This is Sagan Actual," Admiral Southern commanded over the com system. "Launch fighters." Her command initiated all fighter craft to soar into a V-formation headed for Mars.

"Almost home," Francis whispered, a thought every pilot and crewman considered at that very moment.

Chapter 16

"All wings report in!" Captain Mosher commanded as the fighters completed their first pass of Mars.

"This is Eagle One," Francis replied. "We've detected no signals or transmissions, over." The other REOs made similar reports.

"Roger that! Sagan, this is the CAG; all clear... I say again all clear. Fighters form up and commence CAP." Every fighter, save for Rebecca and Francis's, turned about to take positions around the Sagan.

"CAG, this is Eagle One," Rebecca called into her microphone. "We are initiating Mars landing."

"Roger that, Frost. Good hunting... CAG out." With that, Rebecca piloted her fighter into an orbit.

"Sagan, this is Eagle One. Commence with shuttle launch." After confirmation from a Sagan deck officer, two port bays opened on the Sagan's lower hull through which two shuttles, the Drake and Hawking, launched and approached Eagle One's position.

"Keep your eyes peeled to the idiot lights, Recoil," Rebecca said as she positioned the fighter twenty kilometers in front of the lead shuttle.

"You expecting company?" Francis asked, though he knew the main concern shared by all the top brass.

"There aren't supposed to be any weapon systems deployed on Mars, but we can't risk it. If a missile launches, we'll engage it while the shuttles retreat."

"Roger that," Francis replied as he scanned the radar for any blips. The flight went without incident as expected. Rebecca made continuous flybys over the Mars base while the shuttles landed on the runway, their heavy-tread tires having remarkably little trouble managing the sediment that coated the cement construction.

"How do you think our skids will manage the runway?" Francis asked as Rebecca guided their fighter into a final approach.

"Our skids aren't really a worry," she replied. "I just need to slow us down to a maneuverable speed."

"What?"

"Just hang on, Recoil!" Rebecca exclaimed as she guided the ship away from the runway in the direction of a landing pad mostly covered in what appeared like red sand. The fighter jolted to a near stop just shy of the pad when a series of motors activated unseen parts within the fighter's hull.

"Holy crap... is this a Battloid?" Francis asked, his excitement overwhelming.

"A what?"

"A Battloid... you know like a Veritech fighter, from Robotech?"

"What the hell are you blabbering about now?" Rebecca asked as the fighter's twin engines pivoted downward while hover-vents beneath the cockpit provided thrust for a relatively gentle landing.

"Robotech... it's an animated series," Francis said as he enthusiastically looked about at the fighter's visible components.

"This is not a cartoon, Francis. It's real life, so get your head out of the clouds," Rebecca scolded as she shut down the fighter's systems and opened the canopy. The pilot and copilot then scaled down the side of the fighter to stand on the planet's surface. Before taking in the landscape and structures, Francis felt obligated to clarify something.

"Robotech is not a cartoon; it's Anime!"

***

"So far, so good," President Counts said as confirmations of touchdown came in from the shuttles and the lone fighter craft. Admiral Southern, meanwhile, marched about the bridge to relay final commands to each separate science station participating in the operation, which was code-named "Red Dawn."

"The board is green," Admiral Southern finally commanded as she sat in her chair. "Commence operations." President Counts silently stepped towards the admiral as a flurry of communications erupted between the bridge crew and surface teams.

"Well done, Admiral Southern," Clarence remarked quietly.

"Thank you, sir," she replied while nodding at the Commander-in-Chief. "Will you be leaving us now?"

"No, I want to see this through. Wait, am I making you nervous?" He smiled wryly; she didn't miss his jest.

"Mr. President, it's great to have you here," Taryn said before leaning forward and whispering, "but something tells me your eyes should be turned elsewhere."

"Go on, Admiral… I'm all ears."

"Sir, the representatives are holding a press conference within the hour," Taryn said. She grew silent as an aide brought over an inventory checklist for her to sign. The admiral continued once the aide was out of earshot. "You know they're up to something."

"Of course they are, Taryn," Clarence whispered. "They're career politicians. One way or another, Harding and Torres were going to make a move against us. I can't stop being president to baby-sit those two. My place is here." Taryn nodded at his words.

"What if you could be in two places at once?" Taryn asked after a moment of silence passed.

"I'm listening."

"If they want to bully the populace and seize power, they're gonna need help from the delegates on Maximus Prime."

"Very true," Clarence said. "What do you propose?" Taryn turned and smiled at the president before she stood and walked to and picked up the nearest com receiver.

"This is the admiral," Taryn said. "Have Captain Fornoff report to the bridge, on the double." After confirmation of the order came through, Taryn returned to her seat.

"What do you have up your sleeve, Admiral?" Clarence asked, never really doubting Taryn had long ago set contingencies for such a coup.

"When bullies surface... send in the bully-slayer."

***

The shuttles Drake and Hawking landed safely on Mars before the fighter, the latter shuttle retrofitted with a tank for storage of any recovered water. The Drake, meanwhile, carried the crews of Marines, sailors and NCIS agents eager to touch solid ground.

After landing, the crews, clad in standard-issue flight gear and respirators, disembarked and gathered near the fighter; everyone was speechless as human eyes gazed at the Martian landscape for the first time in over two hundred years. Francis felt it looked like a gigantic red desert with wind-whipped dust devils the only occupants save for the landing party. The piercing cry of the increasing wind made for a chilly companion as the party marched towards the base.

"Keep tabs on your O2!" Lieutenant Morris ordered as teams began to break apart. While Morris led his team towards the water tanks, Sergeant Beauchamp, teamed with Corporal Dennison and several other Marines, oversaw the unloading of equipment for inspecting the fuel storage tank. Sarah Beauchamp was well known throughout the ship as she was a star on one of the Sagan's coed rugby teams. Francis, however, had seen the mid-height blond, in an altogether different environment even beyond their brief encounter in the Sagan's maintenance bay; Sarah Beauchamp served as one of the elementary school teachers, one who taught reading to many of the Sagan's youths. For Francis, Sarah's presence served to further highlight the adage, "don't judge a book by its cover."

"Agents, get ready," Special Agent Todd Harrington called out as a small group gathered around the lead investigator. Frost was there along with three others, all of whom donned utility packs and harnesses with a multitude of tools visible: flashlights, knives and other odds and ends. The sight jolted Francis's memory; he suddenly walked off to the fighter's cargo pod and opened the underside panel to remove his gear. By the time he joined the others, Francis donned a webbed Marine utility belt with multiple pouches, a hatchet hanging at his left side. Additionally, Francis carried a dark-stained maple staff, which caused Frost to shake her head once more.

"What the hell is he thinking?" Frost asked quietly as Francis strode within earshot. "At least it doesn't have a Batman belt buckle."

"All right, listen up," Agent Harrington said before finally seeing Francis. Todd simply smiled before continuing. "We don't have much time here. Captain Sanford, Professor Burns... this is my team: Bob Hanley, Heather Harvey and Dan Caufield." Each of the team members nodded in reply to their names before Todd turned to them. "While not an investigator, Professor Burns is a fellow archaeologist and will join in our reconnaissance." Each team member again nodded after Todd's words.

"I hear you studied under Dr. Engelbrecht?" Todd asked, as he again looked over Francis.

"Yes, Sir," Francis replied.

"Well, that's good enough for me. Bob, you and newbie here will take point."

"Roger that," Bob replied as he walked forward to lead the team on towards the main Mars base facility. "You're with me, Francis."

"That's Professor Burns to you," Rebecca said, her irritation palpable. Bob stopped in his tracks, and everyone looked at Rebecca.

"You're amongst anthropologists, Rebecca," Francis said as he patted Rebecca on her shoulder and walked by her. "We don't stand on formality." He then turned back and winked. "Right behind you, Bob."

***

The team made their way east towards the main facility single file, their movements hampered by winds that struggled to find consistency. For Francis, it was a joyous stroll where OCD took a back seat to adrenalin-laced wonder and his eyes fixated on the sand that swallowed his boots with each step. Finally, disappointment returned as Francis's feet touched pavement; the company was now on a walkway, which led to the main structure. After first being concerned with avoiding cracks in the walkway, Francis's attention turned to the cement and steel structure ahead of them, which resembled an elongated octagon.

"The walls and roofing seem surprisingly intact," Francis remarked as the company maneuvered along the pathway leading towards the opposite side of the Mars base's main living space. The remainder of their march passed in silence as the collection of agents, Marines and Francis trudged through undulating sand dunes. Tiring footsteps ultimately led to the main entrance of their destination.

"Oh frak!" Francis exclaimed, voicing everyone's aggravation. A mountain of sand covered the only doorway. Agents Harrington and Hanley spent minutes discussing options while prodding the dunes with telescopic walking sticks as the others searched for other entry options. It was agents Caufield and Harvey who discovered the only other entryway.

"Todd? Over here!" Dan exclaimed into his headset as he and Heather cleared red sand from a partially covered steel slab embedded in the pavement. "What about using this drainage tunnel?"

"Drainage tunnel?" Francis asked. Francis Burns stood horrified at the thought of sewage as the others worked the slab open.

Chapter 17

Francis's forthcoming journey through sewage timed well with a press conference occurring simultaneously on board the Sagan. The Congressional representatives, Harding and Torres, set a press conference for when they assumed the president would be most involved with the Mars landing. Perhaps, if they'd truly considered their perceived adversary, the two legislators would have known better.

The congresswoman and senator were suddenly assigned a new location, the tribunal room, for their press conference, which should have immediately tipped off the Federal legislators that something was afoot. The room itself was wide, but it had little depth. Gray, full-backed chairs, set five rows deep and twenty-four chairs across, covered the bulk of the room's surface area. Before this seating rested a dark, red mahogany conference desk, which contrasted well with the oak slates covering the entire floor. From the conference table, seated in plush, leather executive chairs, Harding and Torres anticipated a coup of quiet yet epic proportions. With backs turned to the judge's dais, the legislators looked on as Navy and Marine Corps personnel filed in. Along with a retinue of press agents, the growing assembly generated an air of excitement and celebration.

"Now is our time," Representative Harding said as she turned and smiled at Torres. Standing, she then hammered her gavel into the accompanying sound block multiple times. "Order! Order!" It took mere seconds more for the room to become deathly quiet.

"Joyous times, indeed, my fellow Americans!" she exclaimed to which a roar of excitement washed over the throng, and cheers reverberated from within the room to the farthest regions of the Sagan until Harding's upraised hands silenced all. "Even now, our teams are stepping upon the surface of Mars, affirming our Nation's life and prosperity... and Earth is just weeks away." Again, a tumultuous roar, laughter and cheers bellowed from the gathered. Harding smiled; she had them. "The president has brought us to a victory over fear and doubt... and we congratulate him and celebrate his leadership." All stood and applauded, including Senator Torres.

"My God, we have them," Antonio whispered as elation overwhelmed him.

"Now, it is up to us," Harding continued after quieting the cheers and clapping and after all returned to their seats. "We must set things in motion, to restore our Nation to its glory. We are even now communicating with the Maximus representatives to craft legislation, which will guarantee our survival and our continued prosperity. Be assured, your representatives are committed to joining President Counts in ushering in a new 'American' century." Though somewhat subdued, another series of cheers sprang from the gathered citizens. Harding raised her hands once again, but she failed to utilize the sudden silence before new voices chimed in beginning with a woman Harding anticipated trouble from.

"Representative Harding... do the Sagan and Maximus legislators plan to hold open-door meetings so the citizenry remains abreast of Constitutional adjustments?" Kristy Mazurek asked after standing above those around her. A lead reporter from the Sagan Trib-une, Kristy's long, red hair and crystalline eyes herald-ed her spirit for and skill in uncovering the best laid plans of politicos.

"We have committees in place to make certain a number of the population is involved in our delibera-tions, Ms. Mazurek," Harding replied quickly. "Now, if I could continue…"

"And will these committees be comprised of more than just your staff, Representative Harding?" an-other reporter asked as he stood from his seat in the front row.

"Stefan," Harding whispered before swallowing hard. The man before her always maintained a jovial smile and commanding presence, which he always used to best those with ulterior motives. "Mr. Mychajliw… chasing conspiracy illusions again I see."

"As I recall, you were censured on several occa-sions for promoting friends over more qualified candi-dates for government posts," Stefan added as he turned and stared at Antonio.

"Those missteps were due to clerical errors, Mr. Mychajliw," Senator Torres.

"Of course," Stefan replied. "Wasn't it your sis-ter who investigated the case?" Senator Torres shot a frightened glance towards Harding who adeptly moved the discussion elsewhere.

"New committees are already being assembled," Harding said after nodding towards the senator. "What's important now is that we look to the future."

"And this future you speak of, will younger vot-ers be locked out of the decision-making process as in prior movements?" said a young woman who pushed through those standing in the back of the room. The woman had long, brunette hair and bright, clear eyes that bore into the representatives. Stefan, Kristy and other members of the media, not to mention the present politicians, knew the woman well mostly for the radio program she started when only sixteen, which was seven years earlier. The radio show bore her name, Chelsea Krost, and through that platform, Chelsea built up a reputation of being a hard-nosed investigator and force for bringing generations together, the latter of which was the last thing Harding needed.

"Unfortunately, we cannot divulge the identities of the committee members, Ms. Krost," Harding replied curtly, an attempt to end further debate. "Now, if everyone will please calm down. As communication with Maximus delegates is ongoing and includes sensitive discussions, we cannot divulge everything planned at this time."

"That's convenient," Chelsea said; the murmurs that spread through the gathered seconds later confirmed that Chelsea was not alone in her frustration and suspicion. Torres sensed the building uproar first; he scoped out the quickest, safest exit for him while Harding continued to stem the raucous. Torres knew his compatriot fought a lost battle.

"Representative Harding is correct in her assertions," a voice said above the collected protest. The voice was sweet, but it carried with it a steel edge that silenced all others. Only the guard stationed at the entrance dared speak now, and that was only to announce the voice's personage.

"All rise!" the guard exclaimed. "The Honorable Christy Fornoff presiding." Captain Fornoff, the Interim Judge Advocate General of the Navy, marched through the gathered, past Harding and Torres, to the dais at the room's back. Donning her dress-blue uniform, her blond hair laying just below her shoulders,

Judge Fornoff outshone everyone in the room. Then, as Christy turned and sat in the leather, wing-backed chair behind her bench, her true strength became apparent through her strong eyes, eyes that reflected hope to the hopeless and justice to the unjust.

"The legislature is within its rights to generate committees as they see fit," Christy continued. All shot vacant stares at Harding and Torres while Harding let slip a wry grin. "Representatives Harding and Torres, when you are ready to begin transmitting information to the Maximus legislators, pass along your correspondence to my bailiff; I will review the materials promptly and inform you when and if the materials will be transmitted." Harding and Torress stood up and turned immediately, horrified.

"Your Honor, you have no right to see our bills!" Torres exclaimed.

"This ship is at DEFCON 1, Senator Torres. As per current UCMJ regulations, all transmissions must be made through either the president or through the Judge Advocate General. If you wish, you can always present your material to the president, if you prefer. This court is adjourned!" Picking up her well-worn, oak gavel, Christy hammered into the complimenting sound block. Harding and Torres approached the bench while the bailiff cleared out the room.

"Your Honor, this is unacceptable!" Harding exclaimed before Christy stopped all protest with a glare.

"I have no doubt that the two of you have been quite busy," Judge Fornoff said, her tone relaxed. "I suggest you meet with President Counts to discuss your plans. I have a feeling that course would be best for everyone. Now… get out of my courtroom."

Chapter 18

"They're friggin nuts," Francis said as he watched several other team members drop down into the sewage pipe. The voices of the descended Marines and NCIS agents, broadcast through their helmet speakers, echoed; it sounded as if the Mars sewage pipes were mammoth in size and filled with opportunities to explore. Francis, however, was not so eager to join in.

Special Agent Harrington, after requesting additional Marine support, was lowered first and followed by Sergeant Zavack. The flow of members into the dark went quickly after that while Francis obsessed. *What contagions would he encounter and bring back to the Sagan and, consequently, inflict upon the entire crew? Would he cause the death of other crew members leading to the removal of his family from the ship, his brothers and sisters jettisoned out an airlock for Francis's actions or inaction?* OCD again seized control.

"Francis, are you okay?" Rebecca asked, her hand now resting on Francis's shoulder. "You can do this," she then whispered after he first jolted at her touch. The OCD beast reflected in her REO's eyes. "Why don't you let me carry your staff, at least until we're underground?"

"Thank you," Francis said, handing over his staff before trudging through the planetary sediment until he stood above the drainage tunnel. His suit filtered out fumes from the atmosphere, which Francis believed hid the stench from what he envisioned was below. Crouching, he saw the top rung of the rusted ladder affixed to the tunnel wall. Slowly, with periodic encouragement from Rebecca and Special Agent Hanley, Francis descended six meters before his boots touch the solidified waste that covered the tunnel floor.

"This way, Professor Burns," Corporal Dennison said as she gently grabbed his arm and led him a few steps from the ladder. Like the other Marines, Leigh held a lantern while the NCIS agents crouched to the ground to conduct tests. "Are you okay," Leigh asked after noticing Francis's blank expression. *The OCD Beast was in control.*

"I'm okay, Corporal," Francis said while he glanced about the tunnel. Though not convinced, Leigh backed away from Francis just as Rebecca approached, the fighter pilot having descended the ladder immediately after Francis.

"Report!" exclaimed Special Agent Harrington, a command that grabbed everyone's attention, save for Francis.

"No radiation signatures whatsoever," Special Agent Harvey said while she continued to scan with a Geiger counter.

"The tunnel's floor is covered in a mix of waste, sand and other particulates," Bob added after running a scan on a handful of sediment with a portable diffraction device. "No particles suggesting toxins in the sediment or air; I'd say we're clear to continue."

"You still plan on burning your suit when we get back, aren't you?" Rebecca asked Francis in a voice sure to be missed by the others.

"Good God, yes," Francis replied as he accepted his staff back from Rebecca and the analyses of the NCIS agents.

"This would be a hell of a place to film a horror movie," Special Agent Caufield remarked as he shined a light down the tunnel's portion that led away from the station above; Caufield's light could not touch the tunnel's end. From above, the sound of crushing metal along with a piercing cry from the wind affirmed Dan's remark. "Definitely a great place for a horror flick."

"Let's move!" a deep, familiar voice commanded, a voice that shook Francis from thoughts of Xenomorph-filled passageways. Just reaching the floor of the tunnel, Lieutenant Mario Williams took command. The Marines marched on in silence while the agents, Rebecca and Francis took positions mid-column. The march lasted a mere five minutes before they reached the first hatch in the tunnel's ceiling.

"That hatch should lead into the station," Todd said as he shined his flashlight about the ceiling in search of fissures or other stress marks. Meanwhile, one of the Marines scaled a cement ladder that reached up to the hatch.

"It won't budge, Sirs" the Marine said before scaling back down.

"Dennison, you got a can-opener?" Zavack asked while keeping her light and gaze on their sole means of entry to the station.

"Always, Master Sergeant," Leigh replied before removing and setting her pack at the base of the ladder. Then, after removing a small sledge, the corporal climbed up and gently tapped on the hatch overhead. She looked back towards Zavack for final clearance. Then, after a quick nod from her master sergeant, Dennison slammed at the hatch twice before opening the portal and showering her comrades with granules of rust and cement. "Heads up!" Dennison then exclaimed before she dropped her sledge and climbed out of the drainage tunnel. Zavack collected the corporal's belongings before climbing the ladder. Drawn by a sudden need to explore, Francis moved to and ascended the ladder until he too stood inside the Mars base.

***

Shadows danced at the edge of Francis's vision, their silhouettes born of the castings of flashlights. Then, as his eyes adjusted to the limited light, Francis took in the whole of the Mars base; the separate shadows suddenly merged to form a dark multifaceted entity, which seemed alive. He marveled as his comrades shuffled about the cavernous room while the huge shadow hovered. Francis felt dread every time a Marine, special agent or fighter pilot disappeared in the darkness, as if the shadow consumed the human. For comfort, Francis tightened his grip on his staff before slamming the butt of the stout stick into the metal flooring. He then reached up to the staff's head and affixed a pen-sized LED light stick into a socket. After hearing the click affirming the light was secure, Francis flicked a switch. The tiny LED bulbs scattered around the light stick cast an intense dome of light, centered on Francis, which illuminated everything in a seven meter radius. The light exposed a network of cement walls and columns, which reached beyond to the ceiling still shrouded in darkness.

"Moria," Francis said as his memory ran through scenes from Peter Jackson's film, *Fellowship of the Ring*; Gandalf again came to mind. "Be on your guard," Francis said quoting one of his favorite lines from the film. "There are older and fouler things than orcs in the deep places of the world." Without another word, Francis marched on regally, the others left in his wake. His procession ended quite abruptly.

"Um... Francis? We're this way," Bob said as he walked in the opposite direction. Francis turned and shuffled onward to catch up to Bob with Rebecca following behind. She simply smiled and shook her head while taking up the rear position. The other teams broke off and scoured their respective destinations searching for evidence of the base's final occupation.

"What the hell went on here?" was asked by nearly everyone in silence as the teams entered room after room only to find thick layers of dust covering total organization. The teams landed with schematics for every room, but the Mars station's crew apparently remodeled and redecorated. The flooring, sure enough, matched the mundane metal decking of the Sagan: cold, sterile and lifeless. Yet, the walls and modified furniture brought warmth to the dwelling. Pictures of families, pets and the station's astronaut's were orderly arranged along the walls; it appeared as if each astronaut decorated her or his own wall. Shreds of gray bunting, made of unidentifiable cloth, still hung over the station's multiple portals. Similarly, the tables were covered with cloth fragments.

"Table cloths?" Rebecca asked to no one in particular as she reached out and brushed away some of the dust covering one of end tables. The fragment of cloth she touched crumbled at her touch. "What the hell went on here?"

"Life," both Bob and Francis replied as they scanned over the photos on the walls. Rebecca walked over to Francis as he pointed to one of the larger groups of photos.

"Look," Francis said as he moved his staff closer to the wall. "These images are of the astronauts alone. All of them, and the images show them aging... over decades it would appear." Bob joined them at

Francis's wall as Francis pointed out one of the astronauts in particular. "See here? Her hair is black; she looks to be mid-aged. Yet in this photo, her hair has grayed considerably."

"And check out the wrinkles in the second photo," Bob added as he leaned in close to exam the photo. "These photos were taken decades apart."

"And they were all taken at the Mars base," Rebecca said as she pointed to the base support columns present in both photos.

"They were stranded here," Francis said, "and left here to die."

"But what ultimately happened to them?" Rebecca asked as she turned and looked about the room, her eyes seeking knowledge beyond sight as she contemplated the possibilities.

"Hanley, you there?" Agent Harrington's voice called out over the com system.

"We're here, Todd."

"I need the professor and the med team in the crew quarters. We've got a body."

Chapter 19

Francis and Rebecca, guided by GPS, hurried on to the crew's quarters while Agent Hanley remained behind to document their findings of the living space they investigated. They crossed through a central maintenance bay while on their trek and came across Corporal Dennison and an engineering crew. Their findings were quite uplifting.

"What do you got there, Corporal?" Rebecca asked as she stopped to shine a light at a dark brown SUV that Dennison was inspecting. The vehicle looked to be in pristine condition.

"You don't know what this is?" Corporal Dennison asked, clearly shocked by the captain's lack of knowledge.

"Now you know what I've been dealing with, Leigh," Francis interjected as he reached out at touched the vehicle. "My God, she's a beauty. It's an Oldsmobile Storm, one of the first vehicles the company designed after its rise from extinction. Along with a new line of Cutlass Supreme, Oldsmobile created vehicles that revolutionized fuel efficiency and safety."

"They built the vehicles with a new polymer coating that helped solidify the frame," Leigh added as she gently ran her fingers down one of the vehicle's panels. "Perfection from the hands that brought us the assembly line."

"Do you three need a moment?" Rebecca asked as she watched her teammates walk about, clearly mesmerized by the SUV. "Wait, I thought Ford first used the assembly line for making cars?"

"No, Olds did," Francis said as he shook his head. His eyes never left the Oldsmobile. "Ford gets most of the credit, but Ransom Olds first used the assembly line in 1901, years before Ford showed up on the scene. Ton for ton, no company has produced as many award-winning and innovative vehicles as Oldsmobile."

"Good to know," Rebecca said before continuing on towards the crew's quarters. "Let's move, Francis."

"Right," he replied before standing and turning towards Corporal Dennison. "Please tell me that this is going back with us?"

"Oh, most definitely," she said, her eyes still fixed on the car. "The Storm's engine appears shot, but I have a spare on the Sagan that will work just nicely. And we definitely have space on the shuttle."

"Happy tinkering," Francis said as he moved off towards Rebecca's now distant light.

***

Francis and Rebecca arrived at the crew quarters to find Petty Officer Ashleigh Fischer and Chief John Williams standing over a cot. Francis could only make out a deteriorated blanket that clearly covered something. Tuning out the conversations of all those present, Francis walked up to the cot and gazed upon the long-dead occupant just as Chief Williams pulled back the cot's blanket.

"Elderly female," Ashleigh reported as she began scribbling notes onto an autopsy form. The mostly skeletal remains were covered in shreds of cloth, the deceased's last vestments. Francis, along with Ashleigh and John, took several minutes to examine the remains for details that would clarify a cause of death.

"No signs of physical trauma," John said as he closely examined the deceased's ribcage, spine and skull.

"At least not physical trauma," Francis added as he looked over the lower extremities. "All deterioration is consistent with old age. No signs of osteoporosis or other maladies."

"What does all that mean in English?" Rebecca asked; she was standing a few meters away not wanting to crowd the investigators.

"It means she likely died from old age," Ashleigh said as the petty officer snipped off a few strands of the deceased's remaining long, red hair. "This should provide some information regarding her diet and overall health at time of death." Ashleigh secured the sample in a plastic bag before then recording some notes, including the comments from Chief Williams and Francis.

"What do we got, Doc?" Agent Harrington asked as he stepped up between John and Ashleigh. Francis, before responding, turned about to observe the entire crew quarters by staff-light. While covered in shredded blankets, the other cots appeared orderly as if unused after having been made.

"She was the last," Francis said as he looked back to Todd. "There's nothing to suggest foul play here." Francis looked down at the deceased and gently rested his hand on the exposed arm. "She died alone."

"Special Agent Harrington, Captain Sanford," Lieutenant Mario Williams said from across the room. "We're about ready to power up the computer systems." Rebecca and Todd approached the main computer terminal where Sergeant Zavack was connecting a portable battery pack to the system.

"Use minimum battery power," Rebecca said as Zavack connected battery leads to the Mars computer. "We don't want to blow the system."

"Not my first rodeo, Captain," the sergeant replied as she crawled under the desk and finished her prep work. "Besides, these power packs don't provide much oomph." Sergeant Zavack went back to conducting a final check of the system as Mario and Rebecca sat at the terminal. Minutes later, power flowed into the computer, the first time in centuries they estimated.

"What information are you hoping to get?" Rebecca asked as Mario flicked on a number of switches. No response came from the controls.

"If we're lucky, they kept logs of their actions and experiments," Mario replied as he continued to attempt the activation of the system. "Nothing yet, Sergeant."

"Damn!" Karen exclaimed as she maneuvered under the terminal to reconfigure the wiring she'd spent the last fifteen minutes on. "How's this?" A series of the terminal's switches glowed red.

"We're hot," Mario said as he flicked on the main power switch. The terminal hummed, a sound proceeded by the smell of a freshly extinguished candle. "Gotta love the smell of centuries old dust burning," Mario joked as he pulled up the directory of files saved to the main hard drive. "Over half of the main drive is filled, Captain, and the files look intact. I recommend we transfer the files to portable drives and then remove the hard drives entirely before we start examining content. We don't want to start opening files and then have a virus or burnout, which I think is a possibility considering how long these systems have been offline."

"You have the ball, Lieutenant," Rebecca replied. "Get it done and transfer everything to the shuttles while we wrap up our investigations. Sarge, you're with me."

"Yes, sir," Sergeant Zavack said before grabbing her tool kit and joining Rebecca. "What do we have left to do, Captain?"

"The Terradome is all that's left," Rebecca replied before activating her com system via her wrist communicator. "Lieutenant Morris, report!"

"One of the tanks was bone-dry, Captain," Shawn Morris said, his voice crackling from interference. "The other tanks combined had just enough to fill the shuttle's storage tank."

"How's the water looking?" Rebecca asked, hopeful.

"It's looking good, Captain," Shawn replied. "Initial tests indicate no contaminants and no visible particulates suggest contamination. We'll wait for a more thorough analysis before final action, of course, but I think we've hit pay dirt."

"How much longer until you've drained the tanks?" Rebecca asked as she made notes into a small tablet.

"Another fifteen minutes and we should be good here."

"Well done, LT!" Rebecca exclaimed. "Update the admiral and then get your team secured for launch."

"Understood. Morris out." Rebecca returned her attention to her tablet while Francis recorded measurements and other info into a notebook. The symmetry of actions by the entire team, fluid and precise, went unabated for minutes until a voice shattered the illusion of order and peace.

"Agent Harvey to command," Agent Heather Harvey called out to her colleagues.

"Go ahead," Todd replied; he lifted his hands up to quiet those in the room.

"We made it into the Terradome, and we've located the other astronauts who were stationed here.

Chapter 20

Agents Harvey and Caufield entered the Terra-dome after first completing a sweep of their assigned rooms. The great, domed structure was constructed of a network of epoxy-covered, steel girders framed around transparent aluminum window panes. With the sun blazing in the sky above, the view in the dome was far from what anyone could have expected.

The light, disjointed by the girders as well as condensation on and fractures in the panes, reflected off of a mix of greenery, plant species of which neither scientist had ever seen. Chirping from the agents' suits indicated the internal suit temperature was adjusting to the outside air; the dome air was over 90 degrees Fahrenheit. Dan reached down and dug his fingers into the rich, dark soil interspersed between weeds, grass, vines and trees.

"It's a silty loam," Dan said as he dropped the soil into his palm scanner. The scanner ignited in a series of lights as its programming took over. "Picking up large amounts of water, potassium and nitrogen."

"Dan, look at this," Heather said as she reached out and touched the broadleaf of the nearest tree. "It's like a palm leaf in texture. But its shape? It looks like some kind of maple." Walking further into the dome, more species were revealed including berry-bearing ferns and trees with a variety of fruit resembling plums, papayas, bananas and apples. Every step brought new discovery, yet one realization overwhelmed all others; a mass of vines extended beyond the panes of the

Terradome, through gaps where caulking once existed. Looking up, Dan and Heather could see leaves blowing in the winds reaching through the dome's gaps. The wind action generated an eerie cry, which again made Dan think of any number of horror flicks. The perfect conditions for their next discovery: nine graves, the last of which was vacant.

***

It took another thirty minutes for Francis, Rebecca and the small core of remaining forces to reach agents Caufield and Harvey, mostly because of their burden: the remains of the astronaut discovered inside the base. Their procession conducted in silence, all present recognized the importance of laying the astronaut with her Mars family. Francis walked along the line of headstones at the head of each grave, each merely a slab of cement long since covered with a mix of red and black sediment. It all seemed mechanical to Francis. The NCIS agents, save for Agent Harrington who helped carry the remains, bagged samples of soil and plants. Kathleen Leary and a squad of Seabees, meanwhile, investigated the foundation of the dome in search of ways to shore it up and rebuild.

"The Martian atmosphere is showing an increased level of hydrocarbons and Ammonia, and the planet's gravity has increased," Francis heard one Seabee report back to the Sagan. Had the terraforming activities succeeded in turning human occupation of the Red Planet into reality? How was gravity increased? Francis pushed away from that thought as he bent down over to the last headstone.

"Angela Marie Kretz," Francis said after he brushed the sediment off the headstone that overlooked the lone empty grave. He recorded the name in his tablet while Sergeant Zavack and Special Agent Harrington lowered Astronaut Kretz's remains into the ground. "I am so sorry, Angela," Francis continued as the bearers climbed out of the grave. "You will be remembered." Memories of tradition, movies and books flooded Francis's mind and pushed Francis to grab a handful of soil and sprinkle granules over Angela's remains. Sergeant Zavack did not miss Francis's words and actions, nor did she fail to notice the welling of tears in his eyes.

"She's at peace, Francis," Karen said as she squatted by Francis and placed a comforting hand on Francis's shoulder. "We'll go on with her bravery in our hearts, and in that she will live on." Karen then looked about as she stood, cognizant of the activities wrapping up around her. "You stay here, Francis. I'll see if I can find shovels so we can finish laying her to rest. As she marched off, Francis looked again to Angela's headstone. He traced the letters of her name with his index finger; it appeared the letters had been ground into the slab with a chisel. Below Angela's name, Francis noticed the engraving of a cross. Standing, lacking words for a eulogy, Francis quietly sang the first verse of Amazing Grace.

His eyes now closed, Francis listened beyond the activities of the present and tried imagining the days when Angela and her teammates monitored and tended to the Terradome's species. He smiled while considering the thrill of terraforming operations, of exploring a world. The knocking of the doors at the dome's entrance jarred Francis from his tranquil thoughts and drew his attention to the wind channeling through the dome's gaps and down through the entranceway. Then, Francis heard a hiss and felt a breeze emanating from between a nearby pane and it's not so supportive girder frame. Francis looked about as layers of dust were stirred up by the growing wind. Malevolent forms soon appeared amidst the gyrated particles of dust and sediment. Once Francis's eyes adjusted to the now flickering LEDs atop his staff, the fantasy fanatic recognized the ever-changing forms, all villains from the stories he read in his youth.

The Winter Witch, the self-proclaimed ruler of Narnia first materialized, her dead-gray eyes sending a shiver up Francis's spine. Modru of Mithgar replaced the witch, his visage causing Francis's stomach to churn before a new shade arose: Takhisis! The Dark Queen seemed to smile at Francis. Was she amused by his attempt to withstand her? The horrors were just beginning.

Ancient evils now flashed before Francis's eyes. Francis gleaned the forms of Counts Dracula and Strahd from dust kicked up nearby. They appeared to stare but for a moment at Francis before they too turned and dissipated into a swirling cloud of particulates. Music then played through Francis ears as the shade of Darth Sidious appeared. Francis knew the music was in his mind alone, the music that often announced Vader's presence. The Emperor stared and laughed at Francis, but the Sith lord's laughter remained silent.

It was then that he heard a soft yet piercing cry just as a large cloud of dust amassed before Francis.

"Isssstarrriii," Francis heard whispered in the air. Then, for but a second, two dark orb-shaped spots flared within the dust, like eyes. Francis grasped his staff with both hands and thrust it in front of him. The LED lights suddenly intensified, bored into the dust cloud and seemed to drive it to the upper reaches of the dome, but any hopes of the cloud's destruction were quickly thwarted. Francis watched as the dust filtered in between the panes of transparent aluminum and the girders where the cloud hovered; the girders seemed to waver in the limited light.

"Issssstarrrriii," voiced the wind once more as others moved about, seemingly unaware of the voice. Francis raised his staff and glanced about the structure. Shadows flickered about the periphery wherever he looked. Francis's breathing quickened.

"Sauron," Francis whispered as he tightened his grip on the staff. "Be gone!"

"Are you all right?" Rebecca called over to her copilot, having heard Francis's last words. She caught a glimpse of Francis's eyes as he scanned about in search of something. Something was wrong; she drew her sidearm and ran to his side, the others still oblivious to Francis's actions.

"Your weapon is of no use against the denizens of darkness," Francis said. He then turned and looked into Rebecca's eyes. Francis's now bloodshot eyes and furrowed forehead chilled Rebecca into true frost. "Run," he whispered before turning back towards some yet unseen foe. "Run! Fall back to the station, now!" Everyone now turned their attention to Francis. "Run!"

"What the hell is going on?" Admiral Southern exclaimed over the com system.

"Something's wrong with Professor Burns, Sir," an aide was heard replying by those on Mars. Back on the Sagan, fears abound of monsters and disease.

"Frost, report!" General Leary exclaimed. He glanced over to Admiral Southern; he knew her concerns. Rebecca, meanwhile, ignored the command.

"Francis, what the hell is wrong?" she asked as she found herself backing up.

"Run!" Francis ordered. Admiral Southern and all aboard listening heard the exchange. For Taryn Southern, it was a moment that boiled down to one thing: her steadfast belief in and trust of Paul Leary.

"And when he shows his worth, you owe me," words spoken earlier by General Leary that now forced Taryn's hand.

"All hands, evacuate the dome!" Admiral Southern commanded over the com system. "That's an order!" Her words preempted the sound of twisting metal; the dome's girders were caving to the air pressure generated by the wind between window panes and through the dome's main entrance. No one in the service ever disobeyed Admiral Southern.

"Fall back to the shadow!" Francis cried out as the others vacated the dome, his words a quote of Gandalf as the mythical wizard stood against the Balrog. The cloud neither approached nor dissipated. It lingered, hovering overhead as if planning its strike, like a monstrous dust devil.

"Francis, move it!" Rebecca called out as she pushed others towards the exit. Her words fell on deaf ears. Francis stood, giving the others time to flee while fragments of girders and window panes dropped about the structure. Rebecca helped a few of her comrades stand after falling debris pinned them to the ground. It was after helping a third person that Rebecca looked back to Francis, which is when she saw the cloud. The mass of wind and sediment started to shift its position, reaching forward only to retreat as Francis shifted his staff to block the cloud's path. *Was it truly alive?* A pane dropped from the dome, landing nearby, which shook Rebecca into reality. She instinctively reached out to her copilot in the only way that seemed workable.

"Francis Aloysius Burns, now! We're clear!" Rebecca's exclamation jarred Francis back to his senses; he turned and sprinted towards the exit, brushing aside falling objects with his staff while the cloud hovered as if awaiting orders to attack. It didn't wait long.

The dome's shifting air pressure took its toll, and the entire back wall of windows collapsed or shattered. The now unobstructed wind drove the cloud forward towards Francis, knocking him to the ground when he was only a meter away from safety. Francis, still bearing his staff, turned onto his back in time to see a support column fall in his direction. Showered by aluminum, steel and rigid plastic debris, Francis froze as he watched the girder fall. His end had come. With his last breath, the Burns raised his staff, setting its base firm against the ground while directing the staff's lit top towards the approaching girder. Another movie quote flashed through Francis's mind just as the opposing forces, staff and girder, met.

"Your staff is broken!"

Francis's staff indeed shattered under the pressure of the girder, but it served its purpose; the girder fell off to the side landing just a meter to the side of Francis. His suit now torn by shards of the staff and falling window fragments, Francis struggled to breathe as his oxygen filtered out into the atmosphere. Through troubled gasps he watched as a collective of support beams above him fell.

"Farewell," Francis said as the beams drew closer; it seemed to take an eternity. Yet, a mere five seconds passed between the time he saw the structure's final collapse commence and the moment everything crashed into the ground. Sergeant Zavack was quicker.

Zavack's strong hands grasped onto Francis's shoulders, and in one powerful thrust backward, she propelled them both back through the main doors. Karen immediately lifted Francis and carried him beyond the threat of the dome's collapse. Their safety assured, she looked over his body for critical wounds. All Karen noticed was Francis unconscious, his breath labored and a slight smile fixed on his face.

Chapter 21

"What do you fear?" the voice asked again, as it had for what seemed like days, maybe weeks. Francis didn't have an answer. He kept marching along the trail, further into the forest of pines, maples, oak and spruce, his footfalls echoed by the carpet of dried leaves and pine needles. Here, it was forever night. Here, it was forever cold, colder than space. A dozen stars provided illumination for Francis as he meandered about the forest trails, but the stars provided no direction though their light seemed familiar. The damp conifers emitted the boldest aromas while the sound of rushing water ahead drowned out all other noise.

"I know this place," Francis said at one point, but recognition failed to surface until the forest revealed the water's source: Niagara Falls. Even in the limited light, the waterfalls reined in magnificence. Thousands of liters, a cavalcade of foam and water, rushed by, a scherzo of sound accompanied by the thunderous roar of the water over the escarpment.

"The Niagara Frontier," Francis said as he turned and looked at the forests east and south of his location. The dawn then rose and passed as the eastern sky burst into flame; Francis witnessed his first sunrise. He averted his eyes westerly to adjust to the light. Before, the darkness shielded Francis's view. Now, the life-giving light of the sun illuminated an ocean of forests, drumlins and canyons, all outlined by the countless autumn leaves whose mix of red, yellow and green hues enraptured Francis Burns. He stepped further west, to start a new journey, which is when the voice returned.

"Your journey ends here," the comforting voice said. "Leave the west to your kin for you have work to do here." Francis stopped and turned once more; the voice seemed right. Francis knew his home was here, but wonder of the west and far-east remained. Yet, duty called.

"What must I do?" he asked the voice, seemingly contented by his fate.

"First, my lad, you must wake."

***

"Are you actually ready to wake?" a new voice asked; it emanated from the western clouds now reaching towards Niagara Falls. This voice was gentle and caring. A westerly wind suddenly slammed into Francis; he awoke as his lungs gasped for oxygen.

"It's about damn time," the new voice said; it seemed comforted as well as comforting. Francis's eyes struggled to open, and his limbs struggled to move. "Relax, Francis. Just rest. Now where was I?" Francis heard the shuffle of book pages before the voice spoke again. "Hobbits really are amazing creatures, as I have said before," the voice said. It was a well-known line from The Fellowship of the Ring, which Francis could not help finishing.

"You can learn all that there is to know about their ways in a month, and yet after a hundred years they can still surprise you at a pinch," Francis said, his voice no more than a whisper. He opened his eyes and focused on the form standing over him; the voice belonged to Rebecca. "Are you actually reading The Lord of the Rings?" he asked, chuckling for a moment.

"Yes, against my better judgment. Now, shut up and listen." Rebecca's words were curt, but there was an unmistakable relief in her voice. She continued to read from *The Fellowship of the Ring* while Francis awakened further, his senses reaching to every corner of the infirmary in which he rested. The room's low ceiling and gray, metal walls evoked memories of prison movies; the room just needed bars to make the image complete. Of course, the addition of the medical equipment added flair to the imagery and quickly turned Francis's thoughts to the scene in the movie *Aliens*, when Sigourney Weaver awakens from fifty-seven years of hyper-sleep onboard an orbiting medical facility. He absently rubbed at his chest as his breathing eased.

"What happened?" Francis asked, his eyes and attention now on Rebecca.

"Everything is all right, Recoil," she replied, setting the book on a nearby table and then taking Francis's hand in hers. "You got clunked on the head pretty good, but you suffered no major injuries. A slight concussion is all." Francis leaned back into his pillow as his growing alertness finally registered Rebecca's assessment; the pain to his head was mild, but indeed present. "Don't worry, they've pumped you full of a lot of pain killers. The pain should be at bay for some time."

"What about the others?" Francis asked, his eyes tuned in once again on Rebecca.

"We're all okay, thanks to you. We're back on the Sagan and Earth-bound once more. You've been out of it for a couple days now. Rest, Francis, and regain your strength. You'll need it for the Earth landing."

"Admiral Southern still intends for me to join the away team?" Francis asked. He never actually believed the admiral trusted him.

"Let's just say she was quite complementary with your actions as was most of the team. You made quite an impression, my friend."

***

"All right, all right," Admiral Southern said as she stepped off the elevator, General Leary by her side with a smile on his face.

"Then say it," Paul said, his eyes focused ever forward.

"You were right, I owe you," Taryn replied, begrudgingly. "Are you ever going to let this go?" she asked just as she stopped in front of President Count's quarters.

"Not anytime soon at least," Paul replied before Taryn knocked on the door.

"Come in," Clarence called out from beyond the door; the admiral and general entered without further chiding. The president sat in an arm chair next to the room's lone window, which offered a view of distant stars and nebulae. "Please have a seat," Clarence added before moving over to one of the chairs around the room's conference table. "Sit-rep?"

"Do you want the good news or the bad news first, Mr. President?" Taryn asked as she and Paul took seats across from Clarence.

"I'm not in the mood for delays, so why don't you hit me with the bad news first," Clarence responded.

"Very well," Taryn said as she slid over a folder that Clarence immediately opened. "We scoured each of the hard drives recovered from the Mars base and have yet to find an uncorrupted file."

"Terabytes of potential data, and you haven't recovered a single file?" Clarence asked, exasperated.

"The shelf life of flash drives and cds is barely a hundred years, Mr. President," General Leary interjected. "Frankly, sir, we're lucky the drives are bootable at all. As it stands, there's still encrypted files that may contain retrievable data. NCIS is still working on those."

"You're good news better be amazing, Admiral," Clarence said as he turned towards the senior naval officer.

"The water we retrieved, while small in quantity, has been successfully treated. It's being added to our reserves as we speak and should comfortably support continued space travel for an additional nine months," she replied before pulling out another file. "And then there is this," she said as she handed Clarence the file.

"What am I looking at, Admiral Southern?" the president asked as he flipped through a series of high-resolution images.

"Those are the first images relayed by our satellite, which successfully attained orbit around Earth approximately three hours ago."

"Since when does Earth have a ring?" Clarence asked as he pointed to a thin, gray line surrounding the planet. "What the heck is this?"

"Our best guess, Mr. President, is that it's a ring of space debris," General Leary said as he stood and leaned over the table. "There's additional metallic signatures scattered about the stratosphere, but the majority of debris is within this thirty meter ring around the equatorial zone, Sir. We believe it's the remains of the satellites and space stations that once orbited the planet.

We're currently scanning the debris field for power signatures; nothing as yet."

"Keep me informed, General Leary," Clarence said as he leaned back in his chair. Paul nodded to Clarence and Taryn before moving towards the door. "And Paul?"

"Yes, Mr. President?" Paul asked as he stopped and looked back.

"Your selection of Professor Burns?" Clarence asked as he stood and approached the general, extending a hand as he drew close. "Well done, Paul. Very well done." Clarence and Paul shook hands before the general nodded to his commanders once more and departed. "You know, we owe General Leary a vacation," Clarence said before taking his seat once more.

"Neither of you are going to let me forget this are you?" Taryn asked rhetorically.

"What do you need from me, Taryn?"

"Just keep those politicos out of my hair like you've been doing, Mr. President. I have too many preparations to make for the Earth landing to contend with trivial concerns."

"Understood, Admiral." Clarence smiled as he poured a glass of water for them both from a pitcher on the conference table. Moments passed while they sipped at the water, each still in conservation mode.

"How's the search for cabinet members?" Taryn asked after finishing her glass.

"Slow, but at least I'm getting great support from the Sagan's reps. Well, support may be a strong word." Clarence ended his statements with a smile and a chuckle.

"So, they're not being too confrontational?" Taryn asked as she refilled her glass. "Any appointments close to confirmation?"

"Not cabinet-wise, but my selection of Judge Fornoff as Chief Justice seems set for confirmation," Clarence replied. The president returned his gaze out the window, stars and distant planets the only objects in sight. "My God, we truly are alone."

"We're not totally alone, Clarence," Taryn said as she set down her glass and flipped through the images. She selected one and slid it over to the president. "We needed to scan into a few fixed points to help plot the more comprehensive studies of the planet. I thought it would help you to see that our Fathers are with us, Mr. President."

Clarence looked at the image before him, which immediately boosted his spirits about the coming mission and the decisions he would need to make. Clear and showing one of America's greatest edifices in pristine condition as if all erosion had ceased, the image showed the glory and splendor of Mount Rushmore. Indeed, President Washington and company were with them.

Chapter 22

Considering the stoic and sterile environment the Sagan's crew lived in, everyone owed some gratitude to Chief Douglas Phillips. Head of Radiological Services in the infirmary, Chief Phillips had a knack for bringing proverbial sunshine to even the darkest days. Every patient became Doug's true friend, and not a sole was allowed to leave his care without smiling at least once. And that smile had to be genuine.

"But all I do is sit in the cockpit, Chief!" Francis exclaimed as he continued to argue. Francis, knew it was a lost cause, but he desperately wanted to change the mind of Chief Phillips.

"Here's the deal, Francis," Doug replied. He was seated at the patient room desk typing notes into his tablet, his back to the wheelchair-bound Francis. "If I find out you got out of that chair and into the cockpit, even just to sit and read a book, I'm gonna superglue your ass to that chair. Do we understand each other?" Doug turned to face Francis as he made that last statement. Francis looked down to his toes in defeat.

"Don't worry, Chief, I'll keep an eye on him," Francis's cousin Kathleen said. She reached over from her chair and patted Francis on the back, an attempt to console her stubborn cousin.

"Listen here, Francis," Doug said as he wheeled across the floor still sitting on his chair and stopping centimeters from Francis. "You and I both know the G-forces fighter crews are exposed to. The injuries you sustained will not heal properly if you are exposed to such force prematurely. You're lucky there's enough time to get you rested and cleared for the Earth mission." Francis, never looking up, nodded in response. "There's also another reason you can't fly until we reach Earth."

"And what's that?" Francis asked as he looked up at his caregiver.

"Because I said so!" Doug Phillips said as he tenderly smacked Francis in the back of the head. Francis smiled. "All right then, Francis. Get the hell outta here so I can have some peace and quiet for once. You can wheel him out now, Kathleen."

"Thanks, Chief," she replied as she pushed Francis out into the passageway that led into the heart of the Sagan.

***

Lieutenant Kristina Willis had the con. The command responsibility could not have come at a better time. Kristina's bridge shift commenced not long before the Sagan's satellite, dubbed 'Scout', secured a high orbit around Earth, and the first images were breathtaking to say the least. After notifying the admiral of the established orbit, Kristina ordered the initiation of Scout's three multispectral scanners. The immediate concern for Kristina's team was to survey Washington D.C. in hopes of finding intact structures and any indication of human activity. Aside from securing images of the still-standing Washington Monument, the capitol scan proved pointless. The live-imaging scanner only revealed an endless cover of pines, spruce and countless deciduous tree species. The admiral's eventual arrival sparked a flood of discussions on where to focus the next series of scans. Aside from a few unique requests of her commanding officer, Kristina was given free rein to explore through Scout's looking glass for answers to the Sagan crew's infinite questions.

"Ops! I want to reposition Scout!" Kristina commanded as she scanned over a projection map of the United States on a nearby monitor.

"Where to, Lieutenant?" one of the science officers asked as he stood next to Kristina.

"If we're looking for a needle in a haystack, let's increase our odds. We're approaching early-autumn. Let's look to the southern states for signs of a habitation, somewhere near a large source of freshwater." Kristina's statement spurred a quick search on the part of the science officer.

"We can't get further south than Florida, which would make Lake Okeechobee a good starting point."

"Make it so!" Kristina commanded as she continued her examination of the map. It took only a few moments before glitches emerged.

"Lieutenant! We are have a problem refocusing the live-image camera," another science officer said as several shift members started pounding away at their keyboards and miscellaneous touch screens. Kristina watched the main monitor as the satellite's real-time image of Florida flipped from between orbital shots of the country to an only slightly tightened view of the lower half of the State of Florida.

"Switch to infrared!" Kristina commanded, and within seconds a tight image of the lake and its surrounding landscapes emerged. A mix of undecipherable blue, red, yellow, green and orange hues now blanketed the monitor, dancing about the edges of a gray space, which depicted the lake itself. "Pan southward to the Everglades." The resulting image displayed a greater variety of hues, which only increased Kristina's questions. "Does Scout's infrared scanner have the ability to capture clear images of life-forms within a small space, say a twenty meter square area?" She asked no one in particular.

"Definitely, Lieutenant," came the reply before one of the senior techs punched in new commands. Now, the image on the main monitor showed the outlines of creatures, quadrupeds and birds. The number of specimens was indeterminable as the heat signatures overlapped and intermingled.

"Search the archives and see if we have infrared images from the same locale before the Sagan's maiden voyage." This command took minutes to carry out, but a comparable image from 2027 was located and displayed next to the current images cast by Scout. The contrast startled Kristina; the diversity of organisms appeared to have nearly quadrupled in three hundred years. "How accurate can we get with this? Can we pick out different species based just on a heat signature?"

"Most definitely, Lieutenant, though scanning into water poses a number of issues," one scientist replied before Kristina cut him off.

"Expand the scope of Scout's scan to fifty meters. I want every animal you find identified ASAP, and get engineering to see if they can get the Live-imager back online!" Kristina's orders received no objections, which allowed her to move unimpeded to a nearby receiver. "Get me the admiral!"

Chapter 23

As with any journey through the Sagan, Kathleen and Francis's path was circuitous and included repeated exposure to smells, everything from burning oil and solder to various foodstuffs. Francis's attention to the smells soon fell away as they neared a sign directing passersby to the flight deck.

"Stop what you're thinking!" Kathleen scolded as she pushed her cousin past the signs. "Admiral Southern and my dad already ordered everyone to keep you clear of the flight deck, so don't try anything."

"Are you kidding? I don't think Mr. Phillips was kidding about gluing my ass to this chair. That's reason enough for me to not push things." They both laughed as they reached an elevator, which Kathleen stopped at. "Where's Rebecca?" Francis asked as she worked the elevator controls.

"She wanted to come, but the admiral has Rebecca organizing an op." Francis felt forgotten. Days stuck in the infirmary with no results from the Mars mission relayed to him left Francis bored and agitated. Kathleen and Rebecca had been his only visitors, and neither had been very forthcoming with details. Francis closed his eyes and thought about the Mars mission again, about the voices he heard. His memories played out against a backdrop of the sound of the chair's wheels rolling across the metal decking until all stopped. He opened his eyes to find them facing the pilot's briefing room just as two pilots exited. The air emanating from the room smelled of pizza.

"Hey, you two, did you leave us any food?" Kathleen asked as the pilots stopped and shook her hand. "Francis, I want you to meet two of the Aces that fly CAP during quiet hours. This is Tony Comito and Scott Schubbe." Roughly the same height, the two pilots bore jovial smiles and clear, friendly eyes.

"It's a pleasure, Professor Burns," Scott said as he shook Francis's hand. Tony then proceeded to push Scott out of the way before shaking Francis's hand.

"Nice to meet you, Professor," Tony said. "Don't start talking with Scott or we'll never get airborne."

"You implying I talk a lot?" Scott asked as he turned abruptly.

"No, I'm saying you never shut up!" Tony exclaimed before returning his attention to Francis. "Great work on Mars, Professor."

"I was lucky, that's all," Francis replied; he could feel himself blushing.

"That's not luck, Professor," Scott interjected before putting his hand on Francis's shoulder. "That was keen observation on your part, and a number of our dear friends are alive because of it." Francis was speechless.

"Come on, see what I said," Tony said as he pushed Scott onward. "By the way, it's my turn to fly point."

"You nearly clipped my plane the last time you were point," Scott replied before pushing Tony into the wall." Francis watched as the two pushed each other about the hall, their joking no longer audible.

"Those two are good friends, and two of the best pilots on board," Kathleen said as she again pushed Francis forward into the briefing room.

"Will they be joining the Earth mission?" Francis asked.

"No. The admiral wants them with Captain Mosher protecting the ship during the mission."

"They're that good?"

"With Rebecca on the planet, there's no one I'd trust more with the Sagan's safety." Kathleen finished her reply just as she and Francis entered the main briefing area, which was packed with pilots and tables of food.

"Ten-hut!" Rebecca ordered; everyone stood and raised their hand in salute. Kathleen, meanwhile, wheeled Francis to the front where Rebecca stood. Once stopped, Kathleen stood at attention and saluted as well. Then, after looking up at Rebecca, Francis saluted; everyone's hands dropped to their sides after Francis lowered his. "Francis Aloysius Burns, on behalf of President Clarence Counts, Admiral Taryn Southern and the crew of the Sagan, I thank you for your service."

"Hear, hear!" a number of the gathered shouted.

"In honor of your actions on Mars," Rebecca continued, "we gathered to share a meal and a movie, or rather a mini-series. At ease!" Everyone sat in their chairs. Kathleen maneuvered Francis to the front row, center aisle.

"What can I get you?" Kathleen asked. "We have the finest selection of genetically-engineered pizza, popcorn, pretzels and soda available."

"Popcorn and some pop would be great," Francis said as Rebecca took the seat next to him." Kathleen retuned moments later and took the seat on his other side.

"Someone hit the lights!" Rebecca exclaimed before she started fidgeting with a universal remote control. "You earned this, Francis," she said before pressing 'Play' just as the lights dimmed. Rebecca then rested her arm on top of Francis's as the 2003 mini-series *Battlestar Galactica* started.

***

Earth no longer danced around the sun alone. A thin but growing ring of ice, metal and rock served as a companion to the planet now, all held in check by the gravitational pull of Earth, moon and sun. At times, the ring sparkled as sunlight danced amongst its array of surfaces and textures. It was almost alive. Yet, death ever shadowed this ring and would continue to do so as a war of machines enveloped this astral environment.

Even as the Sagan and her crew ventured towards Earth, three surviving satellites remained active. Almost living things in their respective quests, each satellite traveled amongst the ring's debris, often powered by inertia alone. All three were guided by the same principle: target and destroy all incoming craft. Once, there were seventeen such devices, each with varying payloads and guidance systems. The remaining three survived through superior fuel sources, hull integrity and arsenals. They would continue their mission until their power was depleted or they were destroyed.

Chapter 24

For Francis, the weeks preceding the Earth landing involved rehab and lectures, the latter of which he provided to crew members centered on the history of Buffalo and the environment of the Niagara Frontier. To Francis, the lectures brought new anxiety. *What if he failed to mention some bit of information that turned out vital to the mission? Would crewmates die as a result? Would the Sagan itself be annihilated for such an oversight? Would Earth become uninhabitable through his words or lack thereof? Would his family be evicted from the Sagan as a result?*

Francis knew these absurd thoughts were OCD's doing, but such recognition failed to curb the thoughts and the resulting rituals he endlessly performed to combat OCD. He did receive some respite as the pilots now routinely met to watch additional episodes of *Battlestar Galactica* as well as other sci-fi productions such as *Star Trek*, *Alien*, and the first two *Terminator* films. Soon, several pilots were investing time in other movies and television series, which led to debates on best shows and characters. All the while, Francis enjoyed the newfound companionship amongst the crew, mostly since it was centered on things he loved. Admiral Southern, meanwhile, grew a bit frustrated as pilots started using jargon from these sci-fi programs more and more. Some of the pilots went so far as to paint the word 'Viper' on their fighters alongside the crafts' tail numbers. Eventually the com officers picked up on the changes and identified the fighters as Vipers. Yet, for all the annoyance Taryn felt over these changes, she could not ignore the reality that her fighter squadron grew more cohesive by the day. They were ready for the coming mission. The Marines and Seabees were likewise prepared.

Kathleen Leary led daily drills with teams of Seabees. Their exercises included repairing construction vehicles, smelting various ores, welding and weapons training, the latter overseen by Marine drill sergeants. The Marines themselves continued their daily combat drills along with a rigorous series of endurance tests, the latter to prepare them for the trek through Upstate New York's woodlands. For the final cog in the preparation machine, all members of the away teams endured lectures by Francis. The Niagara Frontier's flora, fauna and history were ever on the minds of the Sagan's senior staff, and Francis's lectures and presentations seemed the best bet to prepare for it all, no matter how chaotic Francis tended to be. Even Admiral Southern and General Leary sat in to hear Francis's lectures, which often included a blend of legend and science to enrapture the audience.

"The Niagara Frontier's environment has long supported ample resources for habitants, human or otherwise," Francis remarked during one lecture as he tried to illustrate the complexities of landscapes the landing parties would encounter. "The British burned down Buffalo in December of 1813 in retaliation for the American sacking of Newark." The gathered looked over their maps for reference. "Newark was rebuilt and renamed Niagara-on-the-Lake," Francis added, information that the 'class' quickly processed. Francis smiled as he noticed more than a few smiles as Marines and naval personnel pinpointed the location of their maps.

"Even gripped by winter," Francis continued, "Buffalonians were able to regroup and rebuild. Within months, an assortment of structures were erected including a number of taverns, which indicates what?" Francis was in professor mode.

"The British were inept," one Marine called out. "They had the Americans running and didn't follow through." A number of those present nodded in agreement while a clamor started to rise; Francis quickly moved to refocus the discussion.

"The British blundered quite regularly during the War of 1812, not to mention the American Revolution. Yet, Britain's restraint after the burning of Buffalo may have indicated some level of British intelligence. Why?" Francis walked about the front of the room as he waited for a 'student' to engage him in the discussion.

"They knew the woodlands would make further incursions near impossible," Rebecca said as she leaned forward in her desk.

"Exactly!" Francis exclaimed as he continued on with his lecture while simultaneously projecting the next image on the room's screen. "While the battle itself was retaliation, the temptation to enact more damage likely crossed the British commanders' minds. Yet, they undoubtedly recognized that movement through the dense woodlands would make further success highly unlikely. Supply lines would have been hard to maintain. Buffalonians, meanwhile, knew the area and what resided there besides humans. Deer, fish and a host of rodents would have provided sufficient sustenance until supplies arrived from the south and east."

"And how does this help us?" one of the students asked.

"Don't expect there to be a commissary in the area of our camp," Francis said. "Knowing the flora and fauna is a must since hunting, fishing and gathering of edible plants will serve to feed us. Bottom line, there is sufficient food resources for the entire Sagan crew even after winter hits. That said, there's something else to glean from this study. In addition to a harsh, winter climate, we, like the British, must calculate the biological barriers as well." For a second, every face reflected a quizzical expression; Francis couldn't help but smile. "Predators, my dear friends. Predators like bears, wolves and coyotes will fight us for game not to mention control of the region."

"I think a few rounds from our M4's should scare away any predators, Professor," one of the nearest naval officers commented. Francis, ever prepared, pressed a button on the remote, which activated a series of video clips to run through the room's projector. First, the fury of a swarm of army ants on a multitude of non-human species was on full display as even the bulk of large herbivores seemed to evaporate over a matter of seconds, consumed by the insects' wrath. Next, the voracity of piranha, large herbivores again the main prey, showed the dangers of water ways to unwary travelers. More than a few curses were whispered by Francis's audience, but he still didn't end the show. The decimating power of tigers, grizzly bears, panthers, alligators, and sharks were on full display for thirty minutes, each creature showing the fallacy of Humanity's dominance.

"An M4 is an impressive weapon to say the least, but you better hope you don't miss," Francis said after he finally stopped the videos. "Each of these so-called monsters is nothing more than a living thing defending its perceived home and searching for sustenance for itself and its offspring. These animals don't hate us anymore than they love us. They're just looking to survive, period. Anyone of you who drops his or her guard for even a moment will be killed. Be mindful of your surroundings, because these animals know their territories better than any of you know the Sagan. Now, admittedly, I doubt you'll have to worry about alligators and sharks, but black bears and coyotes are certainly a strong possibility. An occasional mountain lion could be a concern, too. A complete list of all potential predators is included in the pamphlet you received this morning. I advise you all to familiarize yourselves with these animals as well as their tracks and behaviors. What you learn and remember now might just save your life later. Any questions?" Not a soul raised a query as their collective silence and wide eyes made clear Francis's point was received. "Then class is dismissed."

**

Tuesday and Friday evenings, like clockwork, the pilots met for drinks, popcorn and a movie. In recent weeks, Francis had joined his new comrades, but his recent injuries made it difficult to stay awake so he no longer attended. This proved fortuitous on the last movie night before the Earth mission.

After a dinner of lab-generated beef, carrots and potatoes, all stewed in thick gravy, the pilots watched Peter Jackson's THE HOBBIT: AN UNEXPECTED JOURNEY. Still the greatest visualization of J.R.R. Tolkien's seminal work, the film brought to life the journey of Bilbo Baggins, a being out of his element who ultimately shows true courage.

It was Lieutenant Jaelah Jenkins who first noticed it.

It started with the dwarves singing of the Misty Mountains and the loss of Erebor. Then later, after the film ended, the assembled pilots listened to Neil Finn's interpretation of the Misty Mountain song that played during the film's credits.

"Isn't that the song that Dr. Burns is always humming?" Jaelah asked. Though amongst the youngest present, Jaelah, call-sign 'J-Doll', was one of the brightest and most observant pilots. The others listened to several more measures of the tune until a number of them nodded in agreement. Jaelah, meanwhile, pulled out her tablet and linked to a digital copy of THE HOBBIT to find the poem behind the tune. Finn's rendition clearly diverted from Tolkien's original verses. "Why don't we create verses for Dr. Burns?" Jaelah asked her compatriots. A few of the gathered looked puzzled, but the rest assented through nodding or a word of agreement. At that point, Jaelah looked about and noticed all eyes were on her. Where to begin? She activated her word processing app before writing down a few words. "Play the song again so we can hear the rhythm." One of the pilots deftly reversed the video back to the song's beginning. Hours later, the pilots compiled verses for a new song, which they ultimately sang and recorded. In the morning, Francis heard for the first time their tune, the recording having been sent to his email. After reading the verses once through, Francis never forgot the song.

Earthward Saga

Traveling through, the cold of dark and Space
 A journey centuries old, no time to waste
Into the unknown, to find our Home

We go together, family through Fate

Orbits reached, and left in our wake
  A mystery to solve, for no voices remained
Generations to pass, and memories to fade
  Still we seek our Home again

Traveling through, the cold of dark and Space
  A journey centuries old, no time to waste
Into the unknown, to reach our Home
  We go together, family through Fate

Passed solar systems, now long forgotten
  Mysteries solved while new puzzles arisen
In search of ores, and water pure
  Our sanctuary growing more a prison

Traveling through, the cold of dark and Space
  A journey centuries old, no time to waste
Into the unknown, to secure our Home
  We go together, family through Fate

Now we near, our journey's end
  Questions remain while forward we go
What calls Earth home? What species reins?
  Until we land, no one knows

Traveling through, the cold of dark and Space
  A journey centuries old, no time to waste
Into the unknown, to reclaim our Home
  We go together, family through Fate

Chapter 25

Francis found himself once again in a conference room surrounded by politicians and military personnel five 'Sagan days' out from the Earth mission, code named *Homeland*. Rebecca and Kathleen, pivotal players in the landing operation, were hard to find in the last week and tight-lipped about the reports coming from the images captured by the satellite, Scout.

Looking around the room, Francis watched as jittery people anxiously awaited the reports for which rumors had spread. Francis himself heard that zombies were sighted along with evidence of crop marks and new pyramids. Francis Burns, remarkably, remained immune to these speculations trusting that any such discoveries would have likely required the assorted leaders to consult Francis, or at the very least, inform him his role in the mission was scrubbed.

"Ten hut!" exclaimed one of the officers, the command bringing everyone to their feet until the president, Admiral Southern and General Leary were seated. Then after a delay of a mere minute, one additional person entered; Francis immediately stood once more at attention at this person's arrival and nodded out of respect. It was the chief anthropologist aboard the Sagan and President of the Academy of Sciences himself, Dr. Aaron Podolefsky, who had entered. A jovial person and accomplished scientist, Dr. Podolefsky waived Francis to take his seat. Dr. Podolefsky was ever a humble man who cared little for titles, his concern rather that every voice be heard and considered.

"The meeting will come to order!" General Leary commanded, his clear, potent voice negating the need for a gavel to capture everyone's attention. Then, the room silent, Admiral Southern stood and took a position to the left of the room's view screen. After Taryn nodded to a nearby tech, the room darkened and the screen erupted with light as a real-time image of Earth consumed the screen's surface.

"All information we are about to discuss is classified as above top secret," Taryn said curtly; no one muttered a word to question the admiral's command. "After completing multiple scans of the planet's surface, we now can confirm that there is no sign of human life on Earth." While many in the room glanced at friends and colleagues, clearly astonished and frightened, no one uttered a single word. The admiral herself took a moment before continuing, herself unnerved by the report she must give. "As of 0600 today, no transmissions of any kind have been received from Earth just as no replies to our hails have been returned." Taryn took another moment to scan the room. She could see the despair in everyone's visage. She knew the report would only worsen with every word, but she knew she owed her crew the truth, the politicians' protests be damned.

"High resolution scans of several metropolitan regions reveal similar conditions: collapsed buildings, no discernable highways and once urban areas completed covered by mixed forests." The admiral flipped through a series of images labeled with city designations, and each image reinforced Taryn's grim revelation. Sky scrapers, monuments, highways, housing developments and schools all appeared decimated by at least a century of neglect; not a single structure seemed immune to time and the weathering it commanded.

Francis sat in awe of the intricate ways that plant life wove amongst the once stolid girders of buildings, most of which had no discernable roofs or intact windows. The only consolation for Francis was that neglect alone and not nuclear war seemed to have caused the decimation of Earth. After completing a viewing of ten American cities, Admiral Southern continued her report.

"Scans throughout the world's largest urban areas revealed similar conditions. There are no signs of any habitation let alone a major urban complex. It would appear, ladies and gentlemen, that Time has wiped clean Humanity's footprints; we are alone. Dr. Podolefsky?"

"Thank you, Admiral," Dr. Podolefsky said as he rose and stood to the left of a newly displayed high-resolution image of Earth. "This is a live shot of Washinton, D.C. taken in 2027. Now, look at the same quadrant taken yesterday at 0900." The viewer, now displaying both images side-by-side, reflected a stark contrast; the recent image showed a swathe of foliage covering what once was an extensive network of roads and highways intersected by relatively small parks, buildings and monuments. Only the Washington monument showed any resilience to the encroaching vegetation as Dr. Podolefsky cycled though twenty images of their nation's capitol. Any buildings captured in the footage were broken apart with no hope of sheltering anyone from even the gentlest rainfall.

"These images are consistent with every city survey conducted through satellite imagery," Aaron said as he removed his glasses and looked over the throng. "My friends, we are alone."

"What of the southwest?" asked one of the majors seated nearby. "You should check those areas. I doubt the dry conditions would have permitted such an extensive growth of vegetation.

"A good question, which brings us to our surveys of southwestern cities, including Los Angeles. Trust me Major, the Academy has done its due diligence. Indeed, vegetation coverage is not quite as extensive in the southwest as it is in the northeast. Yet, the droughts from the time of the Sagan's departure have long since departed. From our analysis, the southwest is in the midst of one of its longest 'wet' periods, and in such humid climates, plants have a destructive power able to decimate kilometers of cement highways and skyscrapers in a matter of decades."

"So much for global warming," the major retorted. "I thought it would take a millennium for the environment to revert this far back to normal?"

"Normal?" Aaron asked. "The damage of global warming is far from over as we are decades away from a complete reversal of the damage caused by humankind. Those estimates you refer to were based on realistic reductions in fossil fuel usage. Instead, Humanity seemingly vanished overnight, halting all fossil fuel consumption. Think about that! Three centuries without human interference and still the ozone has a significant hole over the southern hemisphere. Additionally, the sea levels around the coasts are half a meter higher than they were three hundred years ago. Given the damage to infrastructure in New York City and New Orleans, we estimate that the water levels rose as much as a full meter at its climax, which is well within estimates provided in the early twenty-first century.

"My friends, Earth is repairing itself as if Humanity was but a mere footnote in world history. Let this be a learning experience for us all. Regardless of what caused Humanity's fall, it is clear that the planet has the ability to endure as it will continue doing until the sun goes nova."

"And what are the likely causes of Humanity's fall, Dr. Podolefsky?" President Counts asked, shutting down further distractions by the major.

"Satellite imagery has provided no clues to Humanity's disappearance. A rover launched two days after Scout has landed and begun surveying two kilometers from Fort Niagara. We are awaiting its first round of scans and tests now. I will have an update within the hour. Now if you'll excuse me, I need Dr. Burns' assistance." At a nod from President Counts, Dr. Podolefsky exited the room with Francis close behind.

"It's great to see you, A-Pod," Francis said once the two anthropologists were in the hall and the conference room's door closed. A-Pod, a name Dr. Podolefsky's students used when addressing Aaron, was born out of affection and respect for the man who ever remained down-to-Earth and cordial to everyone. Aaron took Francis's offered hand before leading Francis on towards the rover mission lab.

"Are you all set for the journey, Francis?" Aaron asked as they maneuvered around crew scattered about the hallways.

"All set. What channel do you want my receiver set to?"

"Channel 11, and hourly updates would be optimal," Aaron replied as he turned to face Francis once the two were alone in the hallway. "You and I both know the dangers of our research in the hands of some."

"You're not worried about the admiral, are you?"

"No, Francis. I have every confidence in Admiral Southern as well as General Leary. They would not hold back the truth from the Sagan's population."

"The representatives?" Francis asked, but Aaron simply nodded as a crew member entered the hallway. The two waited for the passerby to be out of earshot before continuing.

"Politicians are a unique bunch," Aaron finally answered. "Fornoff and President Counts have the people's best interests at heart and will fight to keep all informed. But the senator and representative? Look out for them and any representative they send along on the mission. Understood?" Francis nodded his reply before the two continued on to the lab. Once inside, Aaron and Francis approached the main viewer, which relayed images from the camera atop the rover named 'Buster'.

"Dr. Podolefsky, you'll want to see this." One of the engineers said before punching commands into the main control console. In response to the engineer's keystrokes, a new screen popped up which displayed a still image that was grainy.

"What are we looking at?" Aaron asked as he tried to decipher the distorted shapes spread across the image.

"There was a mound positioned near the landing site. We used the mound to check the ground-penetrating radar and ended up with these images when all we anticipated was rocks and roots to show up."

"Wait a minute," Aaron said after watching the engineer scan different parts of the image. "Look in the upper-right corner." Once repositioned, Aaron, the engineer and Francis looked over the shadows and shapes.

"Pan out and refocus," Francis said as he moved closer to the screen. The adjustments were now all too clear to Aaron and Francis. Skeletons, four within the range of the camera, rested next to one another, each set of remains with the individuals' arms positioned across the chest.

"Burial mound," Aaron and Francis said simultaneously.

"You think it's Native American?" Aaron asked, turning to Francis.

"I'm not sure; there were a few burial mounds found in the Niagara Frontier region. What land forms are nearby?"

"It's the smallest of three mounds in the vicinity," the engineer replied.

"To my recollection, there were not any sites with multiple intact burial mounds, at least not in that area," Francis said as he stepped even closer to the screen. "Can you see any markers nearby?" The engineer maneuvered Buster around the mound in search of some sort of marker; one was eventually found in the form of a stone obelisk placed on the eastern side of the mound.

"Scan in closer with the main camera," Aaron commanded to which the engineer zoomed and focused the lens on the eastern most surface of the obelisk. It was inscribed with the words "Our Beloved Departed," and bore a date that seemed much too young for what appeared to be an ancient Native American burial mound born out of the Adena and their antecedents.

"That's one year after the Sagan left Earth," the engineer said upon seeing the obelisk's inscription.

"Scan the mound to the north of this one," Aaron commanded, excitement and fear evident in all three as the rover seemingly crawled towards the next mound. Once there and after a series of codes were punched into the main computer keyboard, a new scan lit up the room's main monitor. Minutes later, after making multiple adjustments to the rover's scanners, the skeletal remains of humans appeared. However, the placement was far from consistent from the earlier mound.

"What the frak!" Francis exclaimed as he looked over the image. There was no symmetry in the placement of those buried in this mound. Well over twice the size of the first, this mound contained nearly five bodies in the space the first mound devoted to one individual.

"Why are their arms and legs intertwined with the other skeletons?" the engineer asked while trying to sharpen the image. Aaron and Francis did not reply instead exchanging looks of alarm. Then, after a time of awkward silence, Aaron picked up a nearby receiver and wasted no time.

"Get me the president, now!" Aaron exclaimed while Francis returned his gaze to the screen and wondered about the new evidence of Humanity's terrifying end.

Chapter 26

"They're mass graves, Mr. President," Dr. Podolefsky said as he pointed out the three mounds, "and each is roughly seven meters deep." With the engineer still operating the room's technologies, President Counts, Admiral Southern, General Leary and Francis alone remained to observe and discuss the incoming data with Dr. Podolefsky.

"The smaller of the mounds includes uniformly placed remains with a small cache of grave goods, likely tokens for each of the mound's occupants," Francis said as he marched up to the projection of the larger mounds, which was cast onto the room's central wall. "No grave material has been detected in the larger mounds and the placement of the various remains is haphazard."

"Which means?" the president asked abruptly to cut off further delays in the scientists' findings.

"Our belief is that the smaller mound was erected first, when nearby communities first experienced a flurry of deaths," Francis said as he stepped closer to the Sagan's leaders. "The larger two mounds were likely built later, when presumably the death-rate increased exponentially, leaving little time for ceremony."

"What would cause such a crisis, to just summarily bury family?" the president asked.

Dr. Podolefsky and Francis cast somber looks towards one another before Dr. Podolefsky answered.

"A contagion," Aaron said, after which all eyes looked to the president of the main scientific community. "It's the most conceivable likelihood given the evidence gathered so far."

"Even in war, burials usually incorporate some organization of the remains," Francis added. "But when plague strikes, mass graves or pyres become essential in order to contain the outbreak."

"I take it there is no way to accurately determine what if any contagion is still present?" Admiral Southern asked as hopes dimmed.

"We have to directly analyze remains on the planet to determine if it was in fact a contagion and to see if the disease remains a threat," Aaron said. "If there was a contagion, we need to determine if it was viral or bacterial before we can really begin investigating treatment options."

"And there is the possibility that whatever caused this supposed contagion died out along with humans," Francis said. "Again, we need to get boots on the ground before we can determine anything. For now, I suggest every member of the landing party be given a course of antibiotics, just as a precaution."

"Is it feasible to keep the landing party on oxygen for the duration until we know for certain?" Clarence asked.

"The shuttles will be able to store a limited supply," Admiral Southern replied. "We can certainly send down air purification units, but what if it's something we can't filter out or create a vaccine for?" No one had an answer for that question.

"Well, is there any other bad news or is there anything good to report?" Paul asked. Again, Aaron and Francis exchanged a knowing look that bespoke of more dire news.

"We've analyzed heat signatures for multiple regions in North America and around the world," Aaron said as he nodded to the engineer. Infrared images suddenly lit up several screens, and some of the images were of the oceans instead of just land. The oceans made the most impressive display; large creatures, lit in heat signatures, dominated the ocean space. "Whales, my friends, and hundreds of them in an area that contained less than fifty at the time the Sagan left Earth. And then there's this." Aaron nodded towards the engineer who proceeded to once again punch away at his keyboard. New images appeared on the viewers, all void of the brilliant colors the infrared provided.

"What are we looking at, Dr. Podolefsky?" Clarence asked.

"That's sonar," Taryn replied; Aaron nodded while he walked up to the nearest viewer.

"Scout is equipped with multiple sensor pods, which included two ocean probes capable of limited sonar capabilities. These shadows here are schools of fish. When added to the infrared images, the ocean tells a remarkable tale." A new image appeared with the mix of hues and shadows from both the infrared and sonar images; a pod of whales appeared surrounded by schools of fish and other life forms. "Our oceans were significantly depleted of life by 2020, and now there is an abundance of life that can only be explained by the absence of Humanity. This is by far the biggest evidence of an abrupt end to human civilization on the planet. There is no other logical explanation for the ocean's resurgence." For long moments the room remained silent until President Counts broke the others' contemplation.

"I have to brief Congress on this. Admiral, you're with me." Clarence and Taryn proceeded to the door, but Clarence hesitated before leaving. "There is to be no discussion of this outside of this core group. Understood?" He turned to face the officers and scientists to assure a response.

"Yes, Sir!" replied everyone after which the president and admiral exited.

***

Francis returned to his bunk after the meeting and looked over his supplies, which he planned to bring on the mission. Aside from general gear of a mess kit, knife and med kit, Francis packed a few books, his tablet, a survival blanket and some non-regulation clothing. Lastly, there was *Glamdring*. Sharpened, oiled and in its scabbard, the sword rested atop the backpack containing all other supplies. Francis sat on his cot, mesmerized momentarily by the blade and the thought of the coming journey. As evening arrived, Francis continued to contemplate the freedom Earth promised. Alone in the barracks, he listened to the president's broadcast regarding the findings Francis and Aaron revealed earlier. Distant voices spoke of the fear that Francis anticipated. He didn't care. One way or another, Earth would bring freedom. By 'Sagan' nighttime, Francis's quarter mates slowly filed into their racks, though Rebecca remained absent. There remained talk of Earth and the possibility of a contagion, but no one approached Francis about it. It was as if he wasn't there until the courier came.

"You're ordered to go to the Admiral's quarters, asap," was the only thing the young woman said. Now months into his life in the military, Francis didn't question the order, and in minutes, he found himself knocking on Admiral Southern's hatch.

"Enter!" came the command, and Francis wasted no time entering the portal. Inside, he found the admiral and Rebecca looking over charts affixed to a light board mounted on a wall.

"That'll be all," Admiral Southern ordered before Rebecca saluted and walked towards the hatch.

"Captain Sanford," Francis said as he saluted his pilot.

"That's Major Sanford," Admiral Southern said even as Rebecca returned the salute and walked on, smiling. "Please, enter, Dr. Burns." Francis did as asked and accepted a glass offered by Taryn. The amber liquid inside, a rare commodity aboard the Sagan, was by no means unknown to Francis. No ship carrying Irishmen would be whiskey-dry.

"Thank you, Admiral," Francis said after taking a sip of the warm whiskey.

"Please sit, Francis," Taryn said as she led him to two chairs seated in front on the room's window. "Take in this view while you can. It's not likely you'll be on board anytime soon after the mission."

"I've had my fill of the stars, Admiral. All I want now for picturesque views is to watch sunrises and sunsets while standing barefoot on real grass." Taryn could not help but feel a kinship with Francis. She too as of late had felt trapped amongst the Sagan's cold, metal sheeting, but command, her command, kept Taryn going. *How did one like Francis, a person unable to serve and subsequently an outcast, keep going?*

"Are you sure you're up for this, Francis?" Taryn finally asked after a cool silence passed between them. A contagion... unknown dangers? There is no shame in backing out."

"I guess we'll soon find out, won't we?" was Francis's response. He then downed his entire glass and smiled. "Damn, that's good." Taryn smirked as she took a draw from her own glass.

"You saved my people and gave us sight we would otherwise not have. Is there anything I can give you in return?" Taryn asked; she hated owing anybody.

"Just get me to Earth, Admiral, and I'll make sure your people get where they need to," Francis said as he stood. Then, setting the glass down, he extended his hand, which Taryn took in kind. After shaking hands, Francis moved towards the door, but he stopped before exiting and turned. There is one thing you can do for me, Taryn," Francis said as he turned and looked back to the admiral. He smirked at the Sagan's commanding officer, and that smirk made Taryn quite uncomfortable.

"Somehow I know I am not going to like this," Taryn replied.

Chapter 27

"These are the days worth living for," Rebecca said as she finished zipping her pack for the mission, now just an hour away from launch. Meanwhile, in the neighboring bunk, Francis zipped closed his backpack attached to which was a long, slender polyurethane bag. "What the hell is that?" she asked her REO.

"Just some survey equipment," Francis replied as he opened another bag resting on his cot. From with that bag he pulled out two items; a book and a short sword. "These are for you, Rebecca, for the journey."

"What the hell," she said as she took the book and looked it over. "The Lord of the Rings Collection?"

"This copy of the series includes notes and details surrounding major characters and historical events that influenced Tolkien's writings." She looked at Francis as he spoke; he simply smiled with his arm outstretched holding the sword.

"You do realize they give us guns, right?" Rebecca asked as she took the sword. Removing the sword from its stiff, leather scabbard, Rebecca lifted the blade towards the light to examine it further. Much like many an ancient Celtic sword, the blade widened just a touch near the tip. The hilt and pommel, made of brass and partially wrapped with cordage, both bore markings from a language Rebecca could not decipher. Upon further inspection, additional lettering was inscribed into the blade itself. "I can't read this. What language is this?"

"It is ancient Elvish, from the times of Gondolin's glory," Francis said as he looked on.

Rebecca grinned as he spoke, simultaneously slashing the blade about to adjust to its surprising lightness. "It reads, 'Sting, Spider's Bane – Hobbit's Charge', and it is yours."

"Thank you, Francis," Rebecca said as she rejoined the sword and scabbard. For a few moments they stared at one another just smiling before Petty Officer Ashleigh Fischer intervened.

"All right, roll up your sleeves please," Ashleigh said before setting down a med pack on a nearby cart and pulling out two syringes and bandages.

"What are those for?" Rebecca asked with little enthusiasm.

"All of us in the landing party are taking this to boost are immune system, a precaution against potential diseases," Ashleigh replied as she first inoculated Rebecca.

"I didn't realize you were going down with us," Rebecca said after receiving the shot.

"I've been elected as the Australian delegate for the landing party; the Admiral wants everyone of the Sagan's host countries represented," Ashleigh said as she swabbed Francis's arm with an antibacterial towellette.

"I can understand sending down a Canadian delegate, but we are nowhere near Australia," Rebecca replied just as Ashleigh poked Francis in the arm.

"Ouch!" Francis exclaimed. "For God's sake, Frost, let her do her job."

"Sorry about that, Francis," Ashleigh said with a light laugh.

"Is there a set time for an Australian landing?" Rebecca asked while ignoring the scowl Francis shot her way.

"Not anytime soon, but we are already planning for a first settlement. We'll be restoring the capitol at Perth in Western Australia before expanding out to other areas. Right now, there are three thousand Australians on board just waiting to get home."

"You're almost there, Ashleigh," Rebecca said. "Good luck."

"You too, Frost," Ashleigh replied before the two shook hands while Francis rubbed his sore arm.

Rebecca and Francis meandered through the bustling ship until they reached the flight deck and, eventually, their fighter. From there, with assistance from deckhands, they stowed away their gear in the pack attached to their parachutes.

"We're not using the storage pod?" Francis had first asked when crew carried his pack up the ladder to his space.

"We're going full armament, Recoil," was Rebecca's response before she hoisted up and secured her own pack. With equipment stowed, the pilot and REO walked about the ship checking all equipment after which they entered the cockpit to begin pre-flight checks. Then in little time, all was set, and Francis's hopes and dreams were mere minutes away from reality, beginning with Rebecca's... Frost's, commands.

"This is the CAG! All fighters check in."

"Eagle two standing by," Captain Mosher replied, and every other fighter pilot in turn gave the same response. The series of responses reminded Francis of Star Wars: A New Hope, just as the Y and X wings prepared to assault the Death Star.

"Air Boss, this is Frost requesting to activate systems," Rebecca reported. "All fighters set. We are good to go."

"You're all clear to begin final flight checks and enter the hanger," responded the Air Boss. "All hands, launch in progress." Immediately, the now familiar warning lights and horns bombarded Francis's hearing and sight. Then, one by one, the fighters were sealed off from the hanger bay and hoisted out until every fighter dangled below the bottom hull of the Sagan. Then, unlike any other time, it was the admiral who commanded the final launch sequence.

"All pilots," Taryn said as she silently berated herself for agreeing to Francis's request. "Launch Vipers!" With Francis humming the theme from Battlestar Galactica in the background, along with a few initial cheers from pilots and REOs alike, Rebecca initiated the launch sequence, her fighter taking the lead. Within fifteen minutes, all fighters were airborne save for two fighters reserved for 'ready alert' action. Then, in record timing, two support shuttles, the Drake and the MacArthur, launched and headed for Earth each escorted by two fighters; the remaining fighters, meanwhile, took support positions around the Sagan. The USS Douglas MacArthur, the first and only *Constitution-Class* shuttle, was twice the Drake's size and bore the heavy machinery needed to fortify Fort Niagara and build infrastructure for Buffalo and Niagara Falls. Crewed mostly by Seabees, the MacArthur took a position thirty kilometers behind the Drake as the Drake was set to land first to test the chosen landing site.

"Frost to Sagan Actual… we're all set here," Rebecca called into her microphone as shuttles and fighters finally took up their assigned positions.

"Sagan Actual to all birds... Operation Homeland is a go," Taryn replied before turning towards her bridge crew to relay other orders. "Helm, extend our orbit by three hundred kilometers."

"Aye-aye, Sir," the helm's officer replied before reprogramming the shuttle's flight computer.

"Ops!" Taryn exclaimed, turning towards the nearby science stations. "I want continued scans of Earth's debris field as well as the airspace along the shuttles' flight plan." Again, Taryn's deck crew responded with the customary 'aye Sir' and head nods before punching away at their keyboards and screening radar and other sensory relays.

As the Sagan commenced its operations, Major Rebecca Sanford led the fighters and shuttles on theirs. The landing zone, a still intact section of what was once Walden Avenue in Cheektowaga, New York, built adjacent to the Buffalo International Airport, was deemed sufficient to withstand the landings of all shuttles and fighters. Widened and reinforced during the early twenty-first century, scans showed the concrete construction was covered by only light vegetation. The landing itself though was the least of Rebecca's concerns. Earth left too many unknowns, and everyone worried about the doom that had befallen their ancestors. A blaring horn emanating from Francis's console suddenly disrupted any thoughts of Earth and its hidden dangers.

"Talk to me, Recoil!" Rebecca commanded.

"Radar is showing two contacts embedded within the debris field," Francis said as he typed commands into his keyboard. "I can't identify the objects nor can I get a good estimate of their size. The images are there one minute and gone the next."

"This is the CAG, we've detected two bogies bearing..."

A new series of warnings lit up across the fighter's consoles accompanied by new sirens. The warnings lit up each fighter so that, from a distance, the Sagan bridge crew saw what amounted to a light show around the fighters and shuttles.

"Recoil! Sit-rep!" Francis didn't miss the urgency, but he was stymied by the new warnings.

"I'm getting some messages from the Scout satellite, but they're not relaying specifics. Wait, I'm getting… oh Frak! Our new friends have nuclear signatures!"

"CAG to fleet! Bogies are nuclear. Say again, bogies are nuclear! Red, lead shuttles to secondary flight path! Jenkins, you're with me. Time to give our bogies a fly-by. All fighters, weapons free!"

"Sagan Actual to Frost; sit-rep!"

"Admiral, we've got multiple contacts, each with a nuclear signature. Suggest you distance yourself from our position."

"Roger that," Taryn replied. "How the hell did Scout miss that? Helm! Fire up port maneuvering thrusters. Turn us about 180 degrees and then ahead full."

"Aye Sir," the helmsman said as he initiated the sequence for adjusting the Sagan.

"The Sagan is leaving, Frost," Francis said after their home was already making progress away from the bogies. "First object is two hundred meters ahead." Those were the last words spoken before each of the two nearest guardian satellites launched a first salvo of missiles.

Chapter 28

"Evasive maneuvers!" Frost commanded as the missiles approached, one each towards the fighters and two missiles towards the Drake. Both Rebecca and Jaelah piloted their respective fighters into a tight formation away from the incoming ordinance, and the missiles diverted in kind, already locked onto the two fighters. "Recoil! Get ready for flares!"

"Roger that," Francis replied, his left hand already positioned over the control to launch the countermeasure.

"Jaelah, I want you to launch flares on my mark and then hightail it to the Drake so you can take out the other missiles. Recoil and I will take care of the satellites."

"Understood, Major," Jaelah replied as she and her REO prepared for the signal.

"Three, two, one, mark!" Frost exclaimed not ten seconds later; four flares answered the command as Frost veered towards the satellites and Jayla towards the Drake after first pushing her thrusters to the max. The flares confused the missiles' programming sufficient to allow Jaelah to escape detection. Yet, after one missile exploded upon contact with a flare, the second missile, which previously followed Jayla's fighter, locked in on Frost and pursued.

"We gotta friend, closing fast," Francis said as his console lit up once more with warning lights and sounds.

"Good. Let's see how agile our friend is in the debris field. You up for a little dancing amongst the stars, Recoil?"

"Ah, did you ever see *The Empire Strikes Back*?" Francis asked as he looked out the cockpit towards the ring of metal the fighter was hurtling into.

"Nope, never saw it," Rebecca calmly replied as she readied herself for maneuvering.

"Let's just say this reminds me of fighters flying through an asteroid field, and most of the ships that went in didn't make it."

"Well, then it's no worries, Recoil. There's not a single asteroid in the field ahead."

"That's not the point!" Francis exclaimed as Rebecca banked hard to port amongst the titanium, iron, copper and aluminum satellite remains; the guardian satellites launched another missile apiece in answer to Frost's actions... one towards Frost and the other towards Jaelah's fighter.

***

"Two missiles incoming, Red," Captain Mosher's REO said just as the shuttles and support craft were entering Earth's stratosphere.

"Roger that," Joe Mosher replied as he shot a quick glance over his shoulder. "Drake and MacArthur, this is Red! Keep true on towards the LZ, and we'll take out the missiles." The shuttle pilots acknowledged Red before continuing on; the fighters, meanwhile, set course for the incoming missiles. It took less than two minutes for the missiles to lock onto Captain Mosher and his wingman's fighters. From there, the fighters led the missiles away from the shuttles ahead and Frost behind.

"Wait another minute and then engage the ordinance," Captain Mosher commanded his wingman, an attempt to give the shuttles more time to flee. When the time passed, it now became simply a battle between missile and fighter. "Break! Break!"

Red flying one direction and his wingman another, the fighters separated the missiles a good distance before launching flares. Unfortunately, neither missile wavered from pursuit of the fighters.

"Frak this!" Joe Mosher exclaimed as he punched the forward thrusters, causing the fighter to jolt to a stop. Not wasting a second, Joe fired up the port thrusters and turned his fighter 180 degrees, his grip tight on his ship's gun triggers the whole time. After completing the turn and expending nearly one hundred rounds, Red punched the main engines, the fighter's nose down, and diverted from the area just as his bullets hit the missile. Joe and his REO smiled as the missile's explosion ignited the sky like fireworks on the Fourth of July. A second explosion added to the display, but this time, Red and his copilot did not celebrate. The other missile had hit and destroyed Red's wingman.

***

"First missile within one hundred meters and closing," Francis said as he expended their remaining flares; the missile ignored every counter-measure. "So much for the flares."

"Never fear, Recoil, just get me a lock on the satellites."

"Yes, Sir!" Francis's reply was followed by his cycling through frequencies to connect with the incoming ordinance. "I can't find the right frequency, but let me try something else!" Francis exclaimed as he sought a different object's connection.

"Move it, Francis! I can't dodge these things much longer!" Rebecca's order echoed through the cockpit as the entire fighter danced about the debris field.

"All right, take us closer to the satellites," Francis said, his voice almost whimsical.

"Are you outta your mind!"

"A little bit," Francis replied. "You have to trust me, Rebecca." Rebecca Sanford silently scolded herself after Francis said 'trust'. She knew she trusted him, more than anyone she had ever flown with. Certainly, she had served with more technically capable REOs, but she knew, now more than ever, that Francis would defend her more than anyone.

"Changing course; hang on," she said as she jerked the stick hard to port and steered towards the nearest satellite.

"This is where things get interesting. Lock onto the two satellites. The moment they launch missiles…fire one of our own at each of them."

"Roger that, Recoil." Less than a minute later, as alarms resounded about the cockpit, both satellites launched a missile towards their fighter, and Rebecca answered both with sidewinders.

"Dive!" Francis exclaimed. Rebecca punched the main thrusters and powered straight down into a rouge debris field fifty meters below their previous position. The g-forces the pilot and REO endured made it impossible to watch the show they set in motion. While Rebecca's sidewinders hit their respective marks, the satellites' missiles, wirelessly reformatted by Francis, pursued the closest objects with heat signatures: the missiles that had been tailing Rebecca and Francis.

While the plunge through the debris field led to surface damage to the fighter, scars from miscellaneous metal shards, they were alive.

"Great job, Francis!" Rebecca cried out as her scanners reflected the loss of all pursuit. Their jubilation was short-lived.

"May-day, May-day! This is the Drake... starboard engine is damaged... we're going down."

Chapter 29

Jaelah Jenkins and her REO picked up the newly launched missile immediately and turned to confront the projectile. Once in range, Jaelah expended her fighter's magazines until the incoming missile was destroyed. Then, within an eye blink, Jaelah's fighter was again gaining on the missiles hurtling towards the shuttles. She listened to the wireless chatter from her fellow pilots not bothering to care about Joe Mosher's target; that missile didn't stand a chance against the captain. Instead, Jaelah focused on the second missile. Lieutenant David Harris, two years Jaelah's senior and Red's wingman, was an accomplished pilot, but he was neither Frost nor Red; she aimed towards him to assist. From the distance, Jaeleh watched Harris maneuver about, trying to get an edge on the missile, but neither man nor missile gained ground. Then, as Jaelah drew within 200 meters of the fight, the missile separated into three warheads, two flying towards Lieutenant Harris's fighter and one towards the Drake.

"Harris!" Jaelah exclaimed, desperately trying to call out a warning or last second advisement. She knew it was over though. Harris too had spotted the separation and chose his final act in a millisecond. He quickly targeted the missile flying towards the Drake and launched just as the two missiles targeting Harris came home. Jaelah, having already pushed her engines full throttle, could only watch as the ordinance sped towards the Drake. Harris's missile gained and struck true, but the resultant explosion launched a wave of projectiles towards the Drake, multiple shards ultimately piercing through the Drake's hull starboard tail section.

It was minutes before Rebecca reached the Drake, Joe and Jaelah having already assessed the shuttle's damage.

"There's no way in hell that will make a landing, Major," Joe said over the com system."

"Roger that, Captain. Kick it into gear and take Jaelah with you," Rebecca replied. Lead the escort of the MacArthur, and I'll look after the Drake.

"Permission to stay, Major Sanford?" Jaelah asked.

"Negative," was the CAG's reply. "If there are ground missile systems, we'll need your fighter to help. We can't afford to lose the MacArthur."

"Understood, Sir," Jaelah responded before steering towards the larger shuttle.

"Drake, this is the CAG. Do you read?"

"Loud and clear, Major," the Drake's pilot replied. "Steering is sluggish, Major, and I'm losing altitude. I gotta set her down soon."

"We read you," Rebecca said, her voice ever clear and charismatic. "CAG to Sagan Actual, do you read?" Only static replied to Rebecca's summons. "We need options, Recoil. We're not going to make the LZ." Ahead, the MacArthur and its escort had begun their decent and final approach. The Drake, meanwhile had just cleared the Atlantic Ocean and was descending over southeastern New York. "Talk to me, Recoil."

"Route 17 is our best option, Frost. Sending coordinates to the Drake now." Positioned less than a half a kilometer from the Drake, Rebecca and Francis were within the blast radius when the starboard engine exploded. Over the com, Francis heard the screams from those on board the shuttle even as shrapnel ripped apart his own ride. Rebecca, after regaining control of their fighter, watched as a number of objects drifted from the Drake. As parachutes quickly deployed from each of the objects, Rebecca knew that some of the Marines and Seabees survived. Then, after a minute of no one exiting the shuttle, one more person jumped with a quickly deploying chute.

"Leary," Rebecca said just as the Drake exploded. This time, the resultant turbulence broke the fighter's spine; the plane plummeted nose first. "Francis, we've gotta bail!" Rebecca exclaimed; there was no reply. Behind her, slammed into the starboard console by the explosion, Francis was unconscious, blood pouring from his nose. "Damn!" Rebecca broke a small panel on her console and pulled the underlying lever after which the canopy was jettisoned. Not ten seconds later Rebecca engaged Francis's ejection seat, then hers. They were less than 4,000 meters above the Earth's surface.

Chapter 30

"Report!" Admiral Southern commanded after the Sagan was well on its way from the Western Hemisphere, the generational ship's only companions a handful of fighters and a debris field filled with the corpses of long-dead satellites.

"Radiation is interfering with communications, Admiral," one of the Ops officers replied.

"Whatever's going on, it sounded like quite the firefight," Kristina added from her post at the science station.

"Launch the ready-alert," Taryn commanded as she walked to Kristina. The com officer acknowledged and relayed the command as Taryn drew within a meter of her science officer. "Frost reported nuclear signatures. Can you confirm?"

"Negative, Admiral," Kristina replied even as she again looked over her console and its multiple indicators. "We're getting no readings from the debris field over the landing zone, and…"

A series of alarms and indicator lights suddenly lit up the entire bridge, and each alarm indicated the same thing.

"Dammit!" Kristina exclaimed. "Nuclear signature detected.

"From where?" Taryn asked. The chilled look she received from Kristina spoke of Armageddon.

"It's coming from the debris field ahead of us," Kristina said.

"Turn us about and make for the moon, ahead full!" Taryn commanded. "Sagan Actual to all fighters! Nuclear signature detected ahead of you. Prepare for evasive maneuvers. You are cleared to fire."

"Sir, I'm not detecting any nuclear readings ahead, Lieutenant Schubbe's REO reported.

"Don't worry at it, rookie, Scott said as he too scanned his console for corroboration of the admiral's findings. "What do ya say, Tony. Last one back to the nest does dishes for a week?"

"We'll have to change your call sign to 'Prune Hands' by the time…

Nuclear warnings sounded throughout every fighter escorting the Sagan. Hidden amongst the debris field, an American defense satellite hummed to life, its nuclear power cell activating all weapon consoles. Detecting the Sagan, beyond the tiny fighter craft, the defense satellite calculated it needed a full response to quell what its parameters calculated as an attack. It launched its entire remaining payload: seven missiles.

The nearest fighter reacted with its guns to take out one missile; a second missile then slammed into the fighter taking out the threat and the crew. Pilots Comito and Schubbe hung back as the rest of the squadron headed towards the Sagan to provide cover.

"All right, Scotty, let's take 'em," Tony said as he banked to port while Lieutenant Schubbe banked starboard. Two of the missiles diverted to follow each of them while the remaining three missiles moved on towards the Sagan.

"Dammit!" Scott exclaimed. "Sagan, three missiles still in pursuit. Take evasive action!" Just as he finished his warning to Admiral Southern, Scott's fighter had turned to face Tony's oncoming fighter. "Ready when you are, Tony."

"Roger," Tony said as he and Scott simultaneously locked onto the missile following the other and fired. The missiles exploded under fire from the fighters' 50-caliber machine guns. The threat destroyed, the teammates flew on to help the Sagan.

The other fighters were not having as much luck. Breaking off into two teams, the fighters converged on the remaining three missiles. At first, the missiles changed targets from the Sagan to the oncoming jet fighters. The missiles, equipped with evasion software, nullified the advantage of the Sagan fighters' numbers. With Tony and Scott still hundreds of meters away, it took just one missile to break free, and one did. Having lined up on the two nearest missiles, one fighter finally locked in and destroyed the ordinanace with its own sidewinders. The resultant explosion, however, cast a shockwave that knocked out the electrical systems in the nearby fighters, which left the last missile to continue on unimpeded.

"Incoming missile!" one of the Ops officers exclaimed. Like well oiled machines, the bridge crew activated the Sagan's only allowed defense: flares, which the missile ignored. Within a minute, the missile slammed into the Sagan's aft hull, shutting down the main thrusters in the process.

On board, the entire Sagan crew was shook to the ground while red emergency lighting lit up the now darkened passageways.

"Ops, Report!" Admiral Southern commanded as she pulled herself up to a standing position. "Sitrep!" It took seconds for one of the few conscious Ops officers to get up and survey the damage alert panels.

"Main thrusters are offline and we have a hull breach in sector four."

"Any more missiles incoming?" the admiral asked, the nearest radar screen offline.

"Radar is sporadic, Admiral, but nothing appears to be following," the Ops officer replied. All about, circuit boards were sparking, and a veil of smoke emanated from more than one console. The admiral had no doubts other decks were battling the same conditions. The crew needed her now.

"All hands, this is your admiral," Taryn said into a nearby receiver. "I want damage and casualty reports ASAP. I want all bulkheads surrounding sector four sealed, and I want all department heads to report in." Putting down the receiver, Taryn helped a nearby crewmember to his feet before calling out to the com station. "Com – relay our status to the squadron. I want a sit-rep now. Tell them to take an escort position around the Sagan and await further instructions."

"Aye, Admiral," the officer replied before executing the orders. Seconds later, another explosion along the aft hull jarred the Sagan and its crew.

"What the hell was that, Ops?" Taryn asked as she regained her balance.

"We have decompression alarms coming aft, from sections four and eight. We also have fire alarms sounding in sectors four, eight and twelve. Admiral, we've also lost aft maneuvering thrusters; we'll be adrift and powerless in little time." Taryn was out of options, but the admiral had one trick left up her sleeve.

"Ops, I want as many people as possible loaded onto the remaining shuttles and evacuated, including the president and the representatives," she commanded before walking over to the helm station. "Set a course for the moon. Use everything the maneuvering thrusters will give you."

"Aye, Sir," her helmsman replied before carrying out the order.

"Com! Send a report to Maximus! And keep trying to reach the landing parties."

"Aye, Sir!" came the reply and the shuffling of many feet amongst the flurry of blinking lights and sirens. All was set save for Taryn's last duty, which she commenced by picking up a nearby receiver.

"All hands, brace for impact!"

Chapter 31

Light filtered in through Rebecca's eyelashes as consciousness fought off sleep. Pain was there all along, and every moment of consciousness brought bits of memory with it. Jerked out of the fighter by the ejection seat, Rebecca had all breath knocked out of her. Struggling to calm and control her breathing once more, she looked about for Francis, but heavy cloud cover limited Rebecca to less than twenty meters of visibility. Worry built for her REO yet all she could do was fall through the clouds, a high pitched whistle, wind spliced by her gear, her only companion. Then, as the clouds thinned, Rebecca got her first glimpse of a true blue sky, and again she was breathless.

Unlike the chilling dark of space or the drab gray of the Sagan's hallways, the sky was warm, inviting. Below, far below, Rebecca soon glimpsed the planet's surface. It looked like a carpet woven with a mix of colored fibers. It was like a carpet of trees whose autumn hues presented like a raging fire, a fire she wanted desperately to embrace.

A strong crosswind slammed into Rebecca seconds before her chute opened, which spun her out of control; the chute released, but its lines enveloped its charge. With a half deployed parachute, Rebecca plummeted on towards the nearing tree cover. Suddenly, her memories returned full, the image of barreling into leaf-caked branches until snared parachute lines and a stout branch stopped her short of the ground and robbed Rebecca of consciousness. The pain she was registering told her there were no serious injuries, but she knew she would bear the pain for some time. It was then, right when Rebecca realized she was safely on the surface, that she heard a number of growls. Her eyes opened wide in time to see a creature vault up to her, the creature's jaws snapping shut centimeters from Rebecca's face. The creature, over a meter in length and covered in thick, charcoal fur, fell back to the ground, cushioned by other similar quadrupeds. The creatures snapped at their fallen and dazed comrade before returning their stares to Rebecca. The growling commenced once more.

Rebecca looked about to figure out a way to distance herself from the creatures, which she assumed were wolves. She was entwined in the chute's cordage and suspended three meters above the ground. Her hands restrained behind her, Rebecca could only wiggle about to try and gain her freedom. The effort only made her situation worse; a branch supporting her broke, and Rebecca's harness dropped a half meter. She was now within reach of the creatures, and they didn't wait. One by one the creatures jumped up at Rebecca, and each time she diverted the attack with a sweep of her head. Each defense, however, lowered Rebecca a few more centimeters. Time was on the creatures' side. Her only hope was that in falling to the ground she could get her hands free and reach her sidearm. Suddenly, the battle was interrupted by a new adversary.

"Here we are, born to be kings, we're the princes of the universe!" cried out a voice standing atop a nearby hill. There stood a hooded and cloaked figure, an extended hand holding out an MP7 player while the other hand grasped a sword. The music played on, and all combatants were transfixed by the long forgotten voices of the rock band, Queen. *"Here we belong,*

fighting to survive in a world with the darkest powers!"
The ensuing music and lyrics, accompanied by bold
electric guitar play, drove the creatures away. The figure moved forward then, walking at a slow pace until
the welcomed interloper stood twenty meters from Rebecca. The figure was a man, Rebecca surmised, who
stood taller than most. The brown hooded cloak he
wore covered the man's eyes. All she could see was a
smirk.

"Who are you?" Rebecca asked once the figure
turned off the music. The question appeared to stymie
the figure, but the smirk soon returned. Rebecca found
comfort in that smirk.

"I am Gandalf, of course," he said in that all too
familiar voice. "And Gandalf means, me." Rebecca
laughed like never before. She could not stop herself,
and soon 'Gandalf' joined in. This went on for a good
minute until Rebecca stopped abruptly.

"Dammit, Francis, cut me loose!"

***

She was beyond angry. All the while Francis,
Glamdring at his side, worked at cutting Rebecca free,
her anger boiled over Francis's vestments. He had shed
his flight suit and indeed the oxygen-supplied helmet
that accompanied the suit. She tried to distract herself
by trying to reach either the Sagan or one of the landing
parties, but all she received for her efforts was static.

"Don't waste your suit's power cell. I couldn't
reach anyone either."

Once down to a few parachute cords, Francis
had Rebecca cling to him to prevent her crashing into
the turf. Once free, she dusted herself off, wiped her

visor clean, and the punched her REO; the force sent him to the ground.

"What the hell was that for?" Francis asked as he rubbed his jaw.

"You never intended to go back to the Sagan. Now that you've breathed the Earth's air, you can't be allowed back in." Quiet for a moment as if to contemplate Rebecca's words, Francis nodded before looking up and responding.

"I guess I could say that my visor was damaged in the firefight, but I won't lie to you. You're right, I never intended to return," he said as he stood and walked to her. "You will never understand the hell I've endured on that ship. I would rather die here and soon, than return to the Sagan. What is your home has always been my prison." Francis walked over to where he had set a non-regulation backpack. It was dark brown in coloring and appeared to be leather of a sort. Attached to the backpack was an oxygen cylinder, which he quickly handed over to Rebecca. "Here. My supply of oxygen, which should provide you with an extended time before you run out of Sagan air."

"And what if I ordered you to put your helmet back on and use this?" In response, Francis reached down to the ground, dug his fingers into the loam soil, and rose, extending a palm's worth of dirt towards Rebecca.

"This is true American soil, Rebecca, not the metal halls of the Sagan. As I am not a member of any branch of service, I answer to no one. I will help you all get to Fort Niagara, but we do it on my terms. Understood?" Before she could answer he walked past her and into the woods, donning and adjusting his backpack as he moved. It was then that she heard it for the first time. The chirping of birds pierced through the air, discordant voices that culminated into an impossible harmony, which played out against the rustling leaves of nearby maple, oak and birch trees. Rebecca then saw her first bird, a chickadee that landed on a low branch of a silver maple not three meters from her. It whistled a happy tune before looking towards Rebecca; the bird cocked its head at a near 30 degree angle as if to consider the human before it. Rebecca found herself holding her breath while examining her new friend, which then continued singing as if to say it trusted the human.

"I see you've found a new REO," Francis said as he emerged from the nearby brush he disappeared into moments before. "Here, hold out your hand," he said as he reached into his bag and pulled out a bag of nuts and seeds he carried. He placed a few of the seeds into the palm of Rebecca's now outstretched hand before slowly stepping back and crouching to the ground.

"What do I do now?" Rebecca asked, looking back to Francis.

"Just stay still and watch," Francis replied. She did as advised and waited almost two minutes before it happened; the chickadee landed on the tips of her fingers and spent another minute looking back and forth between the seeds and Rebecca. Then, the chickadee grabbed the nearest seed and flew off into the trees overhead. Rebecca turned back and laughed. "That's a chickadee, a very inquisitive type of bird found in this region," Francis said as he stood up and approached her. "Come on, we've got to get going." Francis led Rebecca to a nearby tree where, up in the middle braches, rested her chair from the fighter.

"I don't know how you and your chair separated," Francis said as he shed his equipment and cloak. "I'm surprised you didn't break anything."

"I'm in a bit of pain, if that makes you feel better," Rebecca replied as she rubbed at her right shoulder. "The chairs were designed to disengage under certain conditions."

"Such as?"

"How the hell should I know? Do I look like an
engineer, Recoil?"

"I guess not," Francis replied as he climbed until
he reached the chair. It took another fifteen minutes for
him to secure his footing and reach the storage compartment behind the chair, an exact match to the storage
his chair provided. Upon opening the storage area door,
Rebecca's equipment fell out." "Heads up!" Her attention turned towards her helmet's com system, Rebecca
was oblivious to Francis's actions until that moment.
She dove out of the way just in time.

"Are you trying to kill me?" she asked before
starting to open and organize her equipment. Francis,
after climbing down, crouched next to Rebecca and just
took in the surroundings; the sounds, the sights and the
smells.

"What are you doing?" she asked after Francis
closed his eyes and started sniffing repeatedly. He
smiled, but he did not open his eyes.

"The air is so different here. It's lighter… and it
doesn't reek of oil and metal. It's like every scent is
mixed with sugar. It's light and sweet." She took in his
words while scanning out to the surrounding woodlands. While patches of sky could be seen, the network
of tree limbs seemed everywhere.

"How would vehicles make it through here?"
she asked after a time.

"We are actually right along a highway," he said
before pointing off to the north. Do you see where the
brush is thinner and only pine trees stand?" Rebecca

nodded. "Pines and those bush species have shallow root systems, which allowed them to grow there. After a few centimeters is probably a road of blacktop or cement."

"There's just so many trees," she then said. "How do we clear out all of this?"

"Why would we want to clear all this out? I watched a documentary about the continent's indigenous populations. In it, a historian, a Seneca named John Mohawk, remarked on how before Europeans arrived, a squirrel could travel from north to south, the entire span of what became the United States, without ever touching the ground. Maybe destroying the environment back then was what led to Humanity's fall?"

"You're not serious, are you?" Rebecca asked. "So the environment sought revenge by... creating a virus to kill off humans? Or, did Mother Nature conjure a great monster to eradicate our species?"

"Death by Godzilla," Francis quipped, the Blue Oyster Cult song about the King of Monsters now running through his mind.

"Can you be serious for one fraking minute!" Rebecca exclaimed. Francis walked up to within a half a meter of her.

"I have never been more serious, Rebecca," he said. "Our species endured endless plagues because we often found natural remedies to counteract the cause. What if once, when a plague hit, the very plant needed to cure people was eradicated by human development. We destroyed forests across this planet. Think of the potential cures lost in order to house Humanity's ever-growing population. Whether people want to believe it was Karma, a supreme being or just simple probability, there is a great chance that we could have died out simply because we destroyed what could have saved us."

There was truth in Francis's words, and it pained Rebecca to acknowledge it. She looked around, envisioning how the planet must have looked three hundred years earlier, before Humanity's fall. Children playing, families having picnics, couples walking hand in hand through a garden; now there were just trees and grass and bushes and sky. After a lifetime aboard a relatively cramped spaceship, the planet was too quiet.

"So what do we do now and what the hell were those things that attacked me?" Rebecca asked, the tension calmed.

"We find the others. They can't be too far. As for what attacked you, those were coyotes."

"They weren't wolves?" Rebecca asked, her hand absently going to her sidearm.

"No, wolves are bigger, and without rifles, we'd be wise to save ammo for holding off attacking predators. While you are at it, now would be a good time to unpack Sting. You may need it, and thankfully, a sword doesn't need reloading.

Chapter 32

"Horseheads Cemetery," Francis said after scraping away the dried mud from the marker's surface. With the town name carved deep into the stone slab, time and erosion could not eradicate the inscription as they had the names on most of the cemetery's headstones. With a name to work with, Francis removed a map and an old compass from his backpack. The compass, an heirloom passed down through generations of his family, was the only device that worked as it needed no battery or orbiting satellite to relay GPS information. For a moment, Francis thought of his many times Great Grandfather Burns who had managed some of the docks in Buffalo during the late nineteenth century. The nostalgia passed and Francis soon had his index finger scanning for the town name. After finding the name and gauging the distance from the map's key, Francis relayed the bad news. "We're hundreds of kilometers southeast of our objective. We've a long journey ahead, Rebecca. Rebecca?"

Rebecca was lost in observation. The once quiet forest now seemed more alive than any space on the Sagan. Birds, feathered in a rainbow of colors, dodged about the tree branches. Red, yellow, orange, brown and blue birds of all shapes and sizes sang and flew endlessly about them as if Francis and Rebecca were a mere nuisance. It all seemed so magical as disparate voices and songs clashed while simultaneously working back into the harmony she previously heard. Then, the percussion instruments played along.

The shuffling of rodent feet, a red squirrel and a chipmunk, provided the beat for the ever-growing orchestra. A gray squirrel then entered the area, but its accompaniment was not to be heard. The red squirrel chased off the gray while the birds and chipmunk watched, the song temporarily at rest. All the aerial and earth-bound musicians returned to their music once the red squirrel returned.

"That wasn't exactly nice now, was it?" Rebecca asked before moving one step forward. The animals, all walking about the ground or perched on branches turned and stared at Rebecca for one second before scattering into hiding, a few short chirps of alarm the only sound now made. In that moment, Francis looking on in amusement, one blue-colored bird flew an erratic flight pattern that took the bird short distances before it changed course to avoid another bird. Its final obstacle was not as avoidable; the bird flew into a tree and fell unconscious to the ground.

"Great!" Francis exclaimed as he stood and walked over to the knocked out bird. He then gently picked up the bird and inspected its chest, head and wings. "You broke him!"

***

While the forest was dense, Francis never seemed to hesitate long before finding a passageway. Rebecca simply followed her companion, ever northwest, baffled by the Irishman's sense as well as his compassion for the unconscious bird he carried.

"Predators will get him if we leave him," Francis had said when she asked why he carried the bird. It took Francis only a few minutes to find the bird's identity in the field guide he carried: it was a blue jay. It took only seconds more for Francis to name the bird. He named the bird 'Crash'.

Ever onward, Francis continued to find his way, the compass always handy. Uncomfortably free from command, Rebecca continuously took in her surroundings. Everything seemed diverse, sublime. The trees more than anything stood out to Rebecca. Some trees had branches lined with stiff, green needles. Their scent aromatic, these trees frustrated Rebecca a bit for her fingers became caked with a sticky residue almost every time she touched one. Other trees, meanwhile, bore small and large leafs with each tree seeming to favor a different color. Red and yellow hues dominated these trees, though ones baring green leafs were aplenty as well. Francis identified the trees from memory, but his descriptions lacked specifics. The needle trees were 'coniferous' and the leaf-bearing trees were 'deciduous' in nature. Francis's studies were lacking in vegetation so he could not separate a pine from a spruce or an oak from a chestnut. Maples were a bit easier given their leaf shape and Francis's familiarity with the flag of Canada. Yet, what species of maple they encountered was a riddle that time would have to solve. Rebecca's concentration shifted as her feet landed on worn ground.

"A path? There must be…"

"Don't get too excited, Rebecca," Francis cautioned as he continued on. "Humans are not the only creatures capable of engineering feats, particularly roads. This is likely the work of deer." Her hopes dashed, she continued on returning her focus to her guide.

Francis, meanwhile, separated his time between the compass, map and Crash. The bird was slowly improving, evidenced by the periodic jerks of its talons.

When it then turned its head, Francis smiled. "You're all right, my friend," Francis said as he put his index finger in between the bird's talons; it grabbed hold and stared at Francis. Slowly, Francis lifted Crash's body as the bird released its hold of the man's finger. Then, its body perpendicular to Francis's arm, the bird grabbed hold once more and remained upright on its own.

"It seems you have a new friend, Francis," Rebecca said as she approached. Crash tilted his head slightly and appeared to consider the woman's presence before turning back to Francis. "A brown cloak and a friend of animals? You say you're Gandalf, but you're more like Radagast the Brown."

"Indeed," Francis replied before he turned and continued on the path.

**

It caught the man's scent seconds after hearing the crash through the canopy above. Hungry, ever hungry, the creature moved within sight of Francis. It then followed him through the woods, quiet and hidden at all times. The addition of Rebecca rattled its resolve. Yet, the chance for a meal drove the creature onward. Still healing from an earlier wolf attack, the creature moved on hoping for a chance for a meal without the need of a struggle. This human seemed to be the creature's best chance, especially after Francis started carrying around the helpless bird.

Chapter 33

"You *are* going to tell me where we're going, aren't you?" Rebecca asked as they climbed further up the side of a tree-shrouded mountain. Her attention mostly focused on her radio, Rebecca had left the direction of their trek to her REO. She also struggled a bit to see as her helmet's face shield periodically steamed up requiring her to slow her movements.

"Well, since we can't reach anyone with the radios, we need to use the environment to help out," Francis replied as he continued walking until a clearing opened amongst the tree line. There, Francis pulled back the hood of his cloak and peered over a rock ledge the clearing revealed. While Rebecca continued checking different radio channels, static the only response she received, Francis closed his eyes and took in the scents of the region. Subtle hints of wet grass and pine intermixed with other scents, which he could not determine. *So different from the Sagan, so alive.* He pushed past his joy of nature to their collective purpose and gazed out to the horizon.

"What are you looking for?" Rebecca asked.

"That," Francis said as he pointed in the distance to where a flurry of birds rose over the trees in the distance. "I'm willing to bet it's our comrades that scared off those birds."

"And how do you know that?"

"You know, you sound a bit like Darth Vader speaking through the helmet?" Francis joked before responding to her question. "With no radio contact, no smoke from the shuttle wreckage, no voices and no human tracks, the behavior of animals is our best way to locate the others. Come on, let's move." Then, after taking only a few steps, Rebecca in tow, Francis stopped, turned about and drew *Glamdring* half out of its scabbard. Rebecca in turn drew her sidearm and aimed towards the woods they had just emerged from.

"What?" she asked, Rebecca's eyes darting about the bushes and trees looking for any danger. Francis said nothing for a minute, his gaze steady and directed at the exact spot where they exited the woods before reaching the clearing.

"Nothing, just nerves I guess," Francis finally replied as he returned his sword into its home. "Why don't you lead on, Frost. I'm a bit tired."

"What's wrong?" she asked.

"It's time you learned to track." Rebecca knew there was something else, but she trusted Francis enough not to push. Re-holstering her gun, Rebecca started walking downhill towards where the birds scattered from. Francis, meanwhile, removed his backpack and dug into the main compartment for a few seconds before removing a pack of his k-rations. Then, breaking off a piece of a biscuit, he donned his pack before walking off to catch up to Rebecca. Along the way, he dropped the biscuit fragment.

***

"We've lost another two, Sir," Ashleigh reported to General Leary, the strain of their situation evident by her reddened eyes.

"Thank you, Ashleigh," the general replied as he accepted Killian's and Thompson's dog tags. "And the others?"

"Danielson is the only remaining concern, Sir. His right arm's broken, and while I stopped the bleeding from the gash in his leg, he'll need to be carried. There's no way he can continue on his own." Ashleigh's report was not a surprise to Paul; he'd been the one to uncut Danielson from the parachute rigging which stranded Danielson is a pine tree.

"Keep me updated on the hour, Petty Officer. We're down to fifteen able bodies and can't afford to lose anyone else."

Ashleigh nodded her reply before moving back to her patient.

"Lieutenant!" General Leary then commanded, preempting the arrival of Mario Williams. Williams, who had searched the area for survivors, had retrieved Killian and Thompson along with three other Marines, all of whom received critical wounds from the explosion on the Drake. The general and Williams did everything to pull them out, but each knew it was already too late before any of the dead were removed from the crashing shuttle.

"Yes, Sir?" Mario asked. His flight suit torn and helmet shield cracked, Mario had ditched his helmet and stripped to his Combat Utility Uniform. With his sleeves rolled up, Mario looked ready for combat, his muscles tensed and his breath racing.

"Get the Seabees to build a stretcher for Danielson and then get some rest."

"Sir?"

"You've been going full tilt since the landing. I want you rested for tomorrow. Understood?"

"I'm good to go, Sir," Mario replied, uncomfortable at the thought of ceasing his search for wounded.

"The Drake's flight crew was incinerated in the blast leaving only Dennison unaccounted for. We could spend days looking for her, meanwhile, Danielson may bleed out. Not to mention, we have a mission to complete. Understood?"

"Understood, General," Mario replied. He then saluted and turned to walk away when Paul Leary caught his arm.

"When the mission is complete and the rest of the team is safe, you and I will come back and find the corporal no matter how long it takes." While still not happy with the order, Lieutenant Williams nodded before moving off. Alone, Paul Leary looked out to the surrounding mountains for signs of smoke or movement, something to indicate where the fallen were. Inside, he knew Dennison was a survivor, and he smiled at the thought of her marching along in search of others, cursing at the piss-poor construction of the shuttles. Then, after a short, quiet laugh, Paul returned to other concerns. He heard the report over the com system; Rebecca and Francis went down. Rebecca, too, was a survivor, but his nephew, though resilient, was not a serviceman. He was a scientist with limited exposure to anything outside the arboretum. Francis was out there with only his book knowledge as any real guide. *What could a man do with only a book to prepare himself?*

***

There must have been a hundred of them, crows cawing and fluttering about the tree branches, scoping out Leigh Dennison. Her parachute's rigging snagged within the branches of a gigantic, Norway maple, Corporal Dennison was tangled in such a way that she could not reach her knife.

"Would you please shut the hell up!" she cursed at the crows, though her voice, muffled by her helmet's damaged speaker system, only seemed to encourage the birds to caw louder. Pissed, Dennison went on to her fallback position: *Work your way free*. Her arms ensnared within the parachute rigging, Leigh looked to her legs for escape. Suspended nearly fifteen meters off the ground and about six meters from the main tree trunk, Leigh started to swing her legs back and forth, each swing bringing her closer to the meter-thick tree trunk. Back and forth for five minutes she maneuvered while the crows annoyed her with their unintelligible babble.

"I swear, I'm gonna catch and eat every last one of you if you don't shut the hell up!" she exclaimed, her last word coming just as she was able to extend her legs around the tree truck. A good plan, but her suit's slick exterior provided little catching power so she slide off. More than pissed now, she swung again, though this time she looked for something to catch her legs on, and Leigh did find one option. A knot in the tree, where a branch once hung, offered the possibility of purchase. Just a half meter higher than where she straddled the tree previously, the knot would be difficult to reach. Yet, on her first attempt, Leigh secured her legs around the tree, the knot providing her left leg with a solid hold. "Now what, Dennison?" she asked herself before trying to wiggle an arm free. If anything, it seemed that her actions were tightening the rigging. With no other option, Dennison look to her best available weapon; she started tearing at the rigging with her teeth.

"Ah, when you're done eating, do you want some help getting down, or should we just leave you and your company alone?" Francis asked. While the crows flew off, disturbed by the man's arrival, Leigh had an altogether different response.

"Get me the hell down from here, Dumb-ass!"

Chapter 34

"Admiral? Admiral, please wake up!" The words Taryn heard, her name, came like a crescendo in sound, pain and thought. She registered pain to her limbs and chest, and the strength to open her eyes... she could not find.

"Admiral Southern, can you hear me?" Taryn knew the voice, the speaker's name at the tip of her tongue. "Admiral!"

A brilliant light flashed within Taryn's mind. A glimpse of her grasping the arms of her chair and ordering all to brace for impact followed as did the sounds of a horrific creaking, the creaking of metal. Then, one calm image fluttered by in her mind. A moment where the surface of the moon, heightened by the sun's rays, glowed like a star enough to make the rocks and crevices on the Earth's natural satellite seem like they were moving.

"The man on the moon," Taryn whispered before another flash of light overcame her.

"Admiral Southern, can you hear me?" John Williams asked, his booming voice shaking Taryn at last from unconsciousness. She opened her eyes and saw John hovering a half a meter away from where she was strapped down on a stretcher secured to one of the science station consoles. "We got her," he then said turning to someone nearby. John seemed stable before her while all around him objects and people floated about. Suddenly, Taryn felt nauseated; she coughed as if to vomit.

"What? What is, I?" she asked unintelligibly.

"The GRAV-generators are offline, Admiral. Your have an injury to your head and likely have at least a mild concussion; nausea is to be expected," John explained before turning back to speak to an unseen individual. "Get the lieutenant." While others shuffled by, some floating while others walked in stiff strides, Taryn focused on the word 'lieutenant'. Images of her own promotion to lieutenant and her subsequent years as a fighter pilot blew by in her memory. Then, others memories came: her elevation to a major and finally Commander of the Sagan. Admiral? Who was this… Reality and memory collided. She took in a deep breath as Lieutenant Willis appeared.

"Sit-rep, Lieutenant!" Taryn exclaimed, her eyes now focused on the junior officer before her, the sizzling of fried circuits clashing with the muffled conversations occurring around her.

"We've landed on the moon, Admiral. Engines are off-line and we're on backup generators at the moment."

"Casualties?" Taryn asked, fearing the worst.

"All shipboard crew are accounted for. We had two fatalities and multiple injuries that are critical, but we've survived pretty much intact." Taryn closed her eyes to process the report.

"*You are in command, Southern,*" a voice from the past echoed in her mind.

"Hull integrity and life support?" Taryn asked as she again opened her eyes and looked up at Lieutenant Willis.

"Seabees are checking every nut, bolt and support; it looks like the hull is completely secured and resting almost completely level. Life support systems are fully functioning. Once we get the GRAV-generators operational, we'll be relatively back to normal."

"Except we'll be trapped on the moon in a ship that will never fly again," Taryn added. She knew the outcome before the actual landing, though she expected there to be more casualties.

Unless...

"What of the recon teams?" Taryn asked. Kristina's hesitation spoke volumes.

"A number of our fighters were destroyed. Schubbe and Comito have organized the remaining pilots into a CAP. We did evacuate all remaining shuttles as ordered and each was packed with personnel, which helped reduce injuries. But..." Another hesitation on Kristina's part made clear that was the good news.

"The Drake was destroyed, and based on the explosion radius and loss of radio traffic, none likely survived." A moment of pain crawled through Taryn's gut before memories of field missions with Paul brought relief.

"Don't write off the general and his team too soon, Lieutenant. What of the others?"

"Scout was damaged by some shrapnel in the firefight so communications are down temporarily. Engineering is prepping a new communications satellite for launch within the next few hours. Until then, we have no clue if any ship or crew survived." Taryn gagged and coughed uncontrollably at that point, phlegm and blood partially clogging her throat.

"Let it out, Admiral," John said as he pushed past Willis and began rubbing her back. Taryn coughed out the fluids before taking a few deep breaths. When clarity returned and her breathing eased, Taryn asked one final question.

"What of Frost and Professor Burns?"

**

"Just a little further," Leigh said as Francis reached out towards her bound arms with a stout stick, a K-bar affixed to the tip with rope. This time, the fifth attempt, Francis succeeded in reaching the parachute cordage along Leigh's left side.

"Slowly, Recoil," Rebecca said as Francis began to slice away at the rigging. First using two knives to cut out footholds in the tree, Francis climbed to within four meters of Leigh. Once there, his footing secure, Francis waited for Rebecca to lob the makeshift spear to him; he caught it on the third attempt. Now, patience and calm were what Francis looked to as Leigh and he were precariously perched. Cut too quickly and Leigh would likely plummet down the meters of air until she hit the ground, which was a good distance away. What's more, she would possibly take Francis with her. Their goal was to get Leigh loose enough so she could reach her own knife and cut out footholds with which to secure her position.

"A little faster, Francis," Leigh said a minute into his slicing of the cords. "My legs won't last much longer." Strained as he was, his strength divided between maintaining his hold and cutting away the rigging, Francis knew they both would not last much longer; he increased his cutting pressure and speed. Multiple strands gave way and Leigh slide down half a meter before she could stop herself. The freedom she now had allowed her to untangle her left hand, but the action also caused her few supplies to pour out of the satchel she carried.

"Bloo!" Leigh yelled as a small stuffed bear fell from the satchel right past Francis. Reacting, he dropped the spear and grabbed the bear, movement that made him slip a little before Francis regained his hold.

The stiff tree bark grated his wrist, but he held onto the bear. "Oh, thank God," Leigh said as she moved slowly to reach her knife.

"Are you kidding me?" Francis asked, clearly exasperated.

"You carry around a little stuffed turkey, Francis, so don't give me any lip about Bloo," Leigh remarked while Francis dropped Bloo down to Rebecca. "Bloo is too important to…"

Francis and Rebecca never heard why Bloo was too important; the rigging gave way and Leigh dropped. Francis reached out towards her, but he missed her arm by centimeters. He did succeed in slipping off after her though, and Francis fell right after. Rebecca watched it all unfold, helpless. She tossed Bloo to the ground and raised her arms trying to determine how to soften the blow of her plummeting comrades. Leigh acted first.

Her own K-bar free, Leigh slammed the blade into the tree's trunk, and the blade bit deep. The speed of Leigh's descent, however, caused the Marine to still fall, but her momentum slowed appreciably. It gave her time also to grab Francis's leg as he fell. Then, it what seemed an eternity, Francis, his body jerked to a stop, slammed into the trunk with an oomph before falling two more meters to the ground. Leigh then landed on top of him.

"Are you two okay?" Rebecca asked as she pulled Leigh off of Francis. Leigh seemed no worse for wear. Collectively, they tried to pull Francis to his feet, but he waived them off.

"I'm all right, just, just winded," he said as he stared up into the tree canopy above. Francis paid no heed to the colors that marveled him earlier. He simply tried to calm his breath and assess his potential injuries with little movements.

"Not so high as I thought," Leigh commented as she sheathed her knife."

"What?" Francis and Rebecca collectively exclaimed as Leigh picked up and dusted off Bloo. Then, after giving the bear a quick peck on the nose, Leigh turned to find Rebecca and Francis staring at her, Francis while still resting on the ground with his neck in what seemed an impossible angle.

"What?" Leigh asked before she walked on to collect the items that fell from her satchel earlier. "I swear, you two need to lighten up. It's as if..."

Leigh froze mid-sentence before dropping several items in order to arm herself with her sidearm. Rebecca heard the sound of gun on holster and quickly drew her own weapon in turn. Francis, now on his knees, looked in the direction their guns were pointed and saw the creature that held his comrades' attention. A scruffy animal, covered in a mismatch of white, gray and black fur textures, stood at the edge of the woods and stared right back at them. No more than a meter in length, the animal looked emaciated, its ribs clearly showing as if it had not eaten much in months.

"Lower your weapons please," Francis said as he struggled to his feet. "It's been following us for a few hours." Once Rebecca and Leigh had lowered their guns, Francis reached into his pack and removed another biscuit fragment. He then chucked the bit of food over to the animal, which quickly ate the offered morsel.

"What the hell is it?" Rebecca asked, still uncertain about lowering her weapon.

"It's a dog, part Dalmatian from the looks of it," Francis replied as he picked up Crash from where the still-traumatized bird rested on a low-hanging branch of a nearby pine. "Come on, Crash, let's not take a chance with the doggie." Crash looked at Francis as if to consider the man's words, but then the bird returned to its aloofness. Francis simply smiled. "Don't worry about him, the dog is no threat. He's a scavenger."

The small company put thoughts of the dog out of their minds and restarted their trek through woodlands. Francis, after giving the team a marching direction, looked over the dog, a remnant of humanity's impact on Earth. With a torn right ear, ripped up tail, and dried blood covering much of its fur, the dog appeared in bad shape. Yet, the dog's incessant tail wagging exuded a sense of hope and playfulness. Francis couldn't help but smile. Then, after a few moments of watching the dog watch him, Francis dropped the remaining bits of the biscuit on the ground and followed the path taken by his comrades. The dog, after eating up the offered meal, followed close behind now well familiar with the scent of his new benefactor.

Chapter 35

With the sun edging towards its first nocturnal position, Francis pressed onwards. They had already taken two breaks in the last two hours, both as a chance for the company to take in nourishment: Francis taking water from a stream while Rebecca and Leigh ingested treated water through their suits' feed system. This journey had been harder on Rebecca and Leigh given the complications involved in using the suits. Francis, after filling a canteen, simply took drinks as he needed. In little time, the suits would no longer be functioning, their respective air supplies depleted, which is what Francis and all concerned feared. *Was he breathing any toxins already?* A nagging headache certainly had Francis worried, it had from the moment it started two hours past, but he didn't mention it. Fearing the worst, he did not want Rebecca to worry, or worse, feel responsible.

So, onward Francis led them, ever northwest to where he anticipated the others waited. In the interim, Francis marveled at all about him. The water itself tasted sweet and lacked the chorine aroma and aftertaste of the Sagan's water supply. He had already relived himself three times from his water consumption, and still he couldn't seem to get enough. Then there was the woodlands itself, teeming with an array of life, sounds and smells that no books or movies or virtual simulators could prepare one for.

As for animals, creatures large and small ran about as if to investigate the humans. At first it was just a host of chickadees that peeked in at the newcomers. Later, other aerial visitors participated in the observations almost as if Francis and company were an exhibit at a zoo. Birds endlessly called about to one another and new watchers arrived. Francis recognized some of the species: wrens, cardinals, blue jays, seagulls, red-winged blackbirds, crows and doves. The mix of songs these species played was mesmerizing and more than a puzzle. Francis had spent long hours in the arboretum where he rested under the trees while listening to recordings of bird song. The real thing seemed more cohesive in an almost impossible sense. At times, birds would sing collectively as if they could not hear any other bird. A moment later, one bird would play a solo, which the other birds appeared greatly interested in. *Were they communicating something?*

Earth-bound animals soon joined in the fun, and red squirrels seemed the most curious of these creatures. Running within meters of Francis, red squirrels would jump onto the trunks of nearby trees and then turn to stare at Francis as if the humans were unwanted. Chipmunks were the next to surface, but they seemed less concerned with Francis. Aside from a quick glance whenever Francis drew within four meters of them, the chipmunks just went about, scurrying amongst fallen tree limbs and periodically munching on some morsel they uncovered. Grey squirrels also soon showed their faces, but the red squirrels quickly chased their larger cousins off. Francis could not help but laugh whenever the red squirrels went into "beast mode" as he came to call it.

Encounters with larger animals were rare and usually shocking. The first deer they met startled everyone. Hidden amongst a patch of tall grass saturated in sunlight, a fawn rested until Francis walked within a meter of it. Like lightning, the deer vaulted out from its bed and danced about the surrounding trees until it disappeared. Francis, Rebecca and Leigh all watched, awestruck by the agility of the deer, its effortless bounds clearing distances of more than three meters. The sight of the deer stayed with Francis as he marched on, ever northwest. Then, as the sun dipped below the tree line, he began to relish the air about them.

As with the water, the air was sweet. Above, the tree canopy stood, emboldened by the diversity of autumn-turned foliage. Yet, the colorful display in leaves seemed dull by comparison to the woodland's scents. Rich aromas, more diverse and enlivening than words could ever describe, overwhelmed his olfactory sensors. At one point, as one remaining ray of sunlight broke through the maze of branches, leaves and vines, Francis fixated on a dandelion, which until that moment had been nothing more than a photo in a book, at least for Francis. Crouching down to his knees, Rebecca and Leigh standing behind him, Francis leaned down and smelled the dandelion. He immediately sneezed, which drew laughter from his friends, and Francis soon joined in the laughter. Suddenly, his headache still pounding and his eyes watery, Francis grew silent. He turned around and gently rubbed his finger over the dandelion's head. Turning over his hand, Francis observed yellow particulates coating his index finger.

"Aw Frak!"

***

Mario was battling a severe headache, which Ashleigh could not remedy. The lieutenant worked through the pain while setting up a series of lean-tos to ward off a fast approaching storm front, but it was clear to all that Mario was suffering.

"Any guesses?" General Leary asked Ashleigh as she stopped for the first time that day and was documenting what turned out to be the medications she tried and their subsequent effect, or lack thereof, on Mario.

"None, General," Ashleigh replied as she stood to salute; General Leary waved for her to sit before he crouched by her side. "The lieutenant's system is rejecting everything I've given him. Penicillin showed promise at first, but the symptoms came back with a vengeance."

"Can you try anything else?"

"I have a few additional medicines, but I have to give his system time to process the other medicines or..."

In the distance, Mario stumbled before dropping to his knees; everyone ran to him though leaving Ashleigh to maneuver through a host of bodies until she was at Mario's side.

"I'm fine!" the lieutenant exclaimed, one hand resting on the ground while Mario rubbed the palm of the other over his forehead.

"Give them space," Paul commanded; Ashleigh then rubbed Mario's neck, attempting to relieve some pain. "You said the penicillin worked a bit. Can't you just administer another dose?"

"That won't help!" a voice from within the woods exclaimed. Everyone drew their weapons, Mario included, and pointed about at the surrounding trees trying to locate the would-be interloper. With only a residue of sunlight remaining, a hooded and cloaked figure emerged and drew all their focus.

"Let me see your hands, now!" Sergeant Zavack exclaimed as she took point. "Identify yourself!"

"Me, I'm just an Irishman trying to get home," Francis replied as he slowly removed his hood.

Chapter 36

"Come here, boy," General Leary said after pushing past the others and grabbing Francis in a bear hug. "Don't ever scare me like that again, understood?" Francis nodded to his uncle, his eyes teary at seeing family. Kathleen then hugged her cousin while General Leary saluted Dennison and Sanford in turn. "Thank you for keeping these miscreants safe, Major," Paul said to Rebecca.

"Hey!" Leigh and Francis exclaimed to which Rebecca and Paul laughed. They took no additional time to speak as Francis moved off towards Ashleigh.

"What medications do you have in your pack, Ashleigh?" Francis asked the medic as he crouched down by her as she attended Mario.

"Not much, I'm afraid. The doctors included major inoculants for potential diseases, but they seem to have little effect."

"Maybe Mario and I are suffering from something …simple?" Francis asked. Ashleigh frowned in acknowledgement of Francis's self-diagnosis. *Were Francis and Mario infected and dying?*

"What are your symptoms?" she asked Francis.

"Headache, watery eyes and congestion," Francis replied before showing her his pollen-coated finger.

"I'm not a chemist, Dr. Burns," Ashleigh said as she rummaged through her med pack.

"You're our best shot here, Petty Officer," Francis said in an attempt to encourage her. After a few moments, Ashleigh removed a small container of pills and turned towards Francis.

"These sleeping pills have a small amount of Cetirizine, which was used in the past as an allergen suppressor."

"Let's give it a shot," Francis said as he held out his hand. She gave him a pill, which he took with long draws from his canteen. Mario then took a pill and water before nodding his thanks to Ashleigh. Both men became drowsy within fifteen minutes. Then, after another five minutes, both felt their headaches and breathing issues abate.

"Why just us?" Mario asked after taking the pill.

"Not everyone is affected by the same allergens, Lieutenant, and everyone else still has their respirators on," Ashleigh had responded. "And not everyone's symptoms are effectively treated by the same medicine." To her delight, both her patients improved markedly within less than an hour. Meanwhile, Rebecca gave a report to General Leary.

"We lost a few fighters in the landing in addition to the Drake," Rebecca said as she and General Leary walked towards the periphery of the camp. "And I'm guessing your radios have proved as ineffective as ours?" Paul nodded in response to Rebecca.

"We lost a number of Marines in the Drake fire and the landings. Now we have but one serious injury, which is Danielson," General Leary said as he and Major Sanford walked. "Our armament is limited to sidearms, each with one to two reserve clips. I see you escaped with at least a little more weaponry." His last comment came as Paul's eyes rested on the short sword, *Sting*, belted at Rebecca's waist. She smiled.

"A gift from Francis, General," Rebecca said as she rested her palm on *Sting's* hilt.

"Under the circumstances, it's better than a ring," Paul said before smirking at Major Sanford. He immediately cut off any protest. "Our food stores are virtually non-existent, unless you happened to bring any with you."

"Francis and I both packed some K-rations, but not enough to feed everyone. Hell, there's nothing more than some biscuits and rice."

"There's more than enough food to sustain us and everyone on board the Sagan, Uncle Paul," Francis said, half-startling the commanding officers by his sudden appearance. He then yawned before continuing. "The fish species in the rivers and lakes throughout the state are mostly the same species we farm onboard the Sagan in the nursery. Sergeant Zavack!" Francis then called out before Paul or Rebecca could press him.

"And how do you suppose we eat?" Rebecca asked. We don't have the equipment to create an oxygen chamber; we'd have to remove our masks."

"And then we'd all be exposed to the potential contaminates your breathing in right now," Paul added, finishing Rebecca's assessment.

"Like it or not, your oxygen reserves are at a minimum, and they won't last much longer anyways considering the distance left to travel," Francis observed. "We have my oxygen tank to help those who struggle with sinus problems. Any damage done by germs will have to wait for treatment until we reach Fort Niagara." Further discussion was interrupted by Sergeant Zavack's arrival. Quickly, Francis removed his holster, sidearm and reserve clips included, and handed them to Karen. "This will serve better in your hands, Sarge." Karen nodded at Francis before cinching the holster's belt around her upper left thigh and placing the extra clips in a belt pouch.

"You have to do my laundry for a week, Lieu-tenant!" Karen exclaimed, casting a smile to Mario be-fore removing her helmet and shaking out her long hair. "I knew you weren't done yet, Professor," she then said as she turned about. What do you want done with our dead, General?"

"Lacking shovels and time, I would say a pyre, but getting enough dry wood seems doubtful," Paul re-plied as he considered options.

"How about a cairn?" Rebecca asked after a moment of silence. "There certainly are enough rocks in the area with which to cover the fallen."

"See to the cairn, Sergeant," General Leary commanded before shifting focus like only a general could do. "You think you could get a fire going, you two?" he asked Rebecca and Francis.

"On it," they said simultaneously, drawing a smirk out of Paul as they moved off.

"You'll probably need these, Professor Burns," Karen said as she tossed two lighters to Francis. "Con-sider it payment for the gun. Ortega and Neubauer, front and center!" Karen then commanded. In response, two privates quickly followed Zavack. both removing their helmets as then did so. Ernest Ortega, JR, who stood under two meters, was short amongst his Marine peers, but he ever remained *The Devil Dog*. His light brown hair, handsome facial features and artistic gifts provided 'Ernie' with the flash and style that turned all heads aboard the Sagan. However, his muscular phy-sique and devotion to his fellow Marines made him one of the most feared individuals aboard. Francis had not had much contact with Ernie, but what little he knew assured Professor Burns that he would be a defender for all of them during the trek to Fort Niagara. Gordon Paul Neubauer was the night to Ernie's day.

Gordon, also loyal to his fellow Marines, was a rock of a confidant others trusted. He was quiet and thoughtful as if always contemplating some greater ideal. With a medium build and nearly twenty centimeters taller, about the only characteristic he shared with Ernie was having brown hair. Francis watched as both privates walked off with Sergeant Zavack towards where the dead lay, marveling at the Marines' differences and how quickly they cast aside those differences to aid fallen Marines.

"Come on, Recoil," Rebecca said as she stalked off to find wood for the fire. "Those campfires aren't gonna build themselves." Francis wasted no time catching up to Rebecca and helping her gather an ample supply of wood to fuel the fire. After getting the first one lit, Francis convinced Rebecca and his Uncle Paul to allow for three fires as a perimeter to their encampment.

"The fires will draw attention, but three will likely keep any curious apex predators at a distance for at least the night," Francis had argued. Paul and Rebecca didn't question Francis on his motives or assessment, but they did consider a number of predators hidden amongst the woods. In turn, Paul, Rebecca and a number of Seabees also made certain enough spare wood was collected to keep the fires well lit until morning.

As darkness fully descended, the combined force of Marines and naval personnel pulled within the campfire borders, each removing their suits and donning their utility uniforms, which were camouflage-patterned outfits designed specifically for Sagan Marine and Navy personnel. Francis, who sat to the north side of the encampment, watched as the Seabees and Marines moved about attending to their dress and few supplies. Then, as several Marines removed the face shields from their helmets after expending their oxygen reserves, Francis noted the marked resemblance these servicemen bore to earlier generations of American troops. Indeed, the helmets lacked the bulkiness of earlier helmets, but the forest green and olive drab speckled pants and shirts looked as if they were plucked from the past, right out of Vietnam. Later, after Zavack retuned—the fallen now buried under a mound of rock— General Leary assigned watches for the night and informed all that a service would be held in the morning before marching north. Francis, remaining somewhat secluded from the others, looked outward beyond the fires and listened intently for movement. Amidst the snores of some comrades and the conversations of others, Francis heard the snapping of twigs from beyond the reach of firelight.

"Where are you?" Francis asked to himself knowing that creatures great and small watched his every move. Then, as sleep started to overwhelm him, Francis saw a single set of eyes staring at him. The eyes were large and unblinking, and the firelight castings gave the orbs an almost amber glow. Francis had already prepared for this moment. Holding his gaze unflinchingly, Francis stood and unsheathed *Glamdring*. He held the sword up as a challenge to the watcher. For a moment, the unknown creature's eyes diverted attention to the sword's blade, which was now reflecting the firelight. Then, after it seemingly considered the sword and the human, the eyes disappeared though Francis knew the creature remained nearby.

Chapter 37

The night was alive as if it truly were an animal stalking the woodlands. Francis seemed unaffected by this as he fell into a deep sleep soon after resting into the folds of the blankets he pulled from his pack. Rebecca and the others remained awake and vigilant, continually observant of the sights, sounds and smells that emanated from the surrounding darkness, each wrapped in an emergency blanket to ward off the dropping temperatures. Space travel made for an uneventful sleeping environment, the sounds of distant machinery the only real background noise to accompany sleep. Well, that and the snores from bunkmates. Yet here on Earth, every branch that creaked in the wind and every bush rustled by an unseen animal resonated like the shouts of a drill sergeant. Not experienced in these distractions, all but Francis remained up and alert as if awaiting an attack. When Francis did awaken, he found the others sitting around the fires and quiet, the crackling of the fires the only noise in the immediate vicinity. He sat up and turned about watching the others, an anthropologist to the end. Francis smiled each time a distant noise rang out: wind knocked branches, a snapped twig or the piercing call of an unseen animal. Immediately all heads turned towards the sounds while a few of Francis's teammates quickly placed a hand onto their pistol grips. He decided to lighten the mood.

Up from his blankets, Francis moved to his pack and rummaged around in search of his tin whistle, which he brought on the mission. Francis then stepped to the center point between all three fires and stood motionless as he listened to the noise from the surrounding woodlands. The hoot of an owl along with the calls of other birds intermixed with the crackling flames and wind-brushed tree limbs, an orchestral accompaniment for Francis's memories and heartbeat.

Francis suddenly began tapping his foot to a tune only heard in his mind, and all watching marveled at the man's actions as he brought the whistle to his lips and played an Irish jig, one of many tunes he would play that night. Soon many clapped their hands to the rhythm of Francis's playing until laughter and even dancing overwhelmed the gathered.

Paul Leary watched on as the troops celebrated, and he smiled at the festive air now surrounding the stranded company of Marines, Seabees and scientist. In such a little time, they truly became a family. Further contemplation on the general's part ended as his daughter Kathleen pulled him into the dancing.

Francis struggled not to laugh with joy as his family took over the impromptu dance floor, pine needles and dirt in place of the Sagan's hard metal flooring. His joy was short lived.

Its presence was unmistakable; OCD had come. Fleeting, subconscious questions danced about at the edges of Francis's awareness. *Had his actions already put the remnants of Humanity onto a path to destruction? Was there a different path he should have chosen to safely lead them to Fort Niagara? Had they failed to find another Sagan crew member who stowed away on the U.S.S. Drake?*

Francis battled these intrusive thoughts even as he continued to play jigs, which no longer brought solace to him.

***

Like a covert operative, the animal evaded detection by the stationed guards and came to within a meter of where Francis slept. There, as before, the animal found Francis had left biscuit crumbs for it. The dog considered the human for a moment before eating the food. Unnoticed by the dog, Francis opened his eyes and smiled as the animal ate.

"Good doggie," Francis whispered. The dog immediately stopped chewing and stared back at Francis. For minutes neither moved. Then, after a few sniffs of the air, the dog returned to its meal. Once the food was gone, the dog rested on the ground and quietly whimpered until Francis handed out a few more morsels, which the dog quickly ingested right from the human's hand. The exchange continued for some time until the dog finally sidled up to Francis, resting with its back to the anthropologist. Doggie had found a benefactor and its first friend. From the tree above, Crash watched the exchange, ever tilting its head as if in contemplation of unfolding events. The family was growing.

***

"What the Frak!" Rebecca hollered as she jumped up, drew her pistol and sighted in the dog resting within the protection of Francis's arms. The other Marines and sailors were up in a heartbeat, tossing their blankets aside to stand with guns drawn. Francis extended his arm in line with the barrel of Rebecca's weapon.

"Hold your fire, Frost!" he exclaimed. "Everyone, lower your weapons and step back; this dog is not a threat." Everyone did as told while Paul Leary walked closer. Doggie stood up in between Francis and General

Leary, a protective stance to stop the advance on his newfound friend. "Take it easy, Doggie," Francis said reassuringly as he crouched next to the dog and began gently rubbing the animal's back. Doggie sat, now at ease, but he kept an eye on the people around him.

Daylight was wresting control from the night, which allowed all to obtain a good view of the dog, and they were more amazed than concerned with the animal. "Well, since we're all up, shall we see to breakfast?" Francis's question was directed more towards Doggie than anyone else. "You up for fishing, Uncle Paul?"

The general just shook his head not knowing where to begin. "I take it you carried fish hooks and line with you?"

"Oh, most certainly. Who wants to join me?"

"You know how to fish?" Rebecca asked, dumbfounded at Francis's never-ending talents.

"Of course I do," he replied. "I used to practice in the fish nursery, though I doubt the creeks here are as plentiful with game as the Sagan's tanks are." Francis then walked off towards the creek he and Rebecca passed not far from the camp. "Somebody kick up the fires!"

"Francis Aloysius Burns," Paul muttered amidst a stifled laugh. "Zavack!"

"Sir," she replied as she stepped up to her commanding officer.

"Get the teams in motion. Police the camp for all supplies and have one squad tend to the fires."

"Aye, Sir," Karen replied as Paul Leary entered the brush after his nephew while the guards wondered at how the dog got past them.

***

It took Francis less than fifteen minutes to convert two solid branches into fishing poles with twig bobbers. It took another five minutes to find worms under fallen limbs nearby. Francis never bothered to ask Paul if the general knew how to fish. He knew without question his uncle had fished on the Sagan having heard a number of tales from his father about the shenanigans the Burns and Leary kids got into on a regular basis. So, there they sat, fishing on Earth and neither saying a word as the twig bobbers simply floated in the calm creek. Doggie sat between the two Irishmen, the animal's head shifting back and forth until final Paul's line was yanked hard. Slowly, Paul walked backwards until Francis, the pole's line cupped in his hand, could see the rainbow trout caught on the hook. Francis held the fish high for his uncle to see.

"I told you we wouldn't starve," Francis said as he unhooked the fish and lobbed it at his uncle. Paul dropped his pole and tried to grab the fish, but the slippery trout wiggled through the man's hands only to flip around in the grass. Francis then joined in the attempt to snare the fish, but it was Doggie who landed the scaled creature, grabbing the slimy breakfast and walking off a few meters to enjoy the catch. Francis and Paul laughed heartily for a few minutes until the need for food snapped them back to reality. They again cast baited hooks into the creek, but no longer did silence join them.

"We lost a lot these past few days, Francis," Paul said as he watched his bobber. "And God knows we've lost more than we can imagine. No radio contact, and no search planes?"

"You seriously don't think the Sagan is gone?" Francis asked.

"No, the Sagan is up there; the admiral's not done yet, but it may take considerable time for her to reach us. The hard part is how to convince the troops we are going to be all right?"

"Tell them what you just told me, Uncle Paul. They trust and love you more than you will ever realize, besides..."

Both their lines jerked taut, and the fishermen reacted quickly to insure the catch. Dragging the fish ashore and securing the catch to a tree by stabbing the carcasses with his knife, Francis finishes the previous sentence. "Like I was saying, besides we have fish."

Chapter 38

Twelve fish in all they caught, a mix of both rainbow trout and rock bass. It took nearly an hour's time, which was far shorter than Francis expected even though the clear water showed just how plentiful the creek was with fish. Marching back to camp, the two found all prepped for the eventual departure with but one fire alight for cooking. Sergeant Zavack saw to the cooking and distribution of the fish while the general and Francis packed up their own supplies. The camp remained relatively quiet throughout the meal as each person took time to walk by the cairn covering their fallen comrades. Francis stayed away during this time. Even weeks spent amongst the gathered failed to truly make him feel a part of the team, and he in no way wanted to offend the service men and women. Finally, Paul Leary walked to the far side of the cairn before turning to face everyone. The general's words brought comfort and seemed to reenergize everyone towards the journey at hand.

"We shall never forget them, nor shall we forget their sacrifice. Ten-hut!" Everyone stood briskly at the command. "Hand salute!" As one the Marines and naval personnel saluted. They then stood in silence, each reflecting on the fallen and their own hopes and dreams. In that moment, Francis recalled countless movies and Sagan ceremonies he attended. Removing the tin whistle from his pack, Francis breathed warm air into the instrument while playing his hymn of choice over and over in his head. Then, after a few irksome tweaks, Francis played the first verse of Amazing Grace. Afterwards, as the others filtered away from the cairn and back towards the camp, most to help squelch the lone fire, Francis joined his uncle at the cairn's side. It was Francis who started singing first, but Paul Leary joined in immediately, and their voices carried beyond the surrounding encampment and into the nearby valley. Only a call from Crash acknowledged the song as if all the world listened to the first verse of Thomas Moore's *The Minstrel Boy*:

> The Minstrel Boy to the war is gone,
> in the ranks of death you will find him.
>
> His Father's sword he hath girded on,
> and his wild harp slung behind him.
>
> "Land of Song," said the warrior bard,
> "though all the world betrays thee."
>
> "One sword, at least, thy rights shall guard,
> one Faithful harp shall praise thee."

* * *

Francis finished packing his meager supplies before donning his cloak to fight off the growing cold and wind. Then, after quickly scanning nearby deciduous trees, Francis broke off a stout, two-meter long branch from a nearby maple, quickly removing all smaller twigs and branches from it. Francis then stamped the ground with his makeshift walking stick, gauging its weight and density. "Perfect," Francis said before looking to the distance where he planned to lead the others. There, in that moment, Francis's thoughts drifted to memories built upon books and movies. He gazed about the surrounding woodlands while his mind cycled through a stream of images and sounds: families laughing while at a picnic, a young couple hiking along a woodland trail, a solitary log cabin with smoke streaming out of its chimney. Francis could almost smell the charcoal from the imagined fire; he smiled.

"Francis, we're ready," Rebecca said, snapping Francis back to reality.

"Good," he replied. "Well, there's no time like the present for an adventure." It was then, in the silence of his mind, that Francis recalled a flurry of grand music from a number of his favorite movies, epic tunes to suit their quest. Onward did he then walk towards the northwest trailed by a dog, a blue jay, and the remnants of their landing party. Into thickening woodlands did Francis lead his companions, his legs quickly saturated by dew-soaked grass, which made for an uncomfortable and chilly start. Yet, the further they walked between the region's mountains, the more the exertion warmed his body to counteract the moist landscape. Under the tree cover, where the grass was all but absent, Francis and the others found a network of pine needle-covered paths, again something Francis reasoned to be the makings of deer herds migrating through the area. These paths cushioned Francis's feet and made for an easier hike. Then too there was the pine smell that soothed Francis's spirit, helping to eradicate the thought of the Sagan's musty hallways.

They encountered a broad stream two hours into the journey where Francis called for a break to offer a chance for rest and the refilling of canteens. For Francis, it was an opportunity to record images and descriptions of the journey into a new journal he'd brought along. Not much of an artist, Francis drew rough images of trees and other vegetation they encountered as well details of the creeks and the wildlife they'd so far seen: birds, rodents and fish.

"General Leary!" a voice cried out, pressing everyone to alert status. Paul, Francis and company rushed northward to the caller and found Private Neubauer standing near a clearing in the woodlands that offered a view of a northern mountain that shone like the sun had nestled amongst its eastern slope.

"Forest fire?" one of the men asked as all squinted to survey the mountain. Francis, ever pre-pared, removed a monocular from his bag and scanned the mountain's eastern slope thinking the sunrays were simply reflecting off a rock shelf. What he found was a surprise beyond measure.

"What is it, Francis?" General Leary asked his nephew as he strained to see through the now bright sunlight.

"It's like a sea of gold, Uncle Paul," Francis said as he lowered the monocular and turned to his elder. "It's a wide field of corn covering the mountain side, and some bright yellow flowers growing all around it. It's like a horde of gold waiting for its dragon master."

"Sunflowers and golden rod," Paul finally said after he too eyed the corn through the monocular. "More than enough food for this sorry lot, wouldn't you say, Major?" He tossed the eye piece to Rebecca who nodded after assessing the corn.

"We can be there in a few hours if we keep a good pace," Francis said as he picked up his pack. "We all ready?"

It took more than a few hours to traverse the dis-tance between as the ground was saturated; the paths they found more chilly mud than packed dirt. Then, the climb up the mountainside, steep and with no clear an-imal paths to follow, grew precarious as large sections of slick-surfaced shale dominated the ground surface. Yet, perseverance and the desire to secure a wider selection of food brought the Marines and Seabees to the corn field. Unfortunately, the crop was far from what all hoped it would be. Birds, squirrels and other animals had taken a toll on the corn and sunflowers as few cobs and sunflowers were untouched.

"Is any of this safe to eat?" Francis asked as he picked up a half-eaten cob off the ground and looked nearby to where Petty Officer Fischer examined a patch of sunflowers.

"The plants should be fine as long as there's no rot," she replied as she picked out several seeds from the nearest sunflower. "We certainly could use the nutritional variety; these seeds alone are rich in selenium, potassium, calcium, and iron." Ashleigh ate one of the seeds she picked and winced at the bitter taste before swallowing it. She then removed her mess kit from its outer pouch before placing the seeds inside and returning to removing sunflower seeds from nearby flowers.

"Let's get to it!" General Leary commanded, snapping everyone back to reality. "Francis, see how many fish you can catch in the stream we passed half a click back, and take Kathleen and Frost with you." The three nodded and moved off while the general delegated further. "Show us how to extract the seeds, Ashleigh. I don't want us missing anything." Ashleigh quickly showed her comrades how to pluck the seeds and remove kernels from corn cobs. In little time, nearly every service member was at work gathering food. Only Ernie Ortega and the general remained without a task, but that was by design.

"What do you want from me, Sir?" Ernie asked Paul Leary as the two walked a bit away from the others.

"You're the best tinkerer here. I need you to pull pieces from the radios and see if you can get at least one working. With any luck, we'll catch a signal from either the Sagan or at least other landing party members."

"I'm on it, Sir," Ernie said before saluting and moving to their gathered supplies to begin the repair work. Paul, meanwhile, joined Ashleigh and the others pulling seeds and kernels from the remaining plants. By nightfall, three large fires were blazing while everyone consumed a meal of trout and a trail mix of corn and sunflower seeds. Once again the gathered sang songs and danced about celebrating the fresh air and freedom from the colorless halls of the Sagan. Only two were distracted: Francis and Ernie. Ernie diligently worked by firelight piecing together a Frankenstein radio he hoped would allow for a greater range of their audio reach.

On the other hand, Francis, with Doggie lying nearby and Crash perched above in an ancient oak, sat by the fire positioned farthest downhill drawing pictures of animals they saw while also recording the events of their expedition thus far. In truth, Francis was more focused on serving as a sentry, watching the darkness to see the eyes of predators. Not one predator showed that night, which was all the more telling. Francis knew they were plotting, waiting for a moment when the humans were most vulnerable.

Chapter 39

Admiral Taryn Southern now spent Sagan 'evening hours' patrolling the halls to check in with her crew. While the repairs were progressing and the ship had finally been leveled through the ingenuity of the Seabees, a host of problems remained: radio communications with landing parties had not been restored, the fighter squadron had been reduced to four functioning ships, and once artificial gravity had been restored, most halls were near impassible due to the clutter the zero gravity conditions had moved about. Taryn found herself maneuvering through one of the most congested of the halls as she made her way to the sickbay. In addition to the deaths of a few crewmen, a number of naval personnel and Marines suffered severe injuries. Upon entering sickbay, Taryn found the ship's chief occupational therapist, Jennifer Berner, helping one Marine learn to walk with a leg brace. The young therapist, her blond hair tied back in a ponytail, never ceased to smile and always developed an immediate bond with those she aided. The admiral had no doubt Jennifer could single-handedly restore anyone to full health with just her smile.

"Let's try this just one more time," Jennifer said as she supported the Marine who struggled to move the brace's knee joint.

"Seems like you should have these Marines in tiptop shape by tomorrow, Lieutenant Berner," Admiral Southern said as she approached Jennifer and the injured Marine.

"Well maybe not tomorrow, Sir," Jennifer replied. "But they should be good to go by next week. What do you think, Sergeant?"

"Damn straight, Sirs," the Marine said as he took another step with Jennifer's help.

"Good to hear, Sergeant Peters," Admiral Southern said, a smile beaming on her face, a difficult gesture made easier with Jennifer's enthusiastic grin there for support. "Lieutenant, do you have a minute?"

"Yes, Admiral," Jennifer replied. With a quick nod from Lieutenant Berner, an aide took over supporting Sergeant Peters before Jennifer followed the admiral into the hallway outside sickbay. "Is there a problem, Sir?" Jennifer asked once they were out of earshot of other crewmembers.

"I just need a quick update on the injured."

"Yes, Sir. All patients are out of the ICU, and the chief surgeon was able to remove the shrapnel from around Ensign Hart's spinal cord. When she came to, she had regained feeling back in her legs. I've already discussed with her a physical therapy regimen. We won't start for two weeks, but her prognosis is good for a full recovery."

"Thank you, Jennifer. I know they're in good hands. Keep me posted and let me know if you need anything." It was then that Taryn saw Ensign Anselm Jayatilleke seated in the far back corner of the sickbay. With his chair positioned between two comatose patients, Anselm read softly from a hardcover edition of Lloyd C. Douglas' *Magnificent Obsession* while only diverting his eyes periodically in hopes his audience regained consciousness. Anselm's hushed voice was soothing, and every word he spoke seemed to chip away at the shroud of anguish that enveloped the entire ship.

"Admiral," Anselm said as he started to rise to salute Taryn.

"At ease, Ensign," she replied as she waved for him to remain seated. "Please continue reading." Anselm smiled and nodded before he continued on with the next passage in the book. For minutes Taryn listened, taking solace in the rhythm of Anselm's words and gentleness of the man's character, which always brought peace to the Sagan's crew. Without disturbing Anselm further, the admiral walked on and made her way into the hallway to continue her survey of her ship.

Jennifer Berner's report had brought some relief to the Sagan's senior officer, but Taryn knew the ship and crew were far from whole. Taryn's next stop, though, showed things were progressing better than one could hope or expect. Reaching one of the hubs connecting the Sagan's main corridors, the admiral encountered Aaron Podolefsky who seemed excited by the words of one of the Seabees' chief engineers, Lieutenant Michael Horrigan, who stood next to an open service hatch.

"Gentlemen, sit-rep," Taryn commanded.

"Admiral!" they all exclaimed as the group collectively came to attention and saluted, a gesture the admiral returned.

"We've found the answer to our communications problem, Admiral," Lieutenant Horrigan replied before pointing to a nearby metal box secured to the wall just under ceiling height. Painted red, the box had multiple conduits running in and out of its base, each conduit five centimeters in diameter. "Three of the main transmitters sending power to the com relay were damaged in the crash. But since the battery backups were still functioning, it looked as if the relay was fine. It was only after someone crawled through to the transmitters that we had an answer to why we couldn't send or receive transmissions. Since the main problem is just the power supply, we should be able to just re-route power cables from other transmitters to get things fully back online."

"Our communications grid needs a significant amount of power to send and receive transmissions from more than one thousand kilometers away, Admiral," Dr. Podolefsky interjected. The battery backup along with damage to indicator circuits through the ship made it hard to determine what and where the power disruption was."

"And now we know," Taryn said, hope newly kindled by the news. Suddenly, the overhead florescent lights pulsated, with previously offline lights glowing with new life. Then, sparks from nearby junction boxes struck outward forcing everyone to duck and cover. The light show ended a minute later and left the hallway brightly lit over every square centimeter. As the crew members stood up, the sounds of someone crawling emanated from the service tunnel. Seabee chief Bert Danhof emerged from the service hatch answering who fixed the lights. "Tinkering again, Chief?" Taryn asked as she and Bert exchanged salutes.

"Yeah, you could say that, Sir. I found an old junction box with power cables that lead to one of the incinerators. I simply rerouted the wires and bingo... the com relay has a new burst of energy, which should hold steady until we run new lines."

"Can we transmit to Earth?" Taryn asked.

"Most definitely, but I recommend we limit use to low-grade transmissions. Those incinerator lines aren't built for the huge needs of the com relay. Try too much and you're likely to blow the whole grid. What's more, any signal you send will have to be in the clear.

All encoding devices need to be kept offline until new conduits are run."

"Standard operating procedures, Chief," Lieutenant Horrigan replied. "We don't know if there is someone or something listening, so every transmission needs to be encoded."

"With all respect, Sirs," Bert continued, "those encryption devices require too much power. We'd blow the Sagan's whole damn power grid just to say "hello" to any remaining ground troops. Admiral, it's just too risky."

"As is sending messages in the clear," the Admiral replied. "We'd potentially provide strike coordinates to any remaining satellites in orbit not to mention any hostiles on Earth."

"Not necessarily," Michael interjected after some thought. "Chief, with the remaining satellites and drones we have onboard, could you rig a network of satellites and set it up so the last satellite in orbit begins transmitting a message on a loop that spreads throughout the network, but never reaches back to the Sagan?"

"Definitely, Sir. I could do that within the hour, but we wouldn't be able to alter the message nor receive any response without giving our coordinates away."

"So how do we send a message that lets the ground troops know we're here without giving any specific information to any potential enemy listening in?" Taryn considered allowed. Aaron Podolefsky smiled.

***

It was near dawn, the morning air frigid, when Ernie Ortega finished configuring his Frankenstein radio, and he immediately picked up a transmission after connecting one of the surviving batteries.

"General Leary!" Ernie exclaimed the moment he heard the sounds of music streaming in through the radio, and everyone circled around to listen intently for hopes of word of rescue. Yet, the song that played offered no clear message for those gathered, at least not until Francis reached them. It took less than two measures of song for the anthropologist to decipher the message, and he laughed at the simplicity and grandeur of the song chosen.

"No need to get excited, the Thief he kindly spoke," Francis sang in unison with the radio voice. *"There are many here among us, who feel that life is but a joke."* Francis stopped singing then as he realized that his comrades were looking at him as if he'd lost his mind. "It's *All Along the Watchtower*," Francis said, as if that alone should clarify everything. "By Bob Dylan." Still no one seemed to understand. "Only one person I know would use Bob Dylan music to send a message. It's a message from Dr. Podolefsky; the Sagan crew is alive and "watching" for us. Can we send a message back?"

"Earth to Sagan, come in Sagan," Ernie called into the radio. "I think the transmitter is fried. We can only receive incoming messages."

"But at least we know we're not alone," General Leary said as hope surged through the gathered. But then, as if to squelch that hope, the ground began to shake.

Chapter 40

"What the hell is that?" Rebecca exclaimed as everyone's eyes darted around to look for the quake's source.

"The Buffalo region is on top of a major fault line," Francis replied, "but that's no earthquake." Everyone turned to Francis, waiting for clarification; none came. "Let's move," Francis said as he walked off north down the mountain slope.

"Move!" General Leary exclaimed prompting everyone to grab their packs and march off after Francis. Their trek lasted little time until they reached a clearing in the mountain's tree cover. Paul Leary had just reached Francis to ask what was the matter. Francis simply pointed to the expanse of grassland at the foot of the mountain.

"Megafauna," Francis said, his finger pointed to a herd of over one thousand bison now slowing to a stop, many of the herd already grazing on the plush green grass.

"Buffalo," Paul said as all stopped to gaze at the large beasts before them. Young and old bison dwelt amongst the herd whose periphery was guarded by stout males, all seemingly ignoring the grass and watching outwards in search of would be predators. Interspaced between the grasses and sporadic groves of trees were the remains of multiple dwellings, evidenced by collapsed masonry from chimneys and foundations. For long seconds, Francis's imagination took control, and he envisioned a neighborhood filled with grand houses, families walking about and involved in a number of activities: children playing chase, parents barbequing, and dogs barking at passersby. The images abruptly ended, instantly replaced by the herd of bison, an animal once nearly extinct. The bison now seemed the dominant life form.

"We'll have to move west of the herd or the sentries will take us as a threat," Francis said as he again pulled out his monocular to scan the bison herd. "Looks like a number of them are injured; a few even have fresh wounds visible. Something brazen enough to attack bison is certainly not something we want to confront with but a few rounds amongst us."

"What's your guess, Francis? Wolves?"

"I'm not certain, Uncle Paul. Wolves, coyotes and maybe even some mountain lions are a possibility, but there are a lot of bison injured out there. Predators usually isolate the injured, the old and the young. This herd looks like it's been through a war."

"Then guide us around them, Dr. Burns," Paul said patting his nephew on the back.

"Yes, Sir," Francis replied as he restarted his walk down the mountain, now maneuvering through the nearby tree cover to the west.

"Move out!" Paul then ordered, a command quickly answered by the disciplined footfalls of his troops. Yet, the way was hard as Francis guided them down an ever-changing path of thick vine growth, sheer rock cliffs and dense forest growth. Francis took more time selecting his path, choosing ground void of all indications of animal use. The Seabees and Marines remained restless, especially when Francis halted their progress to scan the brush and areas saturated with pine needles for animal foot prints or feces. At those moments, everyone scanned the woodlands for animal activity, their hands ever resting on the butts of their guns. Finally, after nearly two hours of marching, the landscape leveled off and the forest thinned. Yet, new issues arose which impeded the journey.

The foot of the mountain ended abruptly at the start of a bog, which seemed to extend west and surround every mountain in sight, mountains whose summits' diminished noticeably over the kilometers ahead. From Francis's first steps, which sank nearly half a meter into the sluggish earth, the way grew arduous and soon sapped much of the team's energy. Still, they moved onward. Francis, wrapped in his cloak and donning clothing suited to everyday life on the Sagan, quickly chilled as water seeped into his boots and his cloak and pants also soaked up water. He said nothing of his discomfort, not wanting to give Rebecca or anyone else grounds for ridiculing him. What's more, the discomfort slowly ebbed as Francis thought of his heroes. Odysseus and Perseus and the Argonauts first came to mind, men pitted against evil and forced to venture into unforgiving climates. Next, a slew of second millennium heroes and anti-heroes and heroines stirred his memory: Sir Gawain, Joan of Arc and Captain Blood.

Francis then thought of relatively more recent science fiction and fantasy heroes: Lee Adama, Belgarath, Bilbo Baggins, Drizzt Do'Urden, Katniss Everdeen, Luke Skywalker, and Ellen Ripley. Their courage in overwhelming adversity fueled Francis onward until his heart pumped rigorously from the excitement of the journey after which the cold finally abated. For a time, Francis conjured mental images of Aragorn, Strider himself, leading Frodo and company into The Wild. With every step, he seemed to live out more and more of the fantasies that enthralled him since childhood.

The welcomed distraction then abruptly ended as a sound, much like a trumpet, called out in the distance. Instantly Francis grabbed onto his sword's hilt, his eyes darting about the land in search of any possible interlopers. Soon his comrades were up and by his side as additional trumpets sounded. Ahead, a blanket of tall pines blocked any clear line of sight making it impossible to discern who or what lay ahead.

"Arm yourselves!" Francis exclaimed as he pushed on, walking nearly a kilometer at full tilt until a gap in the woods appeared and Francis and company could see out over a wide expanse of grassland. There, amidst a few watering holes, trudged a number of large beasts, covered in what looked like thick brown fur. The beasts, bearing tusks and elongated snouts, turned and seemed to quickly dismiss the humans as a mere annoyance before continuing to rip grass out of the ground to consume. Others of the herd, meanwhile, used their snouts to grab branches from trees, which the animals quickly consumed as their jaws ground down the plants into minute fragments before swallowing. After a few minutes, all members of the company were surrounding Francis, and each person looked on in silence and awe for the pages of books and photos from the Sagan's archives suddenly came alive.

"What are they?" Private Neubauer asked, a question on everyone's mind except for Francis's, for his studies of Native American prehistory made clear what stood before them. All eyes turned to Francis, waiting for an answer.

"Those my lad, are mastodons."

***

"The bastards actually did it," Francis said as he looked out over the herd of mastodons blocking their path; his anger was palpable. "Couldn't leave well enough alone."

"What the hell are you talking about, Francis?" Rebecca asked. She had maneuvered through the assembled to stand at her copilot's side and looked to Francis for answers while all others gazed at the megafauna.

"Scientists of the twenty-first century spent considerable effort cloning animals with the hopes of cross-breeding living animals with genetic material of their prehistoric forebears. The results, at least the results that survived incubation, live short lives and bore characteristics of both the new and extinct species. A few searched for DNA with which to fully restore extinct species: carrier pigeons, megalodon sharks... mastodons and wooly mammoths. What you see before you show no outward signs of crossbreeding, which means they found preserved mastodon DNA."

"That's a good thing though, isn't it?" Rebecca asked looking now out amongst the herd that seemed to repeatedly consider the humans for brief moments before returning to their feast of grass and leaves.

"Species die out for a reason, Rebecca. Reintroducing a species impacts the environment much as any invasive species. The environment and its biologics would need to adjust and would likely require one or more species to leave or die out. Notice the lack of humans?"

"Are you saying that the mastodons caused Humanity to disappear?" Francis turned to look at her before answering.

"I'm saying that I doubt the scientists responsible began or stopped with mastodons. Who knows what else they recovered. It's conceivable that in restoring elements of past biomes, science released a pathogen that wiped out Humanity."

"Talk to me, Francis," General Leary said, interrupting Francis's tirade. "What's the fastest way forward from here? I'm assuming our safest path is not through that herd."

"We definitely don't want to risk a trek amongst the herd," Francis replied. "I suggest we cross over the mountains west and then divert north to Buffalo."

"Agreed," Paul said before turning to Sergeant Zavack. "Get um ready, Sarge."

"Yes, Sir!" Karen exclaimed before reordering the line even as Francis took lead and marched west. The way was difficult as the easiest paths still led him and his comrades through thick brush and up steep climbs at times. The archaeologist in Francis constantly pulled at the young man's thoughts all the while. First, with the mastodons, Francis delved into his memories of textbooks and documentaries to mentally compile a list of extinct species that possibly roamed the planet once more. These thoughts though were sparse as he randomly encountered fingerprints of Humanity: the foundations of homes and bridges, cemeteries covered in weeds and vines, and stone staircases set in what Francis imagined were parts of a New York State or federal park. With almost every step, Francis heard the voices of men, women and children, all in laughter or casual conversation. He envisioned a gleaming sun's rays piercing through leaves, even though the true day sky was cloudy, dreary. His mind's vision conjured an atmosphere of a forest fire, trees burning with light rather than fire. Then, without realizing, Francis stopped walking, his knees and back sore from walking and climbing, to find he stood at the summit of the highest mountain left to climb. The space was thinned of trees, and below he could see herds of mastodons and even smaller herds of what appeared to be bison.

It was a glancing shadow that then caught Francis's eye, and he absentmindedly grabbed a hold of *Glamdring*'s pommel when realization hit: a wolf. Other wolves then appeared, ten in all, and then covertly ran to a fallen bison, which appeared through his monocular to be long-dead and stripped mostly to the bone.

"Will they come after us, you think?" Ashleigh asked. Her voice broke Francis from his long silence. All stood behind him and looked out to the land far below.

"The herds will provide easier prey than us, I think," Francis said. "We should be fine as long as the fires burn bright at night. They'll be curious, but the wolves won't risk an assault on us." Francis then turned to his uncle, his visage strained by his confusion. "The bison and mastodons aren't reacting to the wolves. It's as if they have no fear of predators."

"Perhaps they have not seen the wolves yet?" Paul remarked as he looked out with the aide of the monocular.

"No, Uncle Paul. The wind favors the herds; they would have caught the scent of the wolves long before we saw the wolf pack. Look still, the wolves are not advancing but rather chomping at a stripped carcass when injured animals are nearby. Something's amiss."

It was then the call came, a howl that pierced through the air and stole the breath of every human and beast within earshot. *Glamdring* was out as was every firearm the Marines and Seabees possessed. Again and again the howl returned, and sometimes it was accompanied by others. Yet, the wolves in view did not answer. Instead, their tails curled under their legs before they ran off north while the bison and mastodon charged in tight formations northwest. Francis tightly gripped *Glamdring* with both hands, his eyes darting back towards the eastern woods from where the howl emanated. Once more the howl sounded, and this time its owner was revealed. Twice the size of the largest of the wolves, a fur-shrouded creature emerged from the tree cover. Its coat was steel gray and its stout body toned and unblemished. The creature's head may well have been a wolf except its snout was flared at the nose while its incisor teeth extended like daggers beyond its lower jaw.

"My God," Francis whispered. "A warg."

Chapter 41

"What the hell is a warg?" Karen asked.

"A mythical creature spoken of in Tolkien's work," Francis replied, his eyes never diverting from the creature which he spoke of.

"That doesn't look like a myth to me," Kathleen said as she checked her weapon.

"Thousands of years ago, a larger breed of wolf roamed North America," Francis said as all eyes look down to the creature. "They're known as dire wolves."

"It's not that much bigger than the other wolves," Private Neubauer remarked as he holstered his gun. "I don't understand why one dire wolf would drive off all prey and predators." As if in response, a large host of dire wolves then emerged behind the lead wolf. All were alike in stature save one, which was half a meter longer than the others. Half of the dire wolves ran off after the herds while the largest one and the remaining wolves looked up towards Francis and his companions. After sheathing his sword and retrieving his monocular, Francis zoomed in on the large wolf. Its coat was a mismatch of gray, white and black fur, but the animal's fur was far from Francis's concern. It was the wolf's eyes that drew his attention, and a mere glance told him all: the dire wolf was the creature he saw in the night. For long moments the two stared at one another, man against wolf. Through the monocular, Francis could see the creature baring its teeth, and the man imagined his enemy growling while sizing up Humanity's children.

A deeper part of Francis called out at that moment. It was silent to be sure, but the inward battle cry would not be ignored. Francis dropped his monocular before once more unsheathing *Glamdring*. Then, Francis Aloysius Burns stared down at his new adversary while holding the sword up high.

"Sagan!" Francis cried out while his comrades looked on, confused. "Sagan! Sagan!" He continued on in chant-like fashion, his voice louder with each cry. Frost and Kathleen soon joined in, and in a matter of seconds every Sagan crewmember present accompanied the battle cry. The large dire wolf, indeed the pack leader, turned and growled at his lieutenants who led the other wolves into the woods at the foot of the mountain on which Francis stood. The dire wolf leader delayed his departure, looking up again at the humans, the wolf's eyes focused directly at Francis. Francis lowered *Glamdring* until the sword's tip pointed at the wolf. The challenge given and accepted, the dire wolf leader sprinted into the woods to lead the other dire wolves into combat.

"Damn," General Leary whispered before turning to his nephew. "They're coming after us aren't they?"

"And it won't take them long to catch up," Francis replied.

"And the business with the sword and your battle cry? That beast will be coming for you, won't it, Francis?"

"A necessary move, Uncle Paul. If I didn't challenge them, they'd think us a weak obstacle and would be charging at us as we speak. The challenge likely caught them off guard and bought us some time."

"We are a weak obstacle?" Paul asked his nephew as he rested the palm of his hand on his pistol.

"When you get down to it, we are a weak species. We always were, physically. Yet our minds... our minds made us the apex predator of this world. We learned from our failures and remembered for a long time the sting of defeat. Then, we passed on our knowledge and grew stronger, more lethal. Technology became our major advantage."

"And now we have limited amounts of that technology," General Leary said.

"Flesh to flesh and bone to bone, these wolves are superior to us one to one."

"Then let's make sure they don't catch us one to one," Paul replied. "Major!" he then called out; Rebecca was by his side in seconds. "Take a squad and set up a patrol of the area. We'll set up a camp up at the hill crest ahead." Paul pointed to an outcrop of weathered rock.

"On it, General," Rebecca replied before casting a hard stare at Francis. "You watch your ass, Francis!" she exclaimed before turning and marching off towards the others to select a team. Paul smirked before he set further plans in motion.

"Lieutenant Williams and Sergeant Zavack, front and center." Mario and Karen responded quickly. With Francis in tow, Paul led Mario and Karen away from the others to make plans. "Those beasts will be here soon, and I want all options on the table."

"Fire is our best resource, Uncle Paul," Francis offered. "We set massive camp fires along the perimeter and prepare torches to use in warding them off."

"And if our lines are breached, what then?" Mario asked. "With limited ammunition, we need more rudimentary weaponry."

"Spears and pikes for a start," Zavack added to which Mario nodded in agreement.

"Sharpened stacks spaced between the fires would give us an impromptu palisade that would further hinder the wolves," Mario then said as he scanned the remaining personnel. "It won't take too long."

"Make it so," the general commanded before Williams and Zavack sprinted off to delegate responsibilities. He wasn't done with his nephew though. "You're a civilian, Francis, and our guide. This battle is beyond your training. I want you in the center of the encampment."

"I can fight the wargs, Uncle Paul. You need me."

"I need you to not interfere with my troops. They are trained to work together in operations, and a civilian in their midst would disrupt that. You've done a great job here, Francis, and no one could or would deny that. But if those, *wargs*, attack, things are going to get hairy quick. Your help will be needed in preparations, but once all is ready, I need you in the center of the camp to allow the unit to work well. Is that clear?"

Francis nodded, though his facial expression reflected his disappointment. For the next half hour, Francis carried armloads of wood to fuel the four campfires started at the mountaintop. Meanwhile, Mario, Zavack and several others sharpened the edge of thick branches hammered into the ground with rocks as hammers. Additionally, stout tree limbs upwards of five centimeters in diameter were sharpened to serve as spears. Francis's responsibility for the coming battle would be to rearm his comrades after they expended their ammo and the spear they were provisioned with. He also would be responsible for helping to keep the fires fueled for the night, which was fast approaching as autumn had cut the hours of sunlight down appreciably.

Sore and tired from the exertion, Francis squatted next to the tree where he had placed his gear. After sorting through and pulling out everything he anticipated needing for the coming battle, Francis sat and contemplated his future and what he truly could do to help his comrades. *Would he be a hinderance?*

"Francis, you okay?" Gordon asked as the last rays of sunlight were fading. Francis was sharpening *Glamdring* with a whetstone, and he never remembered unsheathing the weapon.

"I'm okay, just a little distracted." Gordon smiled at the young man before turning about to look upon the others.

"I've heard your voice, Francis," Gordon said, turning back to smile again at Francis. "You're quite good, like a bard of old. A little bit of music would be a welcome change of pace, wouldn't you agree?" Gordon didn't wait for a response. Instead he walked on to add wood to one of the fires.

"Like a bard of old," Francis whispered before he smiled. "Like a bard." Francis considered his audience; Canadians, Australians, and Americans banding together to conquer an enemy. He could think of no common songs of heroism shared by the three nations, which left him to figure out individual tunes, three tunes, to help encourage his fellows in arms who were busily finishing battle preparations. Removing his tin whistle from his sack, Francis ran through song options one more time even as Gordon smiled at Francis knowing the young anthropologist was feeling better, motivated. First, Francis looked east, and his eyes rested upon Ashleigh, the Australian medic. Ashleigh was sorting through her equipment and consolidating the few medical supplies the collective group possessed. It was easy to think of a song for her and Australia, a tune that always brought smiles to listeners' faces. Ashleigh looked up and started to sing along as Francis played *Waltzing Matilda*. Soon others started clapping and singing along; Francis just kept on playing.

Looking northwards, Francis then thought of his Canadian comrades and the peace that long existed between Canada and the United States. While many still sang Matilda's tune, Francis played bars from the Canadian national anthem. The few Canadians there joined in song immediately. Francis ended his tin whistle playing to conduct the singers and urge them to continue. Then, after the two songs seemed in sync, Francis added one last song, which the Americans instantly sang along to: *Over There*.

Aussies, Canadians and Yanks sang collectively, their voices rising higher than the clouds, even drowning out the crackling and popping noises emanating from the now roaring campfires. Smiles and laughter than replaced the singing, and lifted spirits turned back to the task of preparing for an attack. Fear vanished and joy now reigned supreme.

And they all waited. As the heavily clouded sky drowned out the last rays of sunlight and any hint of a moon, all waited for the dire wolves: *Francis's wargs*. It was nearly an hour before the first sets of wolf eyes pierced the darkness, and the first dire wolves were soon joined by what Francis estimated were nearly twenty of the beasts.

"Talk to me, Francis," Paul said as he stepped up next to his nephew.

"This is combat, Uncle Paul, pure and simple. We are not food but rather an invader. The wolves will seek to destroy us to eliminate a perceived threat to their dominion. They will test our lines and look to expose any gaps. And they will not wait long."

Chapter 42

Rebecca had watched with a spark of glee as the light drizzle turned to fluffy snowflakes, which seemed to surf the currents of air that only increased as time passed. Her euphoria helped maintain her upbeat disposition as she walked about the encampment, the temperature plummeting, and interacted with the troops. She could sense their collective fear at the coming battle. Hell, she shared their anxiety at what was her first real conventional ground-battle. *Could training ever truly prepare us for such an encounter?* It didn't help that along with all her responsibilities to the Sagan crew and the approaching enemy, Rebecca also feared for Francis. *At least I had training.* Yet, there they all were standing perimeter around multiple bonfires, fidgeting at every sound, while Francis stood in front of Danielson in the center of the fires seemingly eager to engage the enemy that darted in and out of the shadows at the edge of the firelight. At his feet sat Doggie. The animal, seemingly emboldened by Francis's presence, growled at the dire wolves. Rebecca couldn't help feel that Doggie believed Francis would never let the dire wolves hurt him, and she found herself feeling the same way.

"I wish they'd just get on with it," Petty Officer Blake Northcott said as the once fluffy snow turned wet and intensified. Blake had removed her helmet, which allowed her long blond hair to blow about in the growing breeze. Her blue eyes focused north of the encampment where most of the dire wolves were positioned. The others nodded in silent agreement with Blake, and as the snow started to accumulate to cover their feet, the desire for starting the fight only increased. It was in that moment that a loud squawk resonated through the air denoting the return of Crash. The blue jay flew in and landed on Francis's shoulder before squawking once more.

"The enemy is upon us!" Francis declared as he drew forth *Glamdring*. His warning jolted Doggie into a defensive stance over Danielson while Crash flew up to the tree branches nearby. General Leary had already surmised where the attack would likely come from; the part of their encampment opposite where the majority of dire wolves had gathered. Mario Williams and Karen Zavack, their sidearms at the ready, unloaded multiple rounds into the two wolves that charged the line. The creatures barely flinched as the bullets bit into their hides, and after a few bounds, the dire wolves jumped into the lieutenant and sergeant; the beasts' first mistake.

The dire wolf that leapt at Mario was at a loss as its target, Mario, dropped his weapon, clasped his hands together, and swung them into the dire wolf's maw. The power behind Mario's hit jarred the dire wolf's senses, and after collapsing to the ground, the dire wolf took a second to get to its feet. By then, Mario was already on the attack. Mario jumped onto the dire wolf's back and held tight around its neck as the two rolled around into the growing snow cover. Before anyone could jump to Mario's aid and amidst the beast's snapping jaws and ferocious growls, Lieutenant Williams snapped the dire wolf's neck. Karen's adversary did not suffer such a quick end.

Karen Zavack was the ultimate warrior, ever assessing situations to instantly determine threats and so-

lutions. When bullets clearly failed to deter the dire
wolves, she released her sidearm and readied her two
K-Bar knives. Then, just as the nearest beast leapt at
her, Karen dropped onto her back and drove her blades
into either side of the dire wolf as it landed on top of
her. Before the beast registered the pain of the knife
wounds, Karen had already retracted and stabbed it
twice more. In a last ditch effort to preserve its life, the
dire wolf rolled over, but Karen held fast, methodically
slicing tendons on the beast's limbs until it finally collapsed. Sergeant Zavack finished her adversary off by
slicing its throat before retrieving her discarded weapon.

"Look to your pikes!" Karen commanded as another dire wolf attacked. This one Francis engaged. His
staff cast aside, Francis swung *Glamdring* with the
force of both hands. The dire wolf dodged aside and
avoided the blade altogether, but Francis recovered and
spun to deliver a second swing that sliced a gash along
the dire wolf's flank. The beast growled, seemingly in-
different to the damage, but its life force already ebbed
as blood poured from the wound. Ernie was there then
to pierce the dire wolf through with a pike, giving it but
time for a muffled howl before closing its eyes forever.

Seeing its pack mates defeated, the pack leader
of the dire wolves stepped forward several paces before
leaning back and howling a call, which was then answered from what sounded a great distance to the south
of the encampment.

"Frak!" Francis exclaimed before looking to his
Uncle Paul. "He's called for reinforcements." He
shouted his assessment to the general as a shrill wind
made speech difficult beyond a few meters. The rate of
snowfall increasing with each passing moment, General
Leary looked about for options. Their lines held, but

nearly a score of dire wolves remained in the immediate vicinity while perhaps another score had answered the pack leader's call. He watched Ashleigh tend to wounds Mario and Karen received in their skirmish and realized a cold truth: they could not hold this position.

"Francis and Frost to me!" Paul ordered. In seconds they responded to stand within a meter of their commander. "We need to move, now! Options?"

"We go into the storm, General," Rebecca advised; Francis nodded his head in agreement. "I doubt they would follow, and maybe they wouldn't be able to track us in the snow."

"She's right," Francis responded though he wasn't really certain a dire wolf could not pick up their scent during a blizzard. He simply knew they would not be able to hold their current encampment.

"How the hell do we disperse the dire wolves without expending all our ammunition?" General Leary asked.

"I'll take care of that, General," Blake said. Standing guard within earshot, Petty Officer Northcott, always seemed to organize plans well when abrupt circumstances arose. A Seabee used to constructing things, Blake moved to the nearest bonfire and removed a stout stick from the fire. She then walked beyond the perimeter, just a few strides, and watched for half a minute as several dire wolves drew closer. Then, after locating the biggest clump of beasts, Blake tossed the impromptu torch at the dire wolves. End over end the torch flew, and all the while the dire wolves seemed entranced by the fire's glow. The beasts were in awe and failed to recognize the significance of such a small object. The torch then slapped against the sides of multiple dire wolves, all of whom yelped and scattered, their coats singed by embers that continued to blaze and burn even after separation from the torch itself. Soon, others amongst the Marines and Seabees tossed torches at their enemy while Francis and others added fuel to the fires. After finishing off one pile of reserve fire-wood, Francis turned towards the dire wolves' pack leader, the sole remaining warg within sight. Francis grabbed a torch with which to drive the pack leader away, but the animal sprinted off before Francis could launch the flaming projectile.

"Let's go, Francis!" Rebecca exclaimed. She and the others were securing equipment in preparation for the march into the heart of the approaching storm. Francis started to walk over to join his comrades when it started. With many coniferous trees still bearing leaves, the added weight of the October snow took its toll; limbs started cracking and falling all around.

"Let's move, everyone!" General Leary ordered; Francis and the others obeyed without question.

***

Into the driving snow Francis led the others, and the way grew more difficult with each step. Blinding whiteouts caused by the strengthening western winds made the way slow and forced the troops to stay within arm's length of each other. Again donning helmets and face shields, everyone marched on, memories of the dire wolves keeping all eager to keep going. Lieutenant Mario Williams, tasked with carrying Danielson, main-tained solid footing even as others routinely slipped in the snow. His allergies at bay and again donning his damaged flight suit, Mario remained a stalwart whose example emboldened others to ignore the cold and move on. Zavack, meanwhile, remained ever mobile walking up and down the line to make certain everyone was accounted for. It never ceased to amaze her how Francis, in the darkness, managed to find relatively gentle slopes and clear paths. Aside from an occasional dense clump of trees or brush, Francis always seemed to locate paths that required little of the others save for walking forward.

General Leary, reliant on Zavack's periodic sit-reps, managed the overall pace of their trek. Nearly every thirty minutes he commanded rest stops during which the officers checked everyone for signs of exhaustion or frostbite. Their flight suits and helmets, designed for the cold of space, were holding up well enough. Only those with uniforms torn during the dire wolf encounter and the escape from the Drake seemed impacted to any extent, but constant marching seemed to compensate for any loss of heat.

It was the first rays of sunlight that brought hope. Not so much in the way of a heat wave, the sunlight brought a greater line of sight. Francis and his fellowship had just crested an escarpment, and the outlines of conifers and deciduous trees at a distance brought hope that the snow was subsiding. Indeed, as they emerged from the band of lake-enhanced snow, Francis, Rebecca and the others discovered that the new terrain was only lightly coated with snow.

"Thank God," Paul Leary said as they exited the snow band. "Major, check them over!" he commanded, an order Rebecca saw to immediately. While Mario looked to Danielson, Zavack and Rebecca went one by one to the others to make certain everyone was okay. Paul Leary went to his nephew, more to check in on Francis than for a report.

"How you holding up?" he asked Francis. Paul waited for an answer as Francis shook out snow from his boots and cloak.

"I'm fine, Uncle Paul. We should be able to move at a quicker pace now and hopefully find shelter of some sort." Just then, a howl pierced through the winds and sent shivers down everyone's spine. Francis wasted no time. "Let's move!" he exclaimed, turning as he did and seeing everyone was ready for flight. Onward they marched, not a soul complaining of the endless trek. Marine and Seabee pushed on through thinning woods and minimal snow cover, the latter providing some reassurance they would escape the pursuing dire wolves. Hope though soon disappeared as the sound of rushing water preceded their view of a swollen river that stretched as far as they could see north to south.

Another series of dire wolf howls clarified their predicament. They were trapped.

Chapter 43

"Oh Frak!" Rebecca exclaimed as she and the lead members reached the river. This was nothing they could swim across, at least now as the water ran rapid.

"Options?" General Leary asked without looking to anyone in particular. It was Petty Officer Northcott who answered first.

"We build a bridge," Blake said as she ran north towards a dead silver maple, less than a meter from the water, that reached upwards to a length almost equivalent to the river's width. She reached the tree and felt around the bark, scanning about the tree just as the others caught up to her. "Enough rounds into the base should be enough to fell this tree, General," Blake said, confidence evident in her sweet voice. A renewed series of dire wolf calls pushed the discussion on without any debate.

"Tell us where, Petty Officer," General Leary said as he removed his sidearm.

"Right here," Blake said as she pointed to an area around the base, which faced the river. Kathleen Leary and Blake quickly instructed the Marines and other Seabees on how the systematically strip away the tree's layers, and within a minute, all were set. Francis, left out of the discussion, watched in awe as his cousin, Blake and the other Seabees worked in concert. A first volley of bullets tore into the tree and shattered bark over the area, but the tree held fast and drew no closer towards the river. Yet, the tree's reaction to the bullets provided Kathleen and Blake with all they needed to know.

"Marines fire here, Seabees here, on my mark!" Blake exclaimed after stepping to the tree's side. She then backed away as all readied their weapons. "Three, two, one, mark!" Bullets slammed into the tree, showering the nearest troops with bark. Francis heard cracking coming from the monstrous tree, and soon visible gaps opened near the base and began to reach up towards the hire branches of the silver maple. "Keep up the fire!" Blake commanded, her voice overcoming the bullets. In less than two minutes, amidst a series of magazine reloading, the Marines and Seabees expended all ammunition, but the tree, now tilting further over the river, held fast. A new series of dire wolf cries left no time for critical reflection.

"Come on!" Blake yelled as she ran to the far side of the tree and began pushing hard against the tree. Mario, Ortega and Zavack were there a second after Blake, and soon others arrived to help. There was space for seven to push leaving the others to silently support the effort. The tree, weakened from the gunfire, creaked and cracked under the force of the troops. Slowly it started to lean further towards the water.

"Here they come!" General Leary cried out as he picked up a fallen branch with which to ward off the dire wolves. Francis went to his uncle's side, *Glamdring* out and readied. The general's call encouraged his troops, and they pushed with greater pressure, pressure the tree could not resist. The silver maple plunged into the water and bridged all but two meters of the river.

"Over the bridge!" Zavack yelled as she waved the others on. The sergeant's words pulled at Francis's memory, specifically memories of words spoken by one of his literary heroes.

"Over the bridge," Francis whispered as he looked at *Glamdring* and remembered the flight of the *Fellowship of the Ring*. "The Bridge of Khazad-Dum," Francis then said as Mario and Rebecca carried Danielson across.

"Francis, let's go!" General Leary exclaimed after only Francis and he remained on the wrong side of the river.

"Lead them on, Uncle Paul," Francis said after stepping back from his uncle. Francis held forth *Glamdring*. "This is my hour," Francis said as he backed further from the bridge. "Go." General Leary nodded to his nephew and crossed over the bridge, helping another injured Marine along. Rebecca took a defensive position a meter back from the far side of the bridge, Sting clutched in her right hand.

"Cross, Francis!" she yelled, urging her partner onward. Francis ignored her plea, walking patiently to the center of the bridge, *Glamdring* readied for battle. Suddenly, the cries of dire wolves pierced the chorus of birds, a call that was followed by the emergence of the dire wolf pack leader from the shadows of the woods. The beast's heavy breath and footfalls the only sound it made, the dire wolf approached the bridge, its heartless eyes never straying from Francis. After reaching the bridge, the pack leader pushed at the fallen tree tentatively. Then, certain it was safe, the dire wolf climbed onto the bridge, a growl emanating from its maw. Unwavering, Francis stood his ground in silence as the beast approached. Stymied by the human's resolve, the dire wolf roared, its fetid breath and saliva covering Francis.

"You cannot pass!" Francis roared back, stopping the dire wolf in its tracks. Again, the beast roared as two more dire wolves crept out from the shadows to take positions behind their leader, just feet away from the bridge itself. One of pack leader's underlings vaulted at Francis; the creature's effort was thwarted as Rebecca cast *Sting* end over end, the blade cleaving deeply into the dire wolf's neck. Francis easily dodged the airborne dire wolf, holding onto one of the few remaining branches to maintain his balance as the warg fell into the river. Other dire wolves then stood behind their pack leader, all growling in anger

Its confidence renewed by the closeness of his pack, the leader lunged forward with one paw. Francis dodged the coming appendage, but not fully; dire wolf's claws pierced into his back. Francis screamed in pain, but the scream quickly turned to a battle cry as the human roared in defiance. Now beaming within the sunlight, *Glamdring* shined like crystal and momentarily blinded the beast.

"Burns!" Francis cried as he swung the fabled sword, which sheared off the beast's ear and the surrounding scalp. As the dire wolf howled in pain, its lieutenants climbed onto the bridge to defend their leader. The added weight destabilized the bridged and forced a once unseen crack to radiate around the bridge's center at Francis's feet.

"Francis!" Rebecca cried. Francis did not retreat.

"Fall back to the shadow!" Francis exclaimed as he locked eyes once more with the beast, its head now awash in blood. Again, the dire wolf roared before stepping forward, the others marching in step with their leader. The crack widened.

"I am the heir of Prometheus, wielder of the steel of Hephaestus," Francis decreed. "Darkness and bone will not avail you." The dire wolf roared again, retreating just a step as if in hesitation. The seething of the pack leader's subordinates then emboldened the dire wolf, and it moved forward once more, forcing the crack wider still. The man before the dire wolf answered.

"You... shall not... pass!" Francis exclaimed as he drove *Glamdring*, with all his might, into the widening crack at his feet. The bridge ruptured, and Francis, along with three dire wolves, plunged into the cold rapids as the now two separated halves of the silver maple slammed to the opposite banks, forced by the river's power.

"No!" Rebecca cried as Francis became enveloped in white caps that formed amidst the fractured bridge and splashing combatants. General Leary, still supporting the injured Marine, could only watch as his nephew fell. Now separated by a river, they had a chance to outdistance the dire wolves, but the cost tore at the hearts of Paul, Kathleen and Rebecca. Yet, the reality of the situation brought General Leary to his senses and the needs of the living.

"Let's go, north now!" he commanded. "Zavack, take point."

"Yes, Sir!" she replied. "On me!" Karen then exclaimed as she marched north, turning once to look where Francis fell. Paul, Kathleen and Rebecca stood on the riverbank, scanning for any sign of Francis. They found none. In that moment, Rebecca saw *Glamdring* still embedded into the massive tree truck, which had jammed into the river bank on their side. She ran to riverbank's edge and grabbed the sword's hilt. After jarring the sword back and forth several times, she freed the sword. Backing up to higher ground, Rebecca looked at the etchings on the blade. While the runes were indecipherable to her, she knew, whatever it said, meant a great deal to Francis whom she loved. Rebecca pledged to guard that blade the rest of her life. Paul Leary moved to Rebecca's side and rested his hand on her shoulder knowing no words would soothe her at that moment.

"Come on, we have to hurry before they find another way to cross," Kathleen finally said, pulling on both Rebecca and her father's arms. With great difficulty and regret, they nodded and followed Kathleen, slowly, looking back more than once to where Francis last stood.

Chapter 44

Left with no time to mourn, General Leary's troops marched northward nonstop. Rebecca, helping to cover the rear of their column, moved about in a daze; no training prepared her for the loss of Francis.

"He shouldn't have even been here," she muttered at one point, tears pooling in her eyes. Onward they went, the piles of snow draining their strength whenever it reached up to their calf muscles. The path they forged led finally to a stretch of flat, grassland covered by less than ten centimeters of snow. After a few minutes rest and discussion amongst the officers, General Leary's force was off again northward. Within an hour they reached what had long been sought: an indication of where they were. It was a cemetery with well worn granite headstones, most of which were mostly covered in the snow. Searching throughout the perimeter is where Rebecca located an engraved marker, which identified the ground as the Lancaster Town Cemetery.

"We're about a day's march southeast of the fort," Kathleen said as she scanned a map she carried. Their jubilation was cut short as distant howls were heard.

"Keep moving!" Paul Leary ordered as they trudged on. True, the lessening snow made it easier to move, but that would be true for the dire wolves as well, reasoning that forced the general's hands: they could not stop. Within another hour, and once again in an area of tall grass and few trees, they heard the howls again, howls that were much closer.

"To the trees!" Paul Leary commanded just as the first dire wolves emerged from the southern woodlands. Neither the dire wolves nor General Leary's troops moved after that moment as a terrible growl emanated from the north. North the sound came from, and amidst the cloudy skies above, the thick growth of pines and maples bent, demarking the approach of some unknown beast. Again the growl came, bloodcurdling and high-pitched, all stopped and braced for the monster's emergence and the dire wolves, who still stood still, twisted their heads to see what was coming. Then, in a most impressive display of strength, Leigh's tank, MYO, burst through the woods, its mechanized sounds alerting the world to a hard truth: Humanity, had returned.

"Run!" Paul exclaimed, urging his troops towards the tank. The wolves, seemingly emboldened by the new threat, charged to subdue the humans. It was not to be their day. Sergeant Beauchamp, emerged from the tank through its top hatch, which positioned her behind the tank's heavy machinegun. After peering through binoculars, Sergeant Beauchamp called down orders, which preceded the turning of the tank's canon towards the oncoming dire wolves.

"Take cover!" Beauchamp yelled. Then, seconds after all of Leary's team were prone, the great canon fired, the shell landing between several of the approaching dire wolves. The explosion ripped the beasts to pieces. Sarah Beauchamp then targeted and fired the heavy machinegun, which further tore into the dire wolf ranks. Demoralized and frightened, the dire wolves retreated to southern woods. Seconds later, the tank stopped within meters of General Leary, and everyone stood, smiles beaming. "Can I give any of you a lift?" Sarah asked, her face at first stern. Then after a quick wink, she smiled and everyone laughed.

"We have injured," General Leary said after a moment.

"There's a medical truck not far behind with medics and food," Sarah replied after first saluting. Relieved, Paul Leary looked up at Sarah and simply nodded and said, "take us home."

***

After placing the injured in the tank, and after Leigh took over the controls of her tank, they all proceeded north and northeast, retracing the path plowed by the tank. Just after nightfall, General Leary and his company entered the grounds of Fort Niagara amidst the cheers of personnel that had long awaited word of the Drake's complement. Paul Leary's first order of business was to contact Admiral Southern, a conversation had in secret for which no transcript was ever made. The admiral broadcast an address to those on Earth, praising their heroism and sacrifice, the latter including mention of all those who died in the landings. Its earthworks still existent, Fort Niagara was now bolstered by five separate new buildings, which included two barracks, a mess hall, a depot and a storage building for supplies and munitions.

Lieutenant Judy Miller, short amongst her peers, guided much of the renovations and was responsible for the quick redevelopment of the historic site's rejuvenation. Rebecca, who always liked the feisty Miller, was always amazed at how the short woman with the long brown hair could make even the biggest Marines cringe when giving orders.

"Come on, you three, help get that support beam in place or I'll knock you into next week!" Rebecca heard Miller exclaim at one point to a group of guards standing nearby. It always seemed that the red highlights in Miller's hair stood out most when she was yelling. For that moment, Rebecca smiled.

"Are you all right, Major?" Judy asked Rebecca, pulling the fighter pilot out of her momentary stupor.

"All good here, Lieutenant. How goes construction?"

"Ahead of schedule, I'm happy to say. The teams are pulling all the stops. With no major storms on the horizon, I believe the command center will be set within the week."

"Keep up the great work, Judy," Rebecca said as she returned a salute from Judy.

"We certainly will, Major."

That first night, Rebecca cared little for the tours given of the old Fort Niagara structures that were being rehabbed. Upon arriving at the fort, Rebecca attended a mandatory visit to the chief medical officer, Dr. Richard Ruh. Ruh sensed the major's stress and depression, and asked Rebecca to return within the week for follow-up. She simply nodded and left to the barracks where she picked a cot near a roaring fire and unpacked her gear. Tears welled up when she uncovered a copy of Tolkien's, *The Fellowship of the Ring*. She had promised Francis she would read of Frodo and Samwise, and she meant to keep that promise for the man she now knew she loved. There, resting on her cot, the crackling fire as background noise, Rebecca Sanford read of Bilbo's birthday party, the Prancing Pony, the Ring Wraiths, and Tom Bombadil. With every page a mix of emotions overwhelmed her, fear at the darkness within the story, joy at the triumphs of the heroes, and pain at not being able to discuss the book with Francis.

As others entered the barracks to sleep, Rebecca kept reading, the firelight in the room making for a captivating atmosphere that fit the tale unfolding amongst the book's pages. Late into the night she read, and every moment entrapped her further into the story of Frodo and the Ring until the tale's heroes entered Moria. Rebecca felt the mine an evil place and wished that Frodo's path led elsewhere. Every step into the caverns, placed upon the pages, tore at Rebecca's nerves. Then, she read of the Balrog. Gandalf's words at the Bridge of Khazad-Dum resonated potently, and for a moment she saw Francis in her mind standing against the Balrog. And then Gandalf fell!

"No!" Rebecca cried out, waking some sleeping nearby. Kathleen was there in a moment, holding Rebecca as tears flowed from both women's eyes.

***

Rebecca packed the book away the next morning and focused on helping to prepare the base for more expansion. An alternant fort was simultaneously being built in North Carolina, an effort that aimed at increasing supplies especially with the winter solstice drawing near. Rebecca also made trips to the Sagan, which was quickly being restored and renovated to serve as a stationary base. On one such trip, Joe Mosher sent his father, Bret, to pick up Frost and escort her in one of the few remaining fighters.

"So Joe told me stories of some of the flights you two made amongst a couple asteroid belts," Bret said after attaining a good distance from the landing strip. Rebecca had said few words up to that point, which screamed at Bret that something bothered Rebecca as she monitored from the REO's seat.

"We had a few close calls, but it wasn't too hairy out there," she replied offering little more in way of conversation for the remainder of the flight. When they reached the moon, Rebecca saw the developments underway: a landing pad for fighters and shuttles as well as the beginnings of two hangers to protect ships from space debris.

"This is Red, I'm set for landing," Bret called into his com; Rebecca was startled at that.

"Red?" she asked Joe's father.

"Yeah, Red. I'm the original version," he joked bringing a smile to her face. It was the first genuine smile Rebecca had made in a while. After landing, Rebecca went into the Sagan to attend meetings and provide the admiral with updates of Fort Niagara's progress. It was at dinner the second day back on the Sagan that she met up with Joe Mosher. After a few stiff drinks to toast their fallen comrades, they spoke of their separate journeys.

"Francis would be proud of what we've accomplished," Joe said late in the evening. He knew how Rebecca felt about the anthropologist and was trying to console her in any way possible.

"His last words," she said after moments of silence. "It was as if the book had come alive."

"How did the story end?" Joe asked, his interest captured by the pursuit of the dire wolves.

"I couldn't finish it. It was just too much." Joe could see the pain she was enduring and wondered what could get her through the tough road ahead.

"You should finish it," Joe finally said. "Francis would want you to. It would be a way to share one last thing with him.

The next day, after returning to Fort Niagara, Rebecca thought long about Joe's advice. In a couple days, her friend's advice won out, and Rebecca picked the book back up. More heartache came with the fate of Boromir, but the courage of Samwise and devotion of Aragorn pushed Rebecca on. Within a day, even with her busy schedule, Rebecca finished the tale and quickly started reading the next book in the series, *The Two Towers*. Rebecca found herself excited again and felt as if Francis was in some way there with her. Fate then intervened as Frost read of the 'White Wizard'. Then in one instant, as the seduction and thrill of the story culminated in the revelation of the White Wizard's identity, Rebecca found hope. Gandalf was alive!

Chapter 45

The bitter cold water bit deep into Francis, seeming to sap into the anthropologist's very bones. With the rush of the river water all about, Francis choked on the water as well, which made his predicament more dire. His vision obscured and hearing nullified, he simply drifted along the river's course wondering when Death would take over. Death never came.

Around a bend not four minutes into his water trek, Francis was forced into a cove where the current slacked. The water less than a meter deep, it was easy for Francis to stand, but movement beyond that was difficult. Saturated and cold, Francis looked about for help and found none. He tried to call out to Rebecca, but Francis's voice failed him. Again the thought of Death plagued him. It was then Francis saw he was not alone. He started when he saw the partially submerged warg, the very dire wolf Rebecca had cast *Sting* into. Unmoving, the beast simply lay near the cove's shore, the sword that slew it still embedded in the dire wolf's body. Hope returned.

Francis struggled through the water to the shore where he cast off his pack and cloak. Then, with every ounce of strength he could muster, Francis pushed the dead beast a meter further up onto the shore. The cold biting still, it was memories of Star Wars that provided direction, memories of Han Solo and Luke Skywalker fighting to survive on the desolate ice planet *Hoth*. Pulling *Sting* from the warg's body, Francis stabbed the carcass below the ribcage and cut a gash to the creature's tail like Han Solo gutted the tauntaun. Then after removing his shirt, Francis pulled out the entrails before forcing his own torso into the newly vacated space.

"Wow, these things definitely smell worse on the inside," Francis said remembering Han Solo's famous line about the smell of tauntauns. He then smiled; he had bought time. For long moments he remained there, soaking in the warmth and the stench of the creature's remains, but Francis knew time was limited. While scanning the area for any dangers, he spotted brush and fallen branches that could serve as fuel for a fire. Thought of fire then drove him to check his pockets. However, his fingers were numb making it impossible to gain access. Placing his hands further up into the warg's carcass, Francis waited minutes longer as his fingers thawed. The next attempt was successful; he pulled out the two lighters given to him by Zavack. Hope grew stronger. After again returning to the warmth of the carcass, Francis stood and gathered small branches, weeds and some long grass, but his ultimate attempt to get a fire started, even with the lighters, failed. Searching through his pack brought no additional solutions until he removed his old copy of *The Hobbit*. Stored in a plastic bag, the book was still bone dry. Night upon him, Francis had no choice; he ripped out pages of the book to fuel a fire until larger branches generated flames. In the end, only the book's maps remained.

A fire set and *Sting* at his side, Francis removed his remaining clothing, which he then washed clean in the cold water. For over an hour he huddled naked next to the fire as his clothes dried. The night itself was alive, the rustling of unseen animals constantly jerking Francis to a guarded stance, the fire behind him and *Sting* in his left hand. Each time the rustling ended without any creature emerging from the woods to claim blame. Hungry, Francis looked to the warg for nourishment. After skinning the beast, he skewered pieces of meat on branches which he then held over the fire. In silence and now draped in the warg's hide, Francis looked to the sky where a number of stars shined. It made him feel like a Celt of old, as if he were traveling in an ancestor's shoes. For that brief moment, he smiled. Francis's mind then drifted to thoughts of Rebecca and the others. *Did they make it? Were they safe?* He suddenly felt an overwhelming sense of guilt and loneliness, which pained him greatly. Just then, another rustling in the nearby brush shook Francis back to the reality of his situation.

"Bring it," he said as he dropped his roasting meat, stood and raised his sword. His rush to defense was wasted for it was Doggie who emerged from the darkness. "So much for being alone."

***

Francis and Doggie spent the remainder of the night resting by the fire, feasting on warg meat, while Francis finished cleaning the hide of his adversary. Then, as the first rays of sunlight rose in the east, his clothes now dry, Francis gathered his remaining possessions and walked northwesterly. Francis's plan was not to venture north to Fort Niagara. For now, he sought the city of Buffalo as his refuge. It was not long before he saw the few remaining structures still standing amongst the ruins of the Queen City of Lake Erie. It was the historic grain elevators that still stood, defiant constructions of the mid-nineteenth to early twentieth century that endured the test of Time. With those structures his goal he marched on, Doggie in tow. The howl of a dire wolf, a warg, ended his trek minutes later. Francis turned south to look for his enemy. He knew in his heart it was the warg chieftain that pursued him. The battle would come this day, one against one. Francis turned about to find the most defensible position and selected a grove of pines for his last stand.

"So be it," Francis said as he walked amongst the pines to find the best place to restrict the movements of his much larger adversary. Stabbing *Sting* into the snow-covered ground and placing his pack in the branches of one tree, Francis walked about gathering branches with which to make suitable palisade spikes. After quickly assembling a good supply and an additional howl letting him know the warg was close, Francis bent down and gently cupped Doggie's face in his hands. "This is my battle, dear friend," Francis said before kissing the pungent canine on the forehead. "Go and survive." Doggie licked Francis across his face, and after another howl called through the air, Doggie took several steps towards the direction of the dire wolf's call and growled. Doggie was going nowhere. Contented beyond belief, Francis quickly sharpened the selected branches and embedded each in the ground surrounding his position. Then, *Sting* in hand, he sharpened the ends sticking out of the ground. His defense set, Francis prepared for the battle.

"Wish I had time for a fire," Francis said as he removed his cloak for better maneuverability. In that moment the thought came, that of the Istari and Gandalf. "I am the servant of the Secret Fire, wielder of the flame of Anor," Francis whispered as he pulled out the two lighters he possessed, the words spoken by Gandalf to the Balrog of Morgoth. Just then the warg emerged from the woods and howled once more. The beast was alone, but its visage made clear its immense hatred for

Francis. Francis maneuvered behind all the spikes he placed and held each lighter in the gathered palms of his hands. Doggie stood at the anthropologist's side, growling his contempt for his cousin's species.

"Let's dance, you and I," Francis then said as he thought quickly of his parents, siblings and Rebecca. Then, epic battle scenes racing through his mind, Francis picked his final call to arms, the Northmen's prayer he'd listened to and recited a hundred times watching *The Thirteenth Warrior*:

> Lo there do I see my Father
> Lo there do I see my Mother, my Sisters and my Brothers
> Lo there do I see the line of my people, back to the beginning
> Lo, they do call to me; they bid me take my place amongst them
> In the halls of Valhalla
> Where the Brave, may live, forever

His final words spoken, Francis raised his hands high overhead as the warg, the dire wolves' chieftain, charged. The beast ran through the spikes, showing little signs of slowing. It then leapt over the remaining spikes towards Francis, but Francis Aloysius Burns timed the moment well. He slammed his hands into the dire wolf's face seconds before the great maw could bite into the man. Crushing both lighters a millisecond before flicking the lighters' ignition mechanisms, the dire wolf's face was coated with lighter fluid before the sparks hit. The resulting burns amidst a ball of fire, scorched the beast as it then crashed into the ground, Francis underneath. Winded, Francis rolled away from his adversary while it smothered its face in the snow. It recovered quicker than the human, but Doggie was there before the dire wolf could take advantage. Jumping on the back of his enemy, Doggie bit into the back of the dire wolf's neck. The great beast shook violently, crashing through multiple low-hanging branches of the nearby pines until finally Doggie was tossed off. It was not to be the dire wolf's day, however.

Free of the smaller canine, The dire wolf turned only to have Crash, the long lost blue jay, appear and flutter about in the face of the dire wolf. The great predator swiped paw after paw at the minor nuisance, but Crash easily darted up beyond reach. Finally, the dire wolf successfully batted the bird to the ground, but the delay had already been achieved. Distracted, the dire wolf failed to see Francis approach from behind; *Sting* bit deep into the creature's back. Having suffered lacerations from the dire wolf's claws and teeth, Francis knew he was outmatched, but the aide of his friends gave him hope. Again and again he swung *Sting*, and each time the blade bit into the dire wolf. Most swings were actually launched to block the dire wolf's paws from striking home, but Francis did successfully advance more than once to inflict deep wounds. The enemies fully engaged alone, Doggie and Crash now out of commission, it seemed only a matter of time before one bled to death or struck the fatal blow. It was Francis who erred first. Backed into a thick conglomeration of pines, Francis failed to recover quickly from one swing, which allowed the dire wolf a chance to strike the sword. *Sting* flew out of Francis's hand and landed underneath the dire wolf; Francis was now unarmed.

Darting amongst the pines, the exhausted human could only dodge about as the dire wolf crashed through the stout branches almost effortlessly. It was only when Francis backed into a broken branch that he discovered his last chance. Looking back quickly,

Francis discovered a thick broken branch, which looked like a dagger that had grown out of the tree's side. Turning forward, Francis waited as the dire wolf drew near. And he waited. Then, just as the wolf charged, Francis dropped to the ground. Driven forward by the force of its own motion, the dire wolf, Francis's warg, impaled itself on the branch. The branch drove deep into the creature's chest, piercing its heart. Its strength gone, the animal could only stay there and await life's end.

"I am sorry," Francis said as he stood up to face the creature. All enmity vanished as the combatants stared at one another until the dire wolf breathed its last.

Chapter 46

"I want continued updates, Major," General Leary had commanded when Rebecca left Fort Niagara. The renewal of hope that Francis was alive was shared by few. Yet, enough believed to risk the journey. Edward Slominski, whom everyone called Butch, had retrofitted the Oldsmobile Storm recovered from Mars, but not before Leigh gave the vehicle a new paint job, burnt orange, and named it Sasha. It now ran on tracks, which would provide better traction in the coming storm. With Butch driving the Storm and Leigh driving the tank, Major Sanford set out with a small, heavily armed team to search for any signs of Francis Burns. Long had she discussed the Burns family history with Francis. She knew of his family's connection to the First Ward. It was there she planned to start her search. It was a good call.

Within a kilometer of Buffalo's First Ward, Rebecca sighted smoke from what she assumed was a hearth. They directed the tank and truck towards the area and found their path led to the largest structures any of them had ever seen outside of the Sagan itself.

"This is the Marine A grain elevator," Butch said as he pulled up information from the GPS coordinates. Once at the structure, with darkness approaching and wind-swept snow encroaching from the west, Rebecca and her team disembarked, between them and the Buffalo River stood a mammoth structure, which looked like a series of tubes standing next to one another.

"This structure is amazing," Chief Warrant Officer Bill Zulatowski said as they walked about the nearest section. Bill was tasked with scouting locations for a depot his fellow Seabees and he could use for staging the rebuilding of Buffalo. "We could easily retrofit this structure to store supplies and equipment. I doubt any weather would impact it." Bill put his hand on the grain elevator's exterior and felt its rough surface. "This thing is extraordinary." Everyone joined Bill in staring up to the grain elevator's upper reaches and marveled at its endurance. However, the structure soon lost its grandeur as Rebecca saw her prize, which she ran to.

Hooded and cloaked, Francis stood next to a doorway along the base of the grain elevator, Crash perched on his shoulder and Doggie sitting by the anthropologist's side. He embraced Rebecca lovingly and kissed her for long moments as the others approached, Crash flying to a nearby tree to avoid an entanglement. Then, after separating for air, Francis smiled at Rebecca before saying, "What took you so long?"

***

Francis led Rebecca's team into his shelter, a stout stone structure that seemingly laughed at the harshest of weather. While outside a storm brewed, inside not a wind could be felt, though the piercing cry of the wind did course through the grain elevator periodically.

"You've missed a lot of progress in your absence, Francis," Rebecca said as they sat down to a meal of bread, venison and carrots. The food, cooked over a fire in one of the elevator's side chambers, was a delicious change for Francis.

"I certainly missed out on new food choices," Francis replied as he stuffed himself full of the meat, bread and vegetable. "I don't think I could eat another fish."

"Christy Fornoff was appointed as Chief Justice of the Supreme Court," Leigh said as she too enjoyed the meal. "I'd say the Supreme Court is off to a great start, there's no one better suited for that role."

"We've also set a base in the southeast," Marine Gunnery Sergeant Kevin Rejewski added. The tall, jovial sergeant had joined the team to take samples of sediments for testing in preparation for farming in the coming summer. "We have shipments of a variety of fruits and vegetables arriving every day."

Francis was barely paying attention as he and Rebecca continually locked eyes. Without saying a word, they promised to never spend a day apart again. That night, as everyone slept, Francis and Rebecca shared a sleeping bag and talked well into the night. After she admonished him for the hell he put her through, Rebecca asked endless questions to make sure the man she loved was indeed okay.

"Everything is fine now that you're here," he replied to her after the questions ended. "So, now that all is set and safe, what are your plans?"

"We still have much to do, Francis. Things are far from settled. The Sagan will never fly again so we have no choice but to rebuild here."

"I doubt anyone will complain. I can't see anyone wanting to continue traveling through space now that we're home." Rebecca couldn't argue with that observation. "Have they determined anything that could explain the disappearance of Humanity?" Francis asked after remaining silent for a time.

"Gunnery Sergeant Rejewski has led a number of teams throughout the region to test soil, water and just about everything else that's testable. They haven't found anything yet that could reveal the truth. For now, it seems we have a clean slate to begin with."

"A clean slate sounds good," Francis replied, somehow not stressed by the lack of information regarding Humanity's fall. "Let's just hope we get things right this time.

***

Admiral Southern's daily routine now consisted of monitoring shipments of food and materials between Earth bases and the Sagan. With a new series of satellites orbiting the planet, communications could reach anywhere on Earth, though no plans were in place as yet to expand beyond Fort Niagara and Fort Henson, the latter established in North Carolina outside of what once was Charlotte. With only five fighters still operable, Taryn believed two bases aside from the Sagan was the most she could safely defend.

"So much to do," Taryn said as she discussed defensive measures with Marine Sergeant James Metzger. "You certainly implemented everything quickly, Jim. I thought it was supposed to take another ten days." Ever stoic, James Fitzgerald Metzger took the admiral's praise in stride.

"The crew did an incredible job, Sir. We've finished the full landing pad along the port bow of the Sagan and have everything in place to begin the auxiliary landing pad within the coming month." Alarms suddenly sounded throughout the Sagan, a series of red and yellow lights accompanying the sounds on the bridge.

"Sit-rep!" Taryn commanded as she moved to the tactical station.

"One contact just appeared on radar, Admiral," Kristina Willis reported as she punched away at keys on her control board. "It's definitely not one of our fighters."

"Launch Vipers!" Taryn ordered before turning back to Kristina. "Dimensions?"

"It's approximately ninety percent the size of the Drake, Admiral."

"How the hell did something that large just appear? Where are my Vipers?"

"Jenkins is airborne, ETA two minutes to intercept," Kristina replied as she ran through new sets of data coming through her accessible scanners. "Admiral, scans are detecting what is..."

"Spit it out, Lieutenant!"

"Admiral, I'm detecting a Warp signature." Admiral Southern ran to the console to look over the readings.

"That's not possible," Taryn said. Quickly she grabbed the nearest com headset with which to call out to the unidentified ship within Earth-space. "This is Admiral Southern of the U.S.S. Sagan. Identify yourself or you will be fired upon." Taryn nodded towards Sergeant Metzger who in turn contacted operators of cannons newly installed in a battery one hundred meters south of the Sagan moon base. Certain she would receive no reply, Taryn hoped she could buy some time before an attack. "J-Doll, report! Do you have a visual?" *Is this ship what eradicated Humanity on Earth?*

"Affirmative," Jaelah replied as she positioned her fighter between the moon and the oncoming craft. "Admiral, I have a contact 2000 kilometers out. Looks like a gigantic, overstuffed pumpkin seed." Her report immediately preceded an alarm from the fighter. "Sagan Actual, this is J-Doll! I have a lock. Do I have clearance to engage?"

"Admiral Southern, hold your fire," came the response from the unidentified vessel, something no one anticipated. "This is Captain John W. Rooney of the U.S.S Enterprise. Admiral Southern, do you read?" All eyes turned to Taryn while she mentally went through the operations manual she developed. Seconds passed before her reply finally came.

"Captain Rooney, transmit security clearance immediately." In less than a minute, Kristina relayed that the Enterprise indeed transmitted the correct code to grant orbit clearance. "Hold all weapons!" Taryn commanded. It then took her several long seconds to gather her thoughts. "Captain Rooney, you are cleared to approach and establish orbit."

"Thank you, Admiral," Captain Rooney replied before giving commands, which Taryn heard over the com.

"Captain, how the hell did you, I mean..." Taryn for once was out of words. A female voice then spoke through the com to respond to the admiral's inquiry.

"Admiral, this is Senator Mary Sharp. I was tasked with representing Maximus Prime's Congressional delegation. The Warp-drive was classified years ago, and no one on board the Sagan was read in."

"And why was I not made aware of its existence after President Counts assumed leadership?"

"At that point, Admiral, we all thought it would be a nice surprise." Taryn could not help but smile at the senator's words. It certainly was a welcomed surprise, something the jovial senator was known for: offering surprises to cheer up those in need. Earlier that morning Taryn and President Counts discussed and worried about the sustainability of the Earth settlements. Yet, now with a way to reach Maximus Prime within a short time, those concerns vanished.

"The gesture is appreciated, Senator, and we're glad to have you here. Captain Rooney, how long does the trip take."

"Three weeks, Admiral, give or take a day for solar storms."

"And the name? You just had to go with Enterprise, didn't you?"

"Was there ever any doubt, Admiral Southern."

Taryn laughed at that, and for a moment she thought of Francis and how he would get a kick out of the news. For that moment, there was only one thing she could think of to say to the Enterprise and her crew.

"Welcome home, Captain Rooney and Senator Sharp. Welcome home."

Epilogue

Sagan Logbook

This is the final entry into this log. As of 1800 today, the Sagan will become officially the Sagan Moonbase, a fitting end to a ship that served Humanity well. For the crew lost in transit, both to and from Maximus Prime, we will never forget their sacrifices, without which Humanity would not have survived. As of now, with Fort Niagara and Fort Henson up and running, we've attained a solid foothold with which to recolonize Earth. As for our partner nations, Canada and Australia, a contingent left three weeks past to start rebuilding Niagara Falls, Ontario. Our Canadian allies have already restored power to multiple turbines and have restored Old Fort Erie as a staging ground for future development. My God, they work fast – the Fort's roofs and few dilapidated sides are completely rebuilt and look as if Godzilla himself couldn't breach them.

Ashleigh Fischer, meanwhile, has been elected Governor by the Australians. Two weeks past, she led a resettlement team to Australia, landing at Perth where upon they set about restoring the Parliament House – for the time being, Perth will serve as the capitol. Estimates point towards it taking the better part of two months to shore up the entire structure, but I have no doubt Ashleigh and her countrymen will get it done. I cannot tell you how much of a relief it is to have other nations here to help carry Humanity's torch.

Tomorrow, I will be transferring my Flag to Fort Niagara. New York Senators Kristy Mazurek and Stefan Mychajliw will join me at the fort, while Congresswoman Chelsea Krost will travel to Fort Henson to coordinate the construction of a satellite uplink hub. We will also be joined by New York Governor-elect, Arthur O. Eve VII, who has been a staunch advocate for local-level representation. The newly elected representatives have done a remarkable job of pulling together the people to organize housing, market space and workers to suit immediate needs. The Sagan itself has a number of shops set up to offer trade supplies coming in with each of the Enterprise's return trips. The influx of people from Maximus Prime has certainly filled the void from Sagan crew who left for Earth's surface. I am glad of this for the Sagan was getting a bit empty for my tastes.

President Counts has been busy meeting with government officials. Plans to rebuild Washington D.C. are underway, but there is no intent to have boots on the ground for at least another nine months. Frankly, we are already stretched too thin with two bases of operation, but we'll get there; President Clarence Counts will see to that. Of that I have no doubt; he can move mountains.

Marines under the command of General Paul Leary have fortified Fort Niagara and Fort Henson alike. With the influx of heavy weaponry, the few engagements with dire wolves have been easily handled. I am optimistic these beasts will steer clear of us, though

I have left orders that no one ventures out without an escort of Marines. God knows what else is alive in the frontiers surrounding us.

For supplies, we have initiated a schedule of shuttles between Fort Henson and Fort Niagara. While the Niagara Frontier is stocked with game, the fruits and vegetables from the southern state are needed to keep the populations healthy. We've even launched several loads of food, water and ore to the Sagan. Supplemented by resources from Maximus Prime, we have more than enough to make it through to the next harvest.

With regards to the disappearance of Humanity, we remain puzzled. All about, whether through satellite scans or personal observations on Earth, most structures have long since crumbled to piles of debris covered in vegetation. It seems only structures of the eighteenth and nineteenth centuries survived, and most of those are far from fully intact. From Professor Burns' investigations, many of the buildings were burned to the ground. But he believes such destruction was only after elements of rain, snow and wind collapsed the structures. It's quite eerie to say the least. Ruins are all about, but instead of interest in investigation, most want to wipe the slate clean – remove the rubble and start fresh. Plans are already fixed to recycle metal and brick while discarding all else. Of course Dr. Burns has argued for the preservation of artifacts. Such decisions, however, are far from concluded as Seabee commanders are justifiably hesitant to excavate for fear of releasing asbestos, lead, mercury and other contaminates into the environment [air, water table, etc.]. Records of future decisions to be included in my Fort Niagara log-book.

For now, we are cautiously optimistic of our future endeavors and that whatever eradicated Earth's human populations is gone. Nevertheless, we will continue to monitor the environment and our airspace for any clues as to Humanity's downfall. Here's hoping that this time, we do get it right.

Respectfully,

Admiral Taryn Southern

Meet our Author
Neil O'Donnell

A life-long resident of New York's Niagara Frontier, Neil spent years developing short stories based around his life and homeland. In time, every geographical feature of the Western New York landscape morphed into the scenery of his conjured realm, which readers know as Tropal. While a student at Buffalo State College, O'Donnell started incorporating his studies in Anthropology into his writing, delving deeply into the discord and compromise that arises when societies interact. Ultimately, O'Donnell's personal and educational experiences merged to form tales where individuals and communities overcome scarcity, injustice, and war to find prosperity, equality, and peace.

O'Donnell currently resides in Lancaster, New York, balancing his time between his family, writing, and working as a college instructor and academic advisor. O'Donnell also is striving to raise awareness of Obsessive-Compulsive Disorder (OCD), a disorder he's personally battled since childhood.

www.ingramcontent.com/pod-product-compliance
Lightning Source LLC
Chambersburg PA
CBHW051523260626
47170CB00003B/761